The Man of Her Dreams
By Robie Madison

Three days. One wish. If the Fairy Queen keeps her promise...

Workaholic web designer Megan Jones exudes sensible and practical by day, but in her dreams she truly lives. Her nights are filled with erotic trysts with a dream lover—who also defends her against the dangerous wild stallion of her nightmares.

When she inherits a Victorian-era Welsh locket, she opens it to a shocking revelation. The tiny portrait of a black-haired man with a sardonic smile is none other than the man in her dreams. There's only one way to learn the truth about him—head to her ancestral home town in Wales.

A member of the ancient race of Tylwyth Teg, Owain Deverell has spent the last 170 years suspended between man and beast—punishment for loving a human woman. Weary of his cursed existence, and longing to be more than the object of Megan's dream desire, he strikes a bargain with the Fairy Queen. In exchange for retaining his human form, she grants him three days to win Megan's unconditional love.

Or remain the object of her nightmares. Forever.

Warning: Contains graphic sex, dream sex, picnic sex, magic sex, a meddlesome Fairy Queen, and did we mention sex?

Serengeti Heat
By Vivi Andrews

The fur's about to fly...

Ava Minor is done being the good girl. As the smallest and weakest in a pride of shape-shifting lions where size and strength rule, she's never had any choice but to toe the line. Now, with sexy, nomadic alpha Landon King winning control of the pride, she grabs her one chance to let her inner feline out to play.

Landon would rather focus on reforming the antiquated traditions of his new pride than taking a mate...until the rebellious Ava crosses his path. All his noble intentions go up in flames, incinerated by the heat she exudes—especially when he realizes she's in heat.

Ava, knowing she isn't mate material, is determined to revel in one wild night before she's sent back to her place in the pride pecking order.

Except Landon has no intention of letting his daring, seductive lioness go...

Warning: This book contains sizzling heat, adult language, no-holds-barred cat fights, and hot shifter lovin' with an alpha male who takes inspired leadership all the way to the bedroom.

Kiss and Kin
By Kinsey Holley

Brotherly love? Oh hell no...

On the surface, court reporter Lark Manning looks like the luckiest girl in the world, blessed with great friends and a wonderful family. Underneath, she harbors a hopelessly unrequited love for the sexy werewolf everyone thinks of as her cousin. Taran rarely notices her except to condescend or lecture. He's treated her the same way since she was eight years old, and there's no reason to think he'll ever change.

Taran Lloyd, a detective in the Houston Police Department's Shifters Investigations Unit (SHIU), lives for those rare moments he gets to spend around Lark, torturing himself with what he can't have. Kin only by marriage, she thinks of him as her big brother. He couldn't bear her pity—or her disgust—if she learned he wants her for his mate.

When weres from a rival pack attack her, Lark screams out the first name that comes to mind—Taran. Only this sexy alpha can keep her safe until they find out who wants her dead, and why. But keeping her safe means keeping her close. And the closer they get, the harder it gets for these not-really-cousins to honor their commitment to keep their paws off.

Warning: Contains a heroine with the world's worst poker face, a hero with more honor than sense, and explicit shifter sex that makes you wish werewolves really were part of the gene pool.

Shifting Dreams

A SAMHAIN PUBLISHING, LTD. publication.

Samhain Publishing, Ltd.
577 Mulberry Street, Suite 1520
Macon, GA 31201
www.samhainpublishing.com

Shifting Dreams
Print ISBN: 978-1-60504-606-8
The Man of Her Dreams Copyright © 2010 by Robie Madison
Serengeti Heat Copyright © 2010 by Vivi Andrews
Kiss and Kin Copyright © 2010 by Kinsey Holley

Editing by Angela James
Cover by Natalie Winters

The Man of Her Dreams, ISBN 978-1-60504-614-3
First Samhain Publishing, Ltd. electronic publication: June 2009
Serengeti Heat, ISBN 978-1-60504-613-6
First Samhain Publishing, Ltd. electronic publication: June 2009
Kiss and Kin, ISBN 978-1-60504-612-9
First Samhain Publishing, Ltd. electronic publication: June 2009
First Samhain Publishing, Ltd. print publication: April 2010

Contents

The Man of Her Dreams

Robie Madison

Dedication

To Norma and Tadge—thanks for the unforgettable summer in Wales.

Chapter One

The stallion galloped out of the trees and raced along the grassy edge of the river as if it believed it could outrun the turbulent waters. And maybe it could. Big and black as sin, clearly he'd never been broken.

At the sight of him, Megan Jones' breath caught in her throat. He was definitely untamed. She could tell by the spirited look in his wild eyes. No matter how many people tried, no one would ever control him.

The horse's sleek coat was shiny with sweat from his run. His tousled mane streamed behind him like a ragged cloak in the wind.

Untamed.

Unbroken.

Wild.

And headed straight for her. She felt lightheaded and slightly nauseous.

The really stupid part was, she was in the throes of a nightmare and she knew it. But knowing didn't stop the jolt of fear that pounded through her veins and turned her hands clammy and cold.

She ordered herself to wake up.

The stallion snorted and tossed its head. Probably in disgust, as if to say, "You can't get rid of me that easily."

She'd scream if she thought it would help. But it never had, so she didn't waste her breath. Nor did she try to turn and run away.

That was the really, really stupid part. She wasn't even here. Wherever here was. She only recognized the trees and the river with its grassy bank because she'd visited the place so often. In her nightmares.

In her more rational moments—like when she was awake— she couldn't even be certain that the horse knew she was here. It was as if only her spirit transported to this place—a spirit who suffered from very corporeal anxiety attacks.

Talk about ridiculous. A wild stallion was thundering towards her while she tried to rationalize a nightmare.

The stallion stopped on a dime at least ten feet away from her. The way he always did.

Steam seemed to billow from his heaving sides. He snorted again and stomped one great hoof. Then, without warning, he reared into the air and kicked out his front legs.

A sound that could have been one of awe, caught in Megan's throat.

Knock, knock. Knock, knock.

Distracted for an instant, she looked around, trying to catch a glimpse of what sounded like a woodpecker in one of the nearby trees. Seconds later the stallion dissolved and she was aware of her hand clutching a blanket.

Her grip on the soft wool tightened infinitesimally. Although she was lying in bed and had been asleep, her body still hummed from the adrenaline rush following her dream encounter with the stallion. She took a deep, steadying breath of air and opened her eyes. Not that she was terribly worried about her racing heart—that reaction, at least, was familiar, even if her surroundings were not.

Her immediate impression was of crisp, white walls accented with a splash of pinks and yellows from a bouquet of flowers that sat on a low dresser across from where she lay. At the continued soft, but insistent knock at the door, she sat bolt upright.

"Come in," she said, shoving aside the covers to scramble out of bed.

The moment her sock feet hit the floor, she remembered exactly where she was. Trefriw. Her mother's hometown situated in the Conwy Valley on the edge of the famous mountains of Snowdonia in Wales.

Except for the denim jacket hanging over the back of a chair and her shoes, she was still wearing the outfit she'd worn on the red-eye flight into Manchester, England this morning.

Her conservative, navy blue suitcase lay open at the foot of her bed and her laptop case sat waiting for her on a small desk by the window. As she stood absorbing the details of the room, the door opened and a face peeked in.

"I'm sorry if I woke you, but you did say you didn't want to sleep too late."

At a nod from Megan, the petite, chatty proprietor of the B&B Megan had booked online smiled and stepped into the room. "I brought you a cup of tea and a couple of Welsh cakes." Mrs. Smith indicated the small tray in her hand. "It should tide you over since you missed lunch."

"Thank you," Megan murmured and meant it. The woman's timely appearance had saved her from her worst nightmare. Literally.

With another friendly smile, Mrs. Smith walked across the room, obviously intent on setting the tray on the dresser. Absently rubbing the goose bumps that pricked her arms, Megan stood beside the bed and watched. The nightmare, which had terrorized her since the age of five, always left her disoriented and slightly fearful, though the stallion had never hurt her no matter how often she visited him.

She shook her head over her attempted rationalization. One of many she'd talked herself into over the years. Even though it was her nightmare, Megan always thought of it in terms of her visiting the horse instead the other way around, since the animal seemed so at home beside the river. Her subconscious attempt, perhaps, to both escape and confront the stresses in her life.

"Oh, how beautiful."

Reflexively, Megan's hand reached for her throat even though she remembered taking the locket off before succumbing to the effects of jet lag. She quickly crossed the room, the need to reclaim her inheritance strong within her.

"Early Victorian, isn't it?" Mrs. Smith said, more to herself than Megan, but then glanced Megan's way. "May I?"

After the briefest of hesitations, Megan nodded and Mrs. Smith picked up the fourteen karat gold oval, cradling it in the palm of her hand while the new chain Megan had bought only weeks before dangled between her fingers.

"It's a family heirloom. It originally belonged to my mother's—my great-great-great aunt," Megan said, gesticulating to indicate the Aunt Margaret in question had lived several generations ago. "It was a gift from a beau."

"The hand-etched design is quite exquisite," Mrs. Smith said, her thumb rubbing gently across a flower petal. "It's sad to think the romance ended and this is all your aunt had to remember her young man by."

"How did you know?" Because what Mrs. Smith said was true. According to family legend the beau had courted Aunt Margaret for some time and then suddenly disappeared.

"Surely you're aware of Victorian symbolism."

Megan shook her head. Until a few months ago, the locket had been the property of a relative she'd never met. And, although she'd heard the few details of Aunt Margaret's love story from her mother several times, she knew very little about the locket itself.

Mrs. Smith gently slid the locket into Megan's palm and then pointed to the etching. "The butterfly represents the soul. It's perched on a bouquet of forget-me-nots, which mean remembrance."

"Aunt Margaret never married," Megan confessed. "And apparently she wore the locket every day for the rest of her life."

"How tragic. She must have loved him very much."

The observation startled Megan. For all the times she had heard the love story, she'd never made that connection. Her hand closed around the locket, holding it tight.

"I think I'll have that tea now," she said.

Mrs. Smith took the hint. "Right you are. You can get a decently priced dinner at the pub in town when you're ready to venture out."

"Yes, thank you," Megan said but the door had already closed. Uncurling her fingers, she ignored the tea and the Welsh cakes and examined the locket lying in her hand.

"She must have loved him very much." Had she? Megan wondered.

Running her finger along the rim, Megan easily found the catch and the lid sprang open. Inside was a miniature—a portrait of a man with black hair wearing the unmistakable garb of the early Victorian era. His appearance immediately conjured the image of an untamable romance novel rogue.

Not that she really needed to study the picture to know

what the man looked like. She knew the stubborn jut of his chin. The sardonic upturn of his mouth, as if he challenged life on a daily basis, his aquiline nose, and the fierce brows that hooded his intense blue eyes.

Intimately one might say, because the man in the picture was Owain—the man of her dreams. Mildly sensual when they'd first begun in her mid teens, their encounters had grown bolder and most definitely steamier the older she got.

The dreams, and Owain himself, were also her secret.

He was hers.

Her dream lover.

Her protector against the nightmares.

And then she'd inherited the locket and discovered he'd belonged to someone else.

By early evening she'd showered, changed into a fresh outfit, and logged onto her computer. First, she emailed her parents, informing them of her safe arrival and then checked for any messages from her clients. A website designer by profession, she was enough of a workaholic to miss the distraction of a new job—even if it was a simple update. But there were no messages, which left her with lots of time to think.

And she definitely had questions. One remained uppermost in her mind after her conversation with Mrs. Smith. Namely, why a dead guy who'd supposedly been in love with her great-great-great and so forth aunt was making love to her in her dreams. But despite her desire to pursue her quest, Megan kept stumbling over her own reluctance. A part of her was afraid to learn the answers, which is why she hadn't confronted Owain during one of her dreams.

What if she discovered the truth and the dreams ended?

What if she lost her dream lover and the nightmares took over?

And yet the question of why had compelled her to cross an ocean in search of answers.

Hungry and unwilling to pace her room in frustration any longer, she tucked the locket into her suitcase, grabbed her purse and headed out into the warm June evening. Maybe some time away from those mesmerizing blue eyes and that sardonic smile would clear her head.

Her destination was the nearby pub recommended by Mrs.

Smith. Walking along the main street, she passed the woolen mill for which the village was famous and then wandered down a side street, absorbing the sense of history. Low stone walls and cars—parking seemed to be at a premium—lined either side of the narrow streets. Up ahead she spotted an actual parking lot in front of a long, low building. A sign hanging out front prominently displayed the back end of a woolly sheep. Obviously the owner of The Sheep's Tail had a sense of humor.

Uncertain what to expect, she opened the heavy wooden door and stepped inside. Several people were milling around the bar, which was right across from the entrance, chatting with each other. A bald bartender glanced up and gave her a quick smile and a nod before someone hailed him with another order. A bit intimidated—crowds of strangers weren't really her style—Megan made her way into the larger room off to the right in search of a table.

The place was fairly full. Weaving through the crowd, she spotted a couple of men playing darts near the back of the room and beyond them an empty chair and table. Only she was mistaken. The table wasn't empty at all. A half-finished pint sat on the table top and a man sat in the other chair, his back against the wall.

She looked over, annoyed, though it was hardly his fault that the men playing darts had blocked her view of him. One glimpse and Megan froze mid-step. The air sucked right out of her lungs and she couldn't seem to find her next breath. The man in the chair looked exactly like Owain.

Chapter Two

"Sweetheart."

Megan blinked. The man who looked like Owain was standing beside her left elbow, his forehead creased with concern.

"Sweetheart, you need to breathe."

She frowned. Wasn't breathing supposed to be automatic? But because the man who looked like Owain suggested it, she concentrated on filling her lungs. Her previously oxygen-deprived brain promptly thanked her by making her feel slightly intoxicated. Had The Sheep's Tail put a little something extra in their air?

She swayed on her feet, bumping against the man who looked like Owain. He didn't budge, quickly caught her arm and held her steady. The heat from his palm seemed to burn through her denim jacket, warming her skin. Her breasts tingled and she was suddenly very aware of the proximity of his hand wrapped around her upper arm. All he had to do was flex his fingers and he'd be caressing her rather intimately.

"Megan. Sweetheart, I think you better sit down."

Before she fell down, he meant.

"That's it." He pulled out a chair and helped her to sit. Then he pulled his chair around so he could sit next to her. Thigh to thigh and not once did he let go of her arm.

"Better?"

"What did you say?" she asked.

"I asked if you felt better."

"Before that."

"Before that, what?" His brow creased again, this time in

confusion. A lock of his black hair, which was short at the sides and longer on top, fell across his forehead, making him look exactly like the Victorian bad boy of the locket. But his blue eyes glittered like sunlight on water, just like the Owain of her dreams.

"What did you say before that?"

"That's it."

She shook her head.

"I think you better sit down," he said, repeating another one of his phrases.

She shook her head again.

The ends of his mouth curled up as if he was trying not to grin. His hand slid down her arm, his fingers intertwined with hers and his thumb caressed the back of her hand. He was trying to distract her from noticing the stubborn set of his chin, which looked just like Owain's.

"Sweetheart." His voice grew husky and she detected a lilt that wasn't quite like the Welsh accent she heard when Mrs. Smith spoke. But he sounded just like Owain whispering to her in the darkness.

"Megan. You called me Megan."

He arched one eyebrow. "Well, that's your name, isn't it?"

"Yes, but—" Now she was the one who was confused. Unless... "Owain?"

He tilted his head in a brief nod. "That's right."

She started to shake her head rather emphatically then thought better of it. She could hardly dispute his veracity or that he looked like Owain, except that his features were sharper and more intense.

"How old are you?" He looked to be in his mid-twenties, which made him about five years younger than her.

He grinned. "Old enough to know my name. And yours."

She grabbed the glass of dark amber liquid sitting in the middle of the table and drank.

"Hey, take it easy. That's strong stuff."

He eased the glass out of her hand and set it at the far end of the small table. Then he caught her chin with his free hand and gently turned her head until she faced him and his intense blue eyes. Eyes weighted by experience far greater than his years.

Strong stuff was coming face-to-face with Owain on her first evening in Wales.

"This is—"

"Crazy that you're sitting right here next to me when I've only ever been able to visit you in your dreams."

"Oh. My. God."

Until he said the words out loud, she hadn't quite believed, despite the evidence staring her in the face. She tugged her head free, but couldn't look away. A slow heat burned her face the longer he stared at her. His eyes were definitely Owain's eyes.

Oh my God, he knows about my dreams.

"I don't believe you." She blurted out the words as a purely defensive strategy. Her dreams were private, erotic, and none of his business, despite his claim that he was the Owain who appeared in them.

His smile was slow and sensual, reaching straight up to his eyes. The deep blue color was now diluted with a touch of silver that sparkled with knowledge. Intimate knowledge.

"What do you know about my dreams?" she challenged.

He couldn't possibly know anything about them.

He slid one hand along the back of her chair, leaning his body closer to hers, until his mouth was right next to her ear. "I know the last time I visited you, by the time my hand reached the edge of your nightgown, your sweet pussy was full of cream."

Oh my God, he does know about my dreams.

She couldn't seem to find her next breath. There was no way he could have known such an intimate detail. Unless. Unless he really was the Owain of her dreams.

"Come on." Abruptly he shoved his chair back, stood up, and hauled her to her feet. "We're getting out of here. You need some fresh air."

Still dazed by the unexpected discovery, she allowed herself to be led out of the pub. A soft breeze ruffled her curls, clearing her head a little.

"Hold your horses," she said, pulling free of his grasp.

An instant later, he whirled around to face her. A feeble light spilled from a bulb over the entranceway to the pub, casting Owain's face in shadows. For a second his features looked grim then he shifted into the light and she convinced herself she'd been mistaken. His gaze was heated with desire and he made no secret of the fact that he was studying her.

She swallowed, hard. Was he seeing the Megan he met in their dreams? Or was he trying to rationalize the situation, just as she was?

Even with his clothes on, this man looked exactly like Owain. He admitted he was Owain. Knew her name and that she dreamed about him. Then he'd gone ahead and proven his claim, which could only mean one thing.

"You've known about me all along, haven't you?"

"Yes," he said. "But then you've known about me, too."

That was just her point. She hadn't. Didn't. Despite knowing every intimate detail of this man's naked body, she hadn't known he was a real person. More to the point, he was essentially a stranger to her.

"I don't know your name. Your full name."

He bowed, slightly. "Owain Deverell, Ms. Jones."

He was trying to ruffle her. She refused to be ruffled. "In my dreams your hands—"

Without a word, he held out his hands for her inspection. She reached out and cupped them in hers. They felt strong and amazingly familiar. She brushed her thumbs against the edge of his index finger. He had calluses.

Her thumbs grazed his palms. "What do you do?"

His hands jerked in hers. "I have a farm just outside the village."

A raucous laugh burst from the partially open door of the pub. Muttering something she doubted was either complimentary or in English, he reversed her hold on his right hand and laced his fingers between hers.

"Come with me, Megan Jones. Let me prove I am who I say I am."

She nodded, not relishing another audience and frankly curious. Were she and Owain linked by some sort of psychic bond? Crazy as the theory sounded, it made an odd kind of sense. Owain certainly physically resembled his distant relative, just as her mother often remarked that Megan looked like her Aunt Margaret.

He led her around the side of the building and deep into

the darkness. His pace was confident, suggesting he was familiar with the lay of the land. Less certain of her surroundings, she hesitated slightly when they reached a line of trees. Firm pavement gave way to the soft crunch of leaves and twigs under her feet. When she tripped over an exposed root, Owain caught her easily, but instead of holding her steady, he backed her up against a tree.

"Owain." She whispered the word on the night air. But unlike all those other nights when she'd spoken his name with a sense of frustrated longing, this time her voice was filled with awe. She reached out and skimmed her fingers across his cheek, just to make sure. His skin was warm to the touch and slightly rough with a five o'clock shadow. He was real all right.

Capturing her other hand, he pulled them both behind her around the trunk of the tree. The move forced his body closer to hers. So close his warm breath laced with a hint of ale fanned her face. He groaned low in his throat and his erection nudged her belly.

A cornucopia of sensual experiences assaulted her—the rough bark of the tree against her back, his hard body pressed against her own. She inhaled and caught a heady masculine scent that was all Owain. Only unlike in her dreams it was sharper, more pungent. Oh, yeah, he was definitely the real thing.

Her own breathing grew harsher as a primitive lust surged through her body. Her nipples hardened, pushing against the lace of her bra, demanding to be released from their confines. She suppressed the desire to grin. Dream or real, her reaction to him hadn't changed one iota.

"I'm sorry I dragged you into the woods," he said, though he didn't sound the least bit regretful. "But I couldn't wait any longer. I need to kiss you."

A bolt of heat shot through her as he bent his head. The anticipation alone was enough to induce a heart attack. She'd waited so long, believed it impossible that he was real. His lips touched her jaw right next to her ear, at once tickling her and stirring something deep inside her that hungered for more. Instead of being sated, her hunger grew as he ran a string of kisses along her jawline. Her body trembled each time his lips touched her skin. He might as well have been tracing a path to her core. That's where the fire burned. By the time he reached her mouth, she'd creamed her panties.

On a groan, he rocked his erection against the apex of her thighs. He caught her at just the right angle and her clit welcomed the friction. Demanded more.

"I can smell you, sweetheart." Words whispered in the darkness, only this time it was no dream. His breath mixed with the sweet summer breeze caressed her ear.

Her tiny gasp of longing was all the invitation he needed to slip his tongue inside her mouth. Their dream kisses were absolutely nothing like the real thing. For one, her senses were sharper—she tasted a hint of the bitter ale he'd been drinking and the flavor of Owain himself. For another, there was nothing gentle or teasing about this kiss. His tongue explored her mouth with an exquisite thoroughness. He traced the edges of her teeth and then plunged deeper, stealing her breath and giving her life.

Emotions assaulted her, battering her wits. When at last he broke the kiss, she swore she could hear their hearts hammering a duet between their bodies.

His eyes burned with a hunger that mirrored hers and she decided she'd been cast under a spell of some sort. How else to explain walking into a pub and finding the man of her dreams sitting there as though he'd been waiting for her to arrive? Psychic phenomenon or not, the situation defied any attempt she could make to rationalize it. And suddenly she no longer wanted to. For once in her well-ordered life she wasn't going to ask for explanations or analyze the situation to death. If this was an enchantment, she didn't want to wake up.

He stepped away, pulling her arms from around the tree at the same time. Then he ran his hands up to her shoulders, easing any strain. Despite the small distance, she was still keenly aware of the sexual tension arcing between them.

"I don't think I can stop touching you," he said.

Now that her hands were free, she settled one against his chest. Heat radiated through the soft cotton of his T-shirt. All this clothing between them was an unexpected novelty. An enticement to bare some skin.

"What about me touching you?"

"Dangerous, very dangerous."

"Sounds like fun."

Her fingers caressed his chest, grazing over his nipple. It

hardened on contact. He hissed and she felt the slight tremor of his muscles beneath her fingers. Her lips parted. His descended. Her eyes blinked once and then closed on a sigh. The tiny sound quickly morphed into a whimper of need when his tongue traced a path along her collarbone. She arched her neck, offering him more. He lifted his head instead.

"I like your dress," he said.

It was white and patterned with whimsically styled deep-red flowers. It was one of her favorites, which was why she'd chosen to wear it. But that didn't change the incongruity of his comment given the erotic thoughts tumbling through her brain.

"Except," he continued, "it's far too long."

She frowned. The dress fell to mid-thigh. What was too long about that?

"And it's in my way," he muttered, finally releasing his hold on one of her arms.

The next instant his hand slid beneath the hem. She cried out when his hot, calloused fingers brushed against her bare flesh.

"Hush, sweetheart. I'm going exploring."

That he was. Straight up what was left of her leg to the elastic edge of her modest white panties. She jumped as one long finger slipped beneath the cotton barrier. Not that he noticed.

"This is also in my way," he said, a hint of annoyance in his tone.

Her fingers crushed the thin fabric of his tee. Not that he noticed that, either. He was otherwise occupied. His brow furrowed, his eyes intently focused on her face.

The backs of two of his fingers skimmed against the dampened curls of her mound. She bit her lower lip to keep from screaming in frustration. They'd barely started and yet she was on the verge of falling apart. Thank God for the solid tree trunk at her back.

"Let go, sweetheart."

All too familiar words whispered across the shadows. She groaned softly and shook her head. Her body trembled with the need to find release and yet—

And yet she was close. So close she could swear that this time his fingers would finish the job before she woke from the dream.

She canted her hips, seeking. Barely daring to hope.

And then two long, thick fingers slid through the folds of her labia. Her eyes flew open and she screamed. Or tried to. Because his fingers found their prize and rammed home. Filling her even as his mouth closed over hers, drinking in the climax that ripped through her body.

She didn't dare let go of him even after the fireworks subsided. Was equally glad when he pulled her impossibly closer and she snuggled her face against the softness of his shirt. He kissed the top of her head and slowly, deliberately, withdrew his fingers from her body. She shuddered. Half sated. Half aroused all over again. An instinctive reaction to the erection pressed firmly against her belly.

Megan lifted her head. "But you—"

Chapter Three

"I don't want our first time to be a quick fuck," Owain said with a shake of his head. A sheepish smile tugged at his mouth.

Megan's eyes widened at his earthy frankness, in part because it didn't make sense. "First time?" In her dreams they always lost themselves in each other's bodies. Real life had been no different, only better. Much, much better.

"They were dreams," he said, as if he'd read her mind. "I wasn't really there." He bent closer and brushed his lips against hers. "And you, sweetheart, were definitely not here in my arms."

He was right. As vivid as her dreams with him had been, there was no comparison to the solid, substantial weight of his body so close to hers. It was as if, without her realizing it, she'd been experiencing their dream encounters through fuzzy reception, which had suddenly cleared.

She looked up into Owain's face. No matter what kind of response he'd coaxed from her body—and she always responded—she'd always woken up from her dreams and taken back control of her life. From the look on his face and given what had just happened between them, she had the distinct impression that from the moment she'd spotted him in the pub, her life had spun right out of control.

The idea should terrify her, but it didn't. Now that she'd found him, she wanted this chance with Owain. Wasn't that the real reason she'd flown all the way across the Atlantic in search of him?

"So, um, what are you suggesting?"

He kissed her forehead and stepped back a pace. He did not, she noticed, let go of her.

"I want more. Of you."

She licked her lips, acutely aware of his eyes tracking the movement. He'd given a precise, definitive answer, without really offering a concrete suggestion. He simply continued to stand there, holding her.

"There's always your place, except—"

"You'd come?" His grip on her tightened infinitesimally.

It was difficult to tell if he sounded shocked or awed. Surprised at any rate, which made her smile. It wasn't the response she expected from a twenty-something guy who'd just made her orgasm. In the middle of some woods. Behind a pub. Against a tree.

"You haven't asked me yet," she said.

"I'm afraid to. I'm afraid if I let go, you'll disappear."

She knew the feeling. "I just got here, remember? I'm not going anywhere."

"Promise?"

"Promise."

He let go and she dropped her arm. Neither of them vanished in a puff of smoke, though he did have an idiotic grin on his face.

"My place, huh."

"Except—"

"I think I better walk you back to wherever you're staying," he said. "I want to do this right. I want...I want to ask you out on a date."

She nodded in agreement. A date sounded like a promise of more.

The pub was still crowded, the street beyond deserted. They strolled down the road hand in hand and Megan was suddenly struck by how ordinary it all seemed. The thought scared her a little. It couldn't be this easy, could it?

When they reached the B&B, Owain swung her around to face him. He stared at her for a long moment then his hands came up and framed her face.

"Megan."

"What if this is a dream, too?" she asked. "What if I wake up tomorrow morning and you aren't here?"

"I'll be here." His tone spoke of grim determination.

She smiled. "You can't camp out on Mrs. Smith's doorstep

all night." And as much as her body might have strong opinions on the matter, she wasn't about to invite him in, either.

He pulled her close for a quick kiss. "I'll be here tomorrow morning at ten o'clock. I'll take you for a picnic by the river."

She grasped his wrists when he would have stepped away. "That wasn't asking for a date. That sounded more like an order."

"It's my promise to you, sweetheart. Maybe then I'll believe you're really here."

Somehow, because 'twas for sure he was not paying attention to where he walked, Owain reached his farm. The first thing he saw was the crumbling wall that surrounded the buildings. The place was in a sorry state. He had no business wanting to bring Megan here.

"'Tis a sad day indeed when I spy you drinking swill in a place called The Sheep's Tail," a voice said from the shadows.

A shape detached itself from a tree and strode into the moonlight. At six foot four, the black-haired, rugged-looking man topped Owain by a good five inches, but then Rhys was the Pendragon. And Owain was...

"'Tis the twenty-first century," Owain said with a hint of rebuke in his tone. "Or do you not remember which Elizabeth is on the throne?"

Rhys swore, in Latin. A phrase he'd no doubt learned directly from one of the centurions stationed at a fort that had once been just north of Trefriw. "Careful, young foal or should I say bloody fool?"

Owain stood his ground. While it was true that Rhys had several centuries on him, Owain didn't care for either epithet. "If you've descended from your mountain lair just to pester me—"

"I didn't." Rhys's black eyes flashed in warning. "I came to ask what that bitch Rhiannon wanted of you two nights ago when the full moon showed her face, but I can see plain enough."

While the Pendragon got on well enough with other members of the Tylwyth Teg, he'd never cared much for the Fairy Queen. Not that Owain had had much use for his fair cousin until recently. Two nights ago he'd struck a bargain with her, a fact Rhys no doubt knew full well.

"'Tis because of her I've roamed this stretch of shore along the River Conwy for the past one hundred and seventy years cursed—neither quite mortal nor beast."

Once again the Pendragon swore quite eloquently, this time in English, and Owain had no trouble understanding the insult to his mother, should he be interested in taking offense. "'Tis because you're a halfwit and flouted the code that governs our interaction with the mortal world. And now look at you. As mortal as the woman you are besotted with. Or near enough."

Owain shrugged. He'd intended no insult or disrespect to his friend, who'd been shifting since the age of five when he'd assumed the form of the red dragon. But, since it was also true that the Pendragon was a law unto himself, able to come and go in either of his forms at will, Owain thought Rhys's argument a poor one. While he had one chance to claim a life for himself.

"Time stretches before me in a way you cannot understand and I am trapped, neither a part of the mortal realm nor my own. Had I a choice, I would keep this form."

Rhys's black eyes bore into his. "How much time do you have to win her?"

No. It did not surprise Owain o'er much that Rhys had guessed what he'd done. A form of punishment, any curse could be broken given the right circumstances.

"Until sunset three days from today."

And today was nearly gone. Half of it lost to the curse that bound him to the river. For while he'd anticipated Megan's arrival in the village, he hadn't considered that she might fall asleep before he reached her. When she had, he'd been unable to resist either her subconscious call or the equine form he was forced to assume.

No doubt the Fairy Queen knew well of his folly. And yet, in the end, she'd granted his request for he'd felt the change steal over him the moment Megan had stepped into the pub. For the next couple more days at least he'd remain fully human.

"The bitch's price is no doubt steep," Rhys said.

It had been, but Owain was not about to divulge as much. 'Twas bad enough that Rhiannon had taunted him two nights before.

The Fairy Queen laughed, the noise akin to the tinkle of a sweet bell, but her eyes, sober and searching were on Owain.

"Has your obstinacy over the mortal woman not caused enough trouble between us?" Rhiannon said and reached out to brush one slim hand across the dusting of hair that covered his chest.

Owain did not dare meet his fair cousin's blue-eyed gaze and cursed when his body remembered for him. Though their affair was a thing of the past, Fairy time worked differently then mortal time, which passed much slower than the water flowing down the Conwy.

He considered the fact that she was casting a spell around him, though he couldn't detect one. Whatever the cause, the proximity of her lithesome body and her slim hand on his chest created a sexual tension that snapped between them like the sting of an electric eel. Sharp, painful and yet it made one feel alive.

"I thought," she continued, when he refused to answer, "I made my position quite plain, as is the code that governs our interaction with the mortal realm and those who live in it. And yet it appears you've heeded me not at all. Your actions are unseemly, cousin."

Owain couldn't tell if her voice was filled with pity or displeasure. "She is coming here," he said. "To see me. I would ask a boon that the curse might be broken."

The slightest quiver of her left wing told Owain that Rhiannon was deeply affected by his announcement.

"I should let Arawn deal with you," she said, her tone resentful.

Owain's heart thumped loudly at the sound of that fearsome name. She must be bitter indeed if she was willing to call on the King of the Underworld and ruler of all the Fairies as final arbitrator.

"If I could, I would deny your request," Rhiannon continued when he refused to back down. "It is bad enough she's spent years living in fear of you. I won't let you ruin another mortal's life."

Owain shook his head, ridding himself of the bad memory. And the partial truths behind his cousin's words. He met Rhys's sharp gaze.

"It is done," he said simply.

"Have the last one hundred and seventy years taught you

nothing about the fickleness of a mortal woman's heart?"

Rhys's voice was deadly soft and yet Owain detected a note of genuine curiosity. Unlike some of his other so-called friends, Rhys had stood by him, willingly entering the mortal realm to visit him and keep their friendship alive. Loyalty on Rhys's part demanded that Owain give him some sort of explanation.

"No, not where Megan is concerned."

"And if you fail to win her declaration of love, freely given?"

A grim smile passed across Owain's lips. He reached out and grasped the Pendragon's forearm in an ancient sign of friendship. And of thanks. Whatever the outcome, this was goodbye.

"Then I will have forfeited my ability to be either mortal or fairy." And instead he'd live thereafter as the creature of Megan's nightmares.

A soft breeze warmed the night air and stars twinkled through the trees. Alone at last Owain wandered around the small farm enclosure, seeing the dilapidated buildings for what they were—a testament to his own existence. Condemned to shift forms as easily as he moved between the fairy and mortal realms, he'd never bothered to make much of a place for himself in either.

And now, in less than three days, the choice would be made.

Unable to bring himself to enter the sorry excuse of a cottage, he slumped against the wall of the stable and slid to the ground. His hands shook slightly and he clenched his fists to stop the tremors. This time 'twas mortal weariness such as he'd never experienced before and not the shift between human and equine forms that affected his body. It had taken all his reserves to keep from revealing his all too human frailties to Rhys, though he didn't doubt the Pendragon had had his suspicions, which is why he hadn't lingered to chat. Owain would need to find his bed soon if he was to keep his promise to meet Megan the next morn.

Tipping his head back against the wall, he closed his eyes. This night he'd held Megan Jones in his arms. She'd been a feast for his senses. Satin smooth skin the color of ivory, long limbs and lush curves—in a word, perfection. But it was her hair and eyes that truly fascinated him. Unlike the blue-eyed

Tylwyth Teg, who were either fair as sunshine or, like him, dark as night, Megan's hair and eyes were the color of rich earth.

She was everything his visits to her dreams had promised. And more. More vibrant and alive and yet just as sensual as the shadow-self he encountered in her dreams. In person, she also bore a striking physical resemblance to Margaret. He hadn't expected that, even though he'd always been aware of the familial connection between the two.

He opened his eyes and stared up at the stars.

Megan was not what mortals referred to as a reincarnation of Margaret, now long dead. But his wild alter-ego had been irrevocably drawn to her—or at least to a part of Margaret inside her that still yearned for him. From their first meeting in Megan's dreams, he'd recognized that thread of Margaret's energy running through her and realized what it meant.

Finding Megan Jones had been the promise of a second chance. One he was more than willing to gamble for, because 'twas Megan he wanted now and not Margaret.

Dead tired, Owain stumbled to his feet a smile on his face. Surprised though she'd been this eve to meet him face-to-face at The Sheep's Tail, Megan had responded to him with the same abandon she always did. There was no mistaking her hunger for him or the hope reflected in her eyes that he was as real as she.

For the brief span it took a moth's wing to flutter, he wished he had the time to court her. She deserved no less, yet he had not the days. So he'd best get himself to bed.

He would rise with the dawn. Skilled though she was, the Fairy Queen had been unable to strip him of all his powers. So, he'd use what little ability he still had to transform his abode into a place worthy of his woman. Then he'd visit the pub and collect provisions for a picnic. Thus prepared, he would set about persuading her to join him here where he would show her what they could have together.

And if all went well, she would never have to know what he was because he would have done all he could to protect her. And then he would spend the rest of his life keeping her safe.

Chapter Four

True to his word, Owain appeared on Mrs. Smith's front door step precisely at ten o'clock.

Following a dreamless—at least as far as visits from Owain were concerned—night, the unsteady flutter of her stomach the next morning robbed Megan of an appetite at breakfast. The sight of him standing in the bright morning sunlight stopped her in her tracks. He was dressed all in black, which only intensified the vivid blue of his eyes. He carried an old-fashioned picnic basket in his hand and a red plaid blanket hung over his arm.

My God, last night wasn't a dream. He is real.

She slipped past Mrs. Smith, who'd answered the door, with a quick "goodbye", and followed Owain down the short walkway. At the sidewalk, he reached out and pulled her to a stop then glanced back at the B&B.

"I do not think she approves," he said.

"Who, Mrs. Smith? Nah, she's just curious." Friendly busybody was more like it. "She was concerned because she thought I picked you up at the pub last night." Megan winked at him. "I told her we met online and I'd come over to check you out."

Instead of smiling back like a co-conspirator, Owain's intense blue eyes bore into her. She was equally aware of his warm hand wrapped around her bare arm.

"She has a right to be protective. I feel the same way."

It was an oddly tender thing to say. It also confirmed the decision she'd made earlier this morning. In the light of a new day, her euphoria over coming face-to-face with Owain last night hadn't dimmed. Prepared to look up church records and search graveyards, his invitation was an unexpected chance to realize the absurd fantasy she'd rarely admitted to about dating the man in her dreams.

"Megan?"

She looked up. "Yes?"

"You told Mrs. Smith we met online?" He sounded both puzzled and curious about her white lie.

"Yes, well." She smoothed a hand across his cotton tee. "I could hardly tell her the truth, now could I?"

But she'd finally accepted it herself. An opportunity to spend a day getting to know the real Owain seemed infinitely more important than questioning his connection to the man portrayed in the locket. She hadn't forgotten her investigation so much as postponed it, tucking the heirloom into her purse for safekeeping. She would show it to Owain after their date.

"You rented a car, right?" he asked. "Do you mind driving?"

"Um, sure. Okay."

Had he walked all the way from his farm? She'd assumed he'd driven to the B&B to pick her up, but then, if he had, wouldn't he have left the picnic supplies in his car? Then again, given the haphazard parking practices and limited spaces, maybe he'd simply been practical.

When they reached her car, she unconsciously headed straight for the passenger side, her brain still geared to North American standards. He made a production of gently steering her around to the driver's door and opening it for her. But, before she could get into the car, he pulled her close for a quick kiss. She closed her eyes against the heady infusion of his masculine scent and the hard press of his lips against hers.

A little dazed, she slid into the driver's seat and waited while he stowed the picnic basket and blanket in the back seat and settled himself in the passenger's bucket seat. She fumbled with the seatbelt, keenly aware of him watching her every move. As soon as the mechanism clicked into place, he buckled himself in and then reached over and rested his hand on her thigh. Heat immediately radiated through the thin piece of denim.

"I like what you're wearing this morning."

In a moment of girly insanity, she'd chosen a calf-length denim skirt with a crocheted belt of many colors and a crisp blue-green, short-sleeved shirt.

"Thanks," she said, unable to shift the automatic transmission into drive because his fingers were busy gathering denim. The material inched higher and higher up her leg, making it impossible for her to think left, let alone straight.

"Only it's way too long."

She had trouble suppressing the urge to laugh at his tone of exasperation. Then she had trouble finding her voice and was forced to clear her throat when his index finger traced a pattern across her kneecap.

"I think it's only fair to tell you," she said, "that I have a small problem remembering which side of the road to stay on." During her entire drive the day before, she'd silently chanted the mantra "think left."

His hand stilled. "You do?"

"I do."

"Then I'll investigate later," he said and let go.

The denim slipped into place, once again covering her leg. She wished her ragged breathing and erratic emotions were so easily smoothed over.

After repeating her mantra to make sure she exited her parking spot correctly, she followed Owain's directions easily enough. They headed north out of town. Not far past the spa, an iron-rich spring originally discovered by the Romans, he directed her to turn left into a rough lane.

"The river is on the other side of the main road, isn't it?" She might be directionally challenged on this side of the Atlantic, but the Conwy River was a pretty big landmark to misplace.

"Yes, there's a path just across the road, through the trees. You can park here and we'll walk the rest of the way."

"I can't park in the middle of the lane."

The side of the road was overgrown with waist-high grass and plants, leaving no obvious place to pull over.

"It's all right, it leads to my farm. No one else uses it."

She couldn't detect any innuendo behind this latest piece of personal information. Only that he'd offered it without her asking, which pleased her. She was here on a mission to find the real Owain and she was as hungry for details about his life as she was for the man himself.

The sun was warm on her face once they left the tree line

and set out along a grassy track toward the river. Owain carried the picnic basket and blanket in one hand. He held her hand with the other, lacing his fingers through hers. The hike was an easy one, but Megan was glad she'd worn a sensible pair of canvas runners.

She estimated it took them about half an hour to reach the river. She'd left her watch at the B&B. She wasn't on a schedule or clocking hours for a client. Today, time didn't matter.

When they reached the river, Owain chose a spot under the protective cover of a few trees and spread out the blanket. Feeling as lazy as the soft breeze that teased her hair, Megan toed off her shoes, dumped her purse beside them, and settled down on a corner of the red plaid.

"This is a lovely spot," she said gazing across the river toward the opposite bank. At this point the river widened marginally as its path curved like the upper part of an s.

"Do you think so?" Owain still stood beside the blanket, gazing out at the water. There was a peculiar tone to his voice, as if he didn't quite believe her.

"Yes, it's—" she paused, searching for the right word. "Enchanting."

Rising to her knees, she reached out and curled her fingers around his hand and pulled. He readily sat down beside her.

"Hey," she said, leaning forward to whisper in his ear. "This is the perfect spot, we're all alone."

He nodded, a smile tugging at the corner of his mouth. He reached for her and she didn't resist when he tumbled her back onto the blanket. He wrapped his arms around her to gentle the fall. His torso effectively pinned her down, but left her hands free to roam across his chest. She immediately set to work tugging the hem of his T-shirt out of the waistband of his jeans. The corner of his mouth quirked then he sat up and pulled the tee over his head, tossing it to the far side of the blanket.

"My turn," he said with a wolfish grin.

One by one the buttons on her blouse came undone. Through hooded eyes, she watched him take his sweet time. Her breath caught in her throat whenever the back of his hand brushed against her skin, which was often. He radiated heat with an astonishing intensity, something she'd never realized during their misty encounters in her dreams. Unable to resist, she reached up to explore the fine dusting of hair on his chest that arrowed down beneath the waistband of his pants. Her hand had just settled on his belt when his fingers skimmed across her belly. Ticklish, she laughed and tried to shy away.

"You need to take a few clothes off, sweetheart."

"Owain." She had no intention of denying him. It just awed her to see his tousled black hair and bronze-skinned body, attesting to his work out of doors on his farm, framed by tree branches and the blue sky beyond.

He leaned closer. "I want you, Megan. More than food. More than anything else in the world. I want you out here under the sky where the sunlight heats your skin. Where I can finally see you, touch you, not your shadow-self."

She shivered at the passion lacing his words. Shadow-self, yes, that was a good way to describe Owain when he visited her dreams. She stroked his cheek, noticing for the first time the tiny lines that bracketed his eyes. Her fingers trailed down his blunt jaw, smooth from his morning shave. Simple details she had never been aware of before, but treasured now.

Before she could answer, her stomach rumbled under his hand. A smile quirked her lips. "All right," she said. "But you still have to feed me."

"With pleasure." Yet he paused to trace the edge of lace that cupped her breast. The tip of his finger burned a trail of fire across her skin, heating her blood. She didn't need the sun. His body heat was potent enough to warm her from the inside out.

Flames still licked her skin when, in one fluid movement, he rolled away and pushed himself onto his feet. Pleasantly boneless, she watched the ripple of muscle play across his back as he walked away. Not far, only to the picnic basket, where he hunkered down and opened the lid. The black denim of his jeans hugged his lean frame, curving tight across his derrière.

She bit her lip. In a few minutes his body would be hers to touch and play with. Eagerly, she sat up and shrugged out of her shirt and unhooked her bra then unzipped her skirt and shimmied out of it. After a moment's hesitation, her panties followed. She'd just lain back on the blanket, after setting the pile of clothes beside her shoes and purse, when he turned.

He crouched, transfixed, his blue eyes glowing with unbridled longing. Despite the different venue, that shadow-self of hers he'd mentioned was too used to being bared for his perusal for her to feel embarrassed or shy. No matter what a mirror told her, in his eyes she always felt beautiful.

"Oh, sweetheart, am I going to have fun with you."

At the promise in his words, her nipples tightened and her womb clenched. She flashed him what she hoped was a saucy smile, in spite of the tremble of anticipation running through her veins.

"Does it involve food?"

Without a word, he placed a bunch of red grapes nestled in a paper napkin on the blanket by her shoulder. Then he stood and began to unbuckle his jeans.

She licked her lips, her mouth suddenly dry. It didn't seem to matter that she'd seen him naked countless times over the years. As she watched him unsnap his pants, she had the distinct feeling that the real Owain was going to prove far more potent than the most erotic dreams they'd shared. She was so attuned to his movements that she heard the rasp of the zipper as it slid down. And then, my, oh, my.

He wasn't wearing briefs or boxers. And his penis, finally free of its confines, jutted proudly out from a thatch of black hair.

Her smile turned into a wicked grin. Her hands skimmed up her ribcage and cupped her breasts, taunting him with promises of her own. She stretched lazily. Her arms over her head, her legs slightly apart, and her hips canted upward—her body on display for him.

In record time he tossed his boots toward his tee and shucked his jeans, which landed in the same haphazard pile. She laughed and reached for him as he knelt down beside her. All too easily he grabbed her wrists and within seconds her arms were pinned above her head. He simply shook his head when she squirmed in token resistance and reached for the grapes, dangling them above her mouth. The deep purply red fruit hung temptingly out of reach. She tried to lift her head.

"Hold still," he growled. "I'll feed you."

Obediently, she stopped moving and opened her mouth. It was the height of decadence to lie still and allow another person to take care of her needs. The smooth skin of a grape brushed her lips. She closed her eyes, shutting out her other senses so she could concentrate on the texture and taste of the fruit. She grabbed the grape with her teeth, loosened it from the stem and bit into the juicy pulp. A tangy sweetness erupted on her tongue. He fed her four more grapes in the same manner before the treat disappeared. Reluctantly, she opened her eyes. He'd set the fruit aside and was watching her again.

"Do you want more, sweetheart?"

She nodded. She was very hungry.

His hand fisted around his cock, which seemed to have grown longer since the last time she'd looked. He pumped his hand up and down his thick shaft. The head was as plump and purple as the fruit she'd been eating. Without a word, he straddled her.

Because he still had her arms pinned above her head, his entire body bowed over hers. His thigh muscles contracted in a loose but firm grip around her upper body, holding them both steady. His downy-soft balls scraped along the valley between her breasts as he tilted his hips forward. She ran her tongue across her lips, moistening them. She'd barely finished when the head of his penis bumped against her mouth.

She opened to him, welcoming the musky male smell and the slightly salty taste from the precome that leaked from the tiny slit. She lapped it up, searching for more.

"That's it, sweetheart." His voice was little more than a hoarse whisper.

Tracing the ridge of his glans with her tongue, she sucked another inch of his cock into her mouth. He groaned and his entire body shuddered.

"Easy, easy, sweetheart."

He was the one teasing her ever so slowly with the smell and taste of him. Didn't he remember how well he'd taught her to take his length? Impatient, she gently scraped her teeth along the rigid skin of his shaft and gained another inch for her efforts. Above her, he swore, in at least two languages. If she could, she'd smile right now. Instead she sucked greedily. An instant later he released his hold on his cock and threaded his fingers into her hair. His grip on her scalp tightened infinitesimally. It was the only signal she needed. Closing her eyes, she relaxed her throat muscles at the exact moment he shoved his cock deep inside her mouth. He grunted in satisfaction and she gave herself up to the feast.

Only four controlled, but intense, strokes later, he pulled out. His eyes sparked with a blue fire.

"Too much." His raspy breath caught on each word.

Not enough.

He ignored her silent plea, his hands releasing their hold on her wrists and hair. His legs kept her imprisoned, though, as he slid down her body to kiss her forehead. She nuzzled his neck.

"You didn't finish," she chastised him.

He chuckled. "I was just warming up."

"Could have fooled me," she muttered, but her mock annoyance was lost on him.

"I'm not finished with you yet, sweetheart."

He reached out and plucked several grapes from the stem and she eagerly opened her mouth. He ignored that request too.

"Don't move," he commanded, rising above her.

Then, one by one, he placed the small oval pieces of fruit in a row down her body, ending with a large grape nestled in her bellybutton. Seized by the barely controllable urge to laugh, she tensed. The grapes wobbled, but none of them fell off.

"That's it, sweetheart. Just relax."

Impossible. Especially when he dipped his head and his cock brushed against her mound. Her vaginal muscles tightened spasmodically. Hopefully. And then his tongue licked her breast bone and his teeth nipped her skin as he retrieved the first grape.

"Delicious," he murmured against her bare flesh.

Please. She wanted to whisper the plea, but for what she couldn't name. Goose bumps broke out across her skin and yet she was burning up. All she could see was the top of his dark head and his broad, bare back glistening against the shadow and light cast by the tree. His mouth, intent on exploration, sought and found her breast. His tongue swirled around the areola and then laved her already taut nipple.

She did not want him to stop. She did not want him to suddenly disappear without her knowing how this was going to end. Quite simply, she didn't want it to end.

Another grape disappeared into his mouth before he lavished his attention on her other breast. She wanted to arch her body so he could take more of her into his wicked mouth, but with two grapes still positioned on her stomach, she didn't dare move. And yet, if she didn't hang on to something, she was going to fly apart. A little desperately, she reached up, her fingers skimming the silky texture of his black hair. Instantly his head reared up. His eyes looked almost feral with his lust.

"Not until I'm finished with you." *Which will take a good long time.* He didn't say those words, but she heard them just the same.

"But I need—"

"You'll get your turn, sweetheart. But I've waited too long for this to back off now. Grab the blanket if you have to, just don't touch me."

He waited until she lowered her hands then bent his head to nuzzle the underside of one breast. She clutched the blanket with both hands, certain her knuckles would turn white before he was done. She tried to focus on the tree branch above their heads, but the leaves blurred together in a swatch of green. The only thing she could concentrate on, the only thing that mattered was the man now kneeling between her legs.

Anticipating her reaction, he held her legs down as he bent low and retrieved the last grape from her bellybutton. Her stomach fluttered, but the swirl and dip of his tongue hardly tickled. Besides, she was far too needy to laugh. *Just a little lower, please.*

"Sweetheart."

She blinked, ready to scream with frustration. Her breath caught in her throat when she saw one small, oval grape trapped between the thumb and forefinger of his left hand. His right hand slid up her thigh and delved into the short brown curls of her mound. She was forced to tighten her grip on the blanket when he nestled the piece of fruit securely between her folds.

Then he took his own sweet time repositioning her legs over his broad shoulders. She started panting. His hands smoothed over her stomach, effectively preventing her hips from rearing up into his face. She thought she heard the faint sound of his laughter, but couldn't be sure. All she cared about, all she wanted was for him to eat her.

He licked her folds, slick with her juices.

"Mmm, delicious," he murmured and leaned in for another taste. His tongue skimmed over the grape, pressing the fruit against her clit.

A series of tiny shockwaves rippled through her body. Her

feet pressed against his back as she sought to hang on. Then he licked again, this time pressing the grape harder against her clit. Waves swamped her, drowning her in sensation after sensation as a tsunami built within her.

Finding some hidden strength, she managed to buck against his mouth, demanding more. The edge of his teeth scraped against the delicate folds of her labia then he finally bit into the grape, sucking her clit into his mouth along with the pulpy fruit. She screamed his name as the tidal wave crashed ashore.

Her next coherent thought came as she lay snuggled alongside Owain's hard body. His erection was pressed firmly against her hip, but that wasn't what captured her attention. Except for last night, every other time they'd been together, she'd woken up before they'd reached this part. She brushed the hair on his chest and savored the quiet pleasure touching him brought her. Finally she turned her head slightly and wasn't surprised to discover him watching her. She had the sneaking suspicion he hadn't napped in the aftermath of their lovemaking.

"You can relax," she said. "I told you I wasn't going anywhere."

A gleam entered his eye and he rolled onto his back, pulling her with him. A square foil packet appeared in his hand as if by magic.

"I should hope not, sweetheart. You have work to do."

Chapter Five

Tossing her hair out of her face, Megan contemplated him and the package. He arched an eyebrow. Daring her? Or begging her? In spite of the evidence pressing against her thigh, the latter hardly seemed likely. Even in her dreams, the man had had attitude.

With a grin, she rapidly walked her fingers up his chest and snatched the packet from his hand. He might have promised she'd get her chance, but then he knew darn well she always insisted on equal time to play.

Sliding her body into place, she pushed herself into an upright position. Her still sensitive pussy glided along his rock-hard shaft, soaking it in her juices. The self-satisfied smile quickly left his face to be replaced by a feral glint of hunger. She shuddered with the need to possess him and rubbed her mound against him again. His jaw clenched and he gripped her thighs. She smiled sweetly and shoved his hands away.

"Grab the blanket if you have to," she told him.

His laugh was guttural, but he obeyed. His eyes turned the color of sapphires when she ripped the package open and slowly rolled the condom into place. Resting her hands on his shoulders, she lifted herself into position and, in one swift move, seated herself to the hilt. He hissed with pleasure.

She kept her eyes open, not wanting to miss a single nuance in the expressions that crossed his face as she rode him. Carnal desire vied with a look of reverence that shook her to the core. Sure the sex was good. Better than any they'd shared in her dreams simply because it was with a real person instead of between a pair of shadow-selves. But something else—something she could barely define—was happening to her.

And if the look on his face meant anything, to him, too.

Even though the friction teased her inner walls, she took great delight in slowly pumping his velvety-steel shaft. With each stroke her breasts ached, swinging like weighted pendulums over his face. Her hands slid off his shoulders to the blanket beneath and she bowed her body until her distended nipples were tantalizingly close to his mouth.

The muscles along his neck tightened and his shoulders tensed as he raised his head to capture a bud between his teeth. He pulled gently, sucking more of her breast into his mouth. His tongue laved the sensitive tip, sending an electrical current spiraling through her spine straight to her pussy. She cried out at the sharp intensity of sensation that bombarded her. Her strokes grew shallower and her inner muscles immediately clamped tightly around his shaft. It wasn't long before neither of them could hold back.

On her next down stroke, his hips surged upward causing the head of his cock to bump against her womb. A primal scream burst from her lips and he answered, shouting her name as he rammed into her again. He came, his body so rigid his veins stood out against his skin. Unable to hold back, her orgasm tumbled through her, violently rocking her body. Drained of strength, she collapsed on top of him and his arms caught her in a crushing embrace.

In the silence that followed, she couldn't stop shaking. Some kind of emotional dam seemed to have burst inside her. Random thoughts flitted through her brain, one question uppermost in her mind. How could she go back to her dream world now that she'd been with the real Owain?

Desires and daydreams she'd barely dared to acknowledge surfaced, leaving her feeling vulnerable. Until last night her fantasies of sharing a life with the man in her dreams had seemed impossible. Or so she'd thought.

So she wasn't entirely sorry when Owain gently pulled out of her, even if he didn't let go. She pushed herself away, rolling onto her back. The tips of his fingers touched her chin, forcing her to look his way. He bent and kissed her lightly on the mouth.

"Are you okay?" His look was guarded, even though he hadn't backed off.

She nodded, not trusting herself to speak. She was falling

hard and fast for this incredible man, but she wasn't going to complicate a simple picnic by the river with feelings so new she could hardly express them even to herself. That didn't mean she couldn't at least be honest about one thing. No matter what happened, she was very glad he hadn't faded away like a mist, lost in her dream world.

Needing to reassure herself as much as him, she reached up, pulled his head down and swept her lips across his. Her tongue brushed against the seam of his mouth and he groaned. But that didn't prevent him from ending the kiss before it really got started.

"Hold that thought, sweetheart."

Sliding his arm out from under her, he reached out and grabbed the napkin that held the remains of the grapes before turning away. She realized he was discreetly removing the condom. Another intimate detail they'd never shared as dream lovers.

She stared at the graceful contours of his back. Broad shouldered and lean, there wasn't an ounce of fat on the man. Fascinated, she reached out to touch him, only to be interrupted by her stomach rumbling with hunger. Her appetite finally seemed to have caught up with the new time zone, at least for the moment.

"I need food," she said and sat up.

He twisted his body around to gaze at her. "As my lady wishes."

His callused fingers caressed her stomach. The gesture was achingly intimate, forcefully reminding her yet again of how little time they'd actually spent together.

"There is bread and cheese in the basket."

"And a chicken leg or two or the whole bird?" she asked, hopefully.

He tensed and then slowly shook his head. "I'm a—what you call a vegetarian, Megan."

The urge to laugh overwhelmed her and she shook her head at the irony. Their relationship was in desperate need of less sex and more practical information. Like condoms, food had never been an issue during their erotic dream encounters.

"I'd tell you my favorite meal, but it might gross you out. Let's just say I tend to be a carnivore." Her stomach growled in agreement.

Mock seriousness vied with amusement. "Then you don't like bread and cheese and hardboiled eggs and tomatoes—"

She leaned in and kissed him soundly before he got carried away. "I love bread and cheese and hardboiled eggs and tomatoes and anything else edible you have in that basket. Now, please."

An hour or two hours later—time truly didn't seem important—Megan's stomach was sated and the picnic by the river over.

"I could get used to this," she said, shaking out the blanket. It scared her a little how easily. She was not an impetuous person by nature, and yet here she was in Wales with the man who haunted her dreams. "Do you know when the last time was that I took a day off, let alone a vacation?"

Owain looked up at her from where he squatted in front of the picnic basket packing up the remains of the feast he'd prepared. He'd eaten his share, but he still looked hungry. An answering shiver of awareness zigzagged down her spine.

"Last weekend?" His face was expressionless, except for the indefinable glint in his eye that said he knew his answer was wrong.

"Ha." She folded the blanket in half and half again. "I was finishing some updates for a client."

"A difficult one?"

"The client or the updates?"

He laughed, his eyes sparkling in the sunlight and she suddenly realized she was totally relaxed.

"The client's a perfectionist, but then, so am I. His updates were straightforward, and this is the first day in—"

She paused because she really couldn't remember. Working from home, her time was her own. It wasn't unusual for her to work late into the night or be up early if the mood and the ideas were flowing. Sure she booked time off for an occasional lunch with a friend and visited a gym regularly to work out, but only for a few hours and then she was back in front of her computer.

"It's been a long while." She hugged the blanket, wondering if she could make her life sound more pathetic or, well, lifeless.

He stood up, the picnic basket in one hand, his other hand outstretched toward her. "The day isn't over yet, sweetheart. Will you come back to my farm with me?"

The invitation was irresistible. She wanted—so much. Maybe too much. He'd asked her out for one date. She forced herself not to glance at her purse—at the locket tucked away inside. It was definitely too soon to intrude on the intense connection between them with practical matters. What's more, it was far too soon to talk relationship, especially given the logistics they faced because they lived on different continents. But his invitation was one thing she could take for herself.

"Ye—"

The word lodged in her throat, choking her. Behind Owain's right shoulder, a honking huge horse appeared in the field, galloping straight for her. Terror rooted her feet firmly on the ground. Then the instinct for self-preservation launched her into a wild dash toward safety which, at the moment, equaled Owain. Before she could reach him, he dropped the picnic basket and whirled to face the oncoming menace.

What does he think he's doing?

Seconds later, Megan skidded to a stop directly behind him. Bent double, she rested her hands on her thighs to steady herself. Her pulse pounded against her skin in time to the beat of the horse's hooves across the ground. She forced herself to look up and that's when she realized her fatal mistake. Her heightened state of panic had caused her brain to misread a significant visual cue. The horse hadn't been heading toward her, but him.

"Don't move."

She couldn't seem to suck in a breath of air without feeling as if she were being smothered, let alone move. Besides, he stood between her and a living vision of her worst nightmare.

"It's Heather and Peaseblossom," he continued. His tone was conversational. In fact, from where she was standing, his body appeared totally relaxed. "Heather has a thing for Will Shakespeare."

She shivered. *Is he crazy?* Apparently both of them were, because she was actually listening to his one-sided conversation. That is, while she kept both eyes firmly on the horse.

Peaseblossom—a more unlikely name for a very large, brown, four legged animal she couldn't imagine—halted inches from Owain. It snorted and bobbed its head. Megan felt the rush of air past her left cheek. Her face tingled and she clenched her hands in an effort to keep from bolting.

That kind of realism never entered her nightmares. The color of the horse was wrong, too. And there shouldn't be a rider. But a catalogue of the differences between her dream state and the present situation didn't seem to help. The resemblances—she was standing on the bank of a river facing a horse that seemed to have a mind of its own, despite the rider on its back—were too uncanny. Besides, during her nightmares she knew what was happening wasn't real.

This was, except this time she was with Owain.

"I swear," the young rider said, tightening her grip on the reins. "She's in love with you, Owain."

Then the rider laughed and Megan was certain she was hallucinating because she swore she heard the soft tinkling of bells.

"Peaseblossom never misbehaves when we meet anyone else," Heather continued.

Owain shifted his stance until he totally blocked Megan's view of the horse. The lines of his body were rigid. "What are you doing here?"

It seemed an odd thing to say, especially in anger. He reached out a hand toward the horse, but before he could touch the animal, it tossed its head and pranced a few steps backwards, directly into Megan's line of vision again. Her body jerked and she absently rubbed her arm in an attempt to warm herself up.

The rider smiled down at Owain, not sweetly as Megan half expected, but with a touch of coldness.

"You didn't think I would make this easy for you, did you?"

Damn his cousin.

No doubt the real Heather was back at her farm down the road, unaware that her horse was being ridden by a Fairy Queen bent on causing mischief. Nay, far more than mere mischief if he guessed aright. He was of a mind to call on Arawn regarding this violation of his three-day grace period. But what could the Overlord of the Fairies do? The damage had already been done.

Owain watched Rhiannon and Peaseblossom as they sedately walked away. The effort it took to ignore Megan was agonizing, but he had little choice. The charm he'd muttered when he'd finally touched the horse was simple enough, yet took every ounce of his weakened powers to sustain against his cousin's greater strength.

Rhiannon hadn't been far wrong when she said the mare was in love with him. More like Peaseblossom smelled the wild mate inside him, which only proved the Fairy Queen's powers to disguise his appearance were at most skin deep. A weakness she'd exploited in an attempt to expose him. However, once the charm had cloaked his scent, the mare had shaken her head, her keen interest in him forgotten. Her mission accomplished, his cousin had once again assumed the demure attitude of the teenager she pretended to be and waved goodbye.

When he was certain they wouldn't return, he spun on his heels to face Megan.

"That was a horse." Her words were little more than a whisper of air and she swayed on her feet.

"Yes, sweetheart."

He swung her up into his arms. Her body trembled against his. She gave a small cry as her arms circled his neck and she buried her face against his shoulder. He carried her as far as the nearest tree and then, rather awkwardly, sat down with his back against the trunk.

Megan snuggled closer and then lifted her head. Tear tracks streaked her face. "I'm afraid of horses."

"I know, sweetheart." He murmured the words and rubbed his palm in circles across her back, hoping to calm the tremors that shook her frame. He'd known for years about her fear of horses, but to witness her numbing terror only proved he'd not been wrong to bargain for his mortal looks.

"It's stupid," she said, wiping the tears away. "I've never even been near a horse in my life. This is the first one I've seen up close."

"Hush." He kissed her forehead.

"It was big, but not half as wild as the one in my nightmares."

She seemed determined to tell him about the stallion, so he gritted his teeth and listened. Eventually she stopped talking. They sat quietly together, his arms wrapped tightly around her and he stared at the river.

After residing along this stretch of the Conwy bordering Trefriw for one hundred and seventy years, Owain knew every blade of grass and every dip and turn along the banks of the river. The s-shaped bend up ahead marked the northerly limits of his domain. Perhaps that was why he'd brought Megan here today.

On an eve, he'd often stand under the trees in either of his two forms—it mattered not which—and gazed downriver imagining all the places he was forbidden to visit. No, not simply forbidden. Rhiannon's curse bound him to this spot as much as it bound him to his quasi-mortal and animal forms. The only times he'd been able to leave were when his shadow-self had been compelled to be with Megan in her dreams.

Except for those visits, his was a bleak, lonely existence. One he'd welcome an end to, for the truth was he never wanted to see the Conwy again. Given the chance, he'd willingly follow Megan anywhere she wanted to go.

He'd known her in her dreams since she was a girl. He'd spent today with the woman she'd become. In turns sharp-witted and shy, she possessed a passion for life he could only envy. The same way he admired her courage—for crossing an ocean to find him and for facing a horse, however terrified.

She stopped trembling and seemed much calmer, but he had no way of knowing what harm the Fairy Queen's appearance on a horse had had on her. Or his own hopes. In truth he was less concerned about the single day remaining to him than he was about this night.

Whenever they visited mortal lands, the Tylwyth Teg were, by nature, creatures of the night. These days mortals rarely believed in the Fairy Realm, but 'twas best to guard against discovery. Even in his quasi-mortal state, Owain had preferred to make his forays among mankind during the shadow of darkness, though necessity had led him frequently enough out into the village in the light of day. The Fairy Queen had been bold, showing her face even in disguise, this day. Which meant his usual haunts along the river and his isolated farm were too vulnerable to Rhiannon's influence, especially with the coming night.

Chapter Six

Megan Jones proved to be a stubborn wench and, the vines notwithstanding, the side of Mrs. Smith's house proved a challenge to climb. But Owain conquered the latter with very little call for his meager magic, save to preserve his neck by preventing a fall off the wall. Now he planned to conquer the former.

He stood in Megan's room, the window behind him closed and the draperies drawn. She'd turned on a desk lamp and stood watching him. Her look should be wary, given what he was thinking, but she appeared more amused by his recent athleticism. He would take her over his knee and warm her bottom, if he thought it would do some good. The idea alone stirred his cock and he took a step forward. Her gaze skittered across his form and then her eyes locked with his. In defiance? Probably. The thought heated his blood.

He'd resolved to keep her safe. To that end, he'd faced and mastered the demon automobile that purred like a cat and exhibited the self-same attitude as an independent feline. He'd ushered her into the pub and ordered her supper, only to be told at the end of the meal she was fine, thank you, and goodbye.

Not bloody likely.

"I'm staying," he said, too annoyed to soften his tone.

"All right."

Uncertain, because she agreed too easily, for the second time that day he pulled his T-shirt over his head and tossed it aside. Despite sating his appetite for her only hours before, he was fully aroused. His staff pressed painfully against the buttons of his jeans. And he swore a stream of fire pumped through his veins in place of ordinary blood.

"Owain."

Now she sounded exasperated, which couldn't be a good thing.

"In your bed," he said, in case she had any other odd notions about where he planned to sleep this night. Or what he planned to do.

"Does that mean you want me to take my clothes off?"

The question caught him mid-stride. He'd teased himself this noon with the barest hint of her soft skin by undoing each of the tiny buttons on her blouse. He'd missed the chance to uncover the rest of her beautiful body when she'd laid herself bare for him. Not that he regretted her eagerness, which had matched his own for a taste of her. But this eve neither of them was in a hurry.

"Yes, sweetheart. Take off your clothes for me."

She did, a little self-consciously. Willing and yet apparently unaware of how potent his need for her was. His heart thumped erratically against his chest as piece by piece her clothing came off, revealing the woman he knew so well underneath.

She shimmied out of her skirt, folding it and adding it to the blouse and bra she'd already piled on the edge of the desk. He loved watching her neat, economical movements, so different from his own haphazard negligence. His eyes skimmed the intriguing curves of her silhouette and his hands itched to rub the softness of her belly. He could tell from the way she hesitated, from the way her eyes darted to his flat abdomen that she perceived the slight roundness to be an imperfection.

"Sweetheart."

Her head jerked up and her hands fell away from the elastic waistband of her panties.

"Come here."

A flame warmed the brown of her eyes as she complied with his command. He circled his fingers around one of her wrists and settled her hand on his groin.

"Do you see?" he whispered, leaning forward so his erection filled her hand. "Do you see what the sight of you does to me?"

He heard the slight catch in her breath and then a roaring filled his ears as her fingers squeezed his cock. She made short work of the buttons on his jeans. Within seconds his hard length spilled into her waiting hands, for somewhere along the way she'd added the other. Wrapping her fingers around his girth, she stroked him long and hard.

By the hounds of hell. He wouldn't last if she kept that up. And yet he would die if she stopped.

She didn't stop. In desperation, he shoved his jeans to his thighs. Her laugh was warm and wrapped itself around his heart, but she obliged and cupped his aching balls. He bowed his head, burying his nose in her silky hair. A faint fruity essence teased his senses. Needing more, he reached for her. Her breasts were firm handfuls a man could play with. His thumbs circled her dusky-rose areolas, teasing the tips. She whimpered with a need of her own, her breath warm against his skin and he knew playtime was over.

He nudged her chin up and kissed her soft upon the lips. They parted beneath his, but he resisted the invitation. "Sweetheart."

She blinked up at him, her hands still firmly gripping his cock. Her tongue darted out to moisten her lips. Then the tip of one finger slid over his slit and found the drop of precome. She brought her finger to her lips and tasted him.

By the hounds of hell. He grabbed the waistband of her panties and ripped them from her body.

"Yes, please." She smiled at him, making him doubt either one of them had control of the situation.

"On the bed, sweetheart. On your hands and knees."

Flushed with excitement, she stroked his cock one last time before turning on her heels and walking over to the bed. He fumbled in his pants pocket for a foil wrapper, damning the shake in his hand. When he looked up, his jeans hit the floor.

She was on her hands and knees on the bed, all right, displaying the firm globes of her buttocks for his perusal. She rested on her forearms so her cheeks were high in the air and her legs were slightly apart, allowing him a clear view of her dewy sex.

He ripped open the packet and sheathed himself, not daring to move until he'd protected them both. A moment later he stepped forward. His hands locked around her waist and his tip nudged her slick entrance and he rejoiced. 'Twas his second night spent entirely in mortal form. And this was an almost perfect reenactment of one of the rare daydreams he'd allowed himself about being mortal and with Megan—his woman wet and ready for him and an entire night to enjoy her. Unable to hold back a second longer he slammed into her, savoring the slap of his balls against the soft flesh of her thighs. Her muscles instantly contracted around his shaft.

"So tight for me, sweetheart." And he needed to rein himself in else he'd shoot like a falling star.

Overeager, she wiggled her bottom against him, her urgent moans begging him to take her. Slowly, he rocked against her, matching the rhythm of her own thrusts, which pushed his cock deeper inside her. Soon she was panting, her pussy muscles clenching spasmodically and with each stroke his balls tightened. Neither of them would last long at this rate. 'Twas a good thing the night was young.

"That's right, sweetheart. Show me."

"Owain, please."

She sounded desperate. No more than he, but at the moment nothing would please him more than to please his lady. He slid a hand between the soft curls of her mound and found her folds, wet with her juices. He nuzzled deeper until he discovered her nub. She bucked beneath him. He held her fast, his finger circling her clit, while his cock nudged her womb.

"Show me," he whispered once more, when her body drew tighter than the string of a lute.

She cried out, the heat inside her igniting an answering blaze within him. Cream gushed from her core, coating his already slick cock. Unable to ride out the flash fire that swept through him, he reared back and thrust into her hard and fast. The walls of her pussy clenched around him, feeding sensation after sensation straight through his cock. The eroticism of the moment pushed him higher until he spurted, the jolt slamming through his entire body.

Somehow he managed to crawl onto the bed and tuck her within his embrace. Her fingers stroked his arm.

"That was perfect," she murmured and kissed his hand.

No, he thought. Perfect would be a life with Megan Jones.

Megan woke to the sound of a soft snore in her ear. A

muscled arm anchored her next to a very warm, very naked male body. It had been a good long while since she'd had a man *in* her bed instead of invading her dreams. She turned her head slightly and gazed on tousled hair and long, black eyelashes that rested against high cheekbones. Even asleep, Owain Deverell managed to look like an unrepentant bad boy.

She reached out and skimmed her fingers across his shoulder. *Mine.* The possessive thought skittered through her mind and made her wonder at the possibilities. Forty-eight hours ago she'd arrived intent on searching for explanations. She still didn't know *what* Owain Deverell's relationship was, exactly, to the man portrayed in the locket or *why* he appeared in her dreams. But, after spending the day with him, there were definite things she knew about the man sleeping beside her.

He was in turns serious and playful. A vegetarian sure of his convictions, he hadn't minded at all when she'd ordered fish and chips at the pub last night. And he was protective of her. Fiercely so, which was a nice way of saying he'd been arrogant and highhanded. He'd refused to discuss options and her arguments that she'd be fine and wasn't scared anymore had fallen on deaf ears. He'd snuck into her room at the B&B anyway.

And realistically, how could she say "no" to having the real man in her bed instead of his shadow-self visiting her in her dreams? She couldn't. She hadn't.

He'd held her all night long. Made love to her so many times she'd lost count. And in the middle of the night, she'd been very glad he was there, so she wouldn't lie staring wide-eyed at the ceiling wondering if their encounter with a horse yesterday afternoon would trigger one of her nightmares.

She shifted, intending to carefully ease out of bed without disturbing him, when his arm tightened around her imperceptibly. Immediately giving up the struggle her head sank back onto the pillow and she turned to look at him. His blue eyes blazed with undisguised heat, even though the rest of his body hadn't moved a muscle.

"Good morning, sweetheart."

He gripped the edge of the sheet and pulled it back. A shiver raced across her skin when his hand settled possessively over her exposed breast.

"Owain."

Her nipple was already taut and aching. Then his thumb rubbed across the bud, sending the ache straight to her womb. He chuckled and propped himself onto his elbow so he could look down at her.

"I see you are a wanton."

Before she could think of a suitable comeback, much less voice it, he bent his head and brushed his lips across her own. She opened to him and his teeth nipped her lower lip. A tiny whimper of need escaped from her mouth and she clutched his shoulder. She shouldn't want him this much so soon after last night. But she did and she reveled in the fact that he was here and not some fading memory from a dream.

"What is it, sweetheart?"

She blinked and looked up at him, suddenly aware that he'd stopped his seduction and was watching her.

"I was just thinking. I could get used to this."

"You mean this?" He flicked her nipple again.

She groaned and nodded.

"Or this?" He slid his palm along her ribcage and across her stomach until his fingers touched the edge of her curls.

Her grip on his shoulder tightened. "Lower."

He grinned. "Demanding wench, aren't you?"

In answer, she slid her legs apart. He bowed his head until his forehead touched the pillow beside her.

"You're already wet for me, aren't you?"

"Why don't you see for yourself?" She tilted her hips in invitation.

He drew a sharp breath at the challenge, but his fingers delved between her folds. It was her turn to gasp as he found and stroked her clit. He murmured rough words, his voice raspy with desires that stirred her blood. He scraped his teeth along her shoulder and then his tongue soothed away the sharp pain. Her hips jerked in response to the contrasting sensations, seeking more of the pleasure he promised.

"Mine," he whispered against her ear.

Then his tongue traced a warm path along her collarbone, tantalizing her skin. He didn't waste time, invading her mouth with promises, his tongue diving deep, her senses dizzy with possibilities. She clutched his shoulder like a lifeline, her thoughts little more than dancing wisps of cloud.

"Owain."

His name was a hoarse cry from her lips as he rammed two fingers inside her pussy. Her hips canted upward, so that his second stroke went deeper.

"Hold still, sweetheart."

She shook her head at his idiotic suggestion. A sweet tension was coiling itself within her and she didn't want to let go. She cried out in frustration and clamped her hand on his wrist when his fingers dared to retreat from their exquisite torture. Her vaginal muscles contracted, desperately seeking the fullness she needed to take her the distance.

After a short tussle, he pulled his wrist free and neatly pinned her arm to the bed. She kicked out her leg in exasperation. Hampered by the covers, her move lost its impact, especially when he neatly slid his leg between hers. His rock-hard thigh rubbed against her mound and she bucked.

"That's it, sweetheart."

And then his cock was there, nudging the entrance to her pussy. His body covered her, skin-on-skin, the heat merely stoking the fire burning in her veins.

"Yes—"

Her "please" was lost as his mouth clamped down on hers again and his cock drove deep inside her. Despite the preceding frenzy, his thrusts were slow and deliberate. His velvety-steel length abraded the sensitive walls of her pussy driving her wild with want. The friction spiraled tighter and tighter within her. She arched against him.

He muttered a curse and released his hold on her arm to clamp his hand on her buttock, pulling her closer against him. And then he began to pump in earnest, deep, swift strokes that ratcheted the tension and caused her pussy muscles to spasm rhythmically around his thick length. She closed her eyes, hoping to lose herself in the sensations inundating her.

"Look at *me*."

The harsh command shocked her into opening her eyes and focusing on him. His face was taut, his eyes wild like a stormy sea. Her orgasm burst upon her and she was lost, her world narrowed to the scent of her man and the texture of his skin. Owain buried his head in the curve of her shoulder, her name a sharp cry on his lips. When he came, his body shuddered under the force of his own passion.

She turned her head and kissed his sweat-soaked skin. "That was quite a good morning."

Owain lifted his head, shifted his weight off her and grinned. "Do you think the neighbors heard?"

A wave of heat that had nothing to do with recent activities washed up her neck and face. *Oh lord.* She closed her eyes as she recalled just how vocal she'd been the night before. Owain kissed her eyelids.

Refusing to open her eyes, she shook her head. "We can't leave the room. Ever."

He chuckled. "I like the sound of that, do you mean it?"

She shook her head and opened her eyes. "We have to get out of here, right now."

"I was teasing, sweetheart. No one heard us."

He sounded very sure and she glared at him suspiciously.

"How do you know? And forget it. Even if you're right and no one heard us, this is a B&B. We have no supplies and we can't even go to the bathroom without leaving the room."

He frowned, but his eyes were full of laughter. "Serious problems indeed. I have a solution."

"It better not involve climbing walls."

"It involves going to my farm. Interested?"

Unable to stop herself, she reached up and caressed his face. "Very interested. But it still better not involve climbing walls."

"Then I suggest you go to the bathroom," he said, neatly avoiding her concern. "I need to pick up a few supplies. I'll meet you at my farm in—"

"Half an hour."

He bent his head and kissed her. "You are definitely a wanton, Megan Jones. Half an hour, then."

She put on her robe, grabbed her toiletries bag and a change of clothes. But when she reached the door she paused and looked back. Her heart thudded in quiet joy at the sight of him lounging in the bed.

"See you soon, sweetheart," he said with a lazy smile.

"Okay. Just don't let Mrs. Smith see you leave."

Owain was gone by the time she slipped back into her room fifteen minutes later showered and dressed. The rumpled sheets were a dead giveaway, though, that he'd been there. She resisted the urge to rush to the window and check the wall. Instead, she quickly made the bed and tidied the rest of the room, impatient to be gone. A pang of guilt assailed her, though, at the sight of her laptop lying neglected inside its case on the desk. She had yet to check her email for return messages from her parents.

Considering how often she'd commented that her computer was her lifeline to the world, it was amazing how little she missed being connected. Grinning, she grabbed her purse and headed out the door and down the stairs. The tantalizing smell of fresh baking wafted past her, reminding her she hadn't eaten yet.

"There you are, dear."

Megan swiveled around at the bottom of the stairs and came face-to-face with Mrs. Smith coming down the hall and groaned inwardly. Here she'd told Owain to be careful and she'd been the one to get caught. She murmured a return greeting and edged toward the front door.

"We missed you at breakfast, so I thought you might like a cup of tea before you go out."

She wouldn't, but when she saw the steaming cup and saucer in Mrs. Smith's hand, she knew she couldn't refuse. "Thank you, that sounds lovely."

"Right in here, dear," Mrs. Smith said and led the way into a cozy sitting area set aside for guests that she'd been shown during her brief tour the day she'd arrived. Since it was so late in the morning, Megan had the room to herself.

Having set the cup and saucer on a low, round table, Mrs. Smith left with a friendly nod. Megan sat on the edge of one of the easy chairs and stared at the cup of tea and the wedge of lemon tucked on the saucer. She might as well drink it. Ignoring the lemon, she picked up the teacup only to pause as Mrs. Smith laughed and the soft, tinkling sound of bells floated in from the hallway. Then she heard the creak of the kitchen door and the gruff voice of Mrs. Smith's English-born husband and the clatter of pans.

Shaking her head, she sipped her tea and glanced at the assortment of tourist pamphlets and Welsh heritage books that filled a nearby wire rack. Thus far she hadn't seen much of Trefriw, let alone Wales. She grinned. But she had seen a great deal of Owain Deverell.

Her gaze flicked over a booklet on the history of the Conwy valley, one on Welsh place names and one on the red dragon, the national symbol of Wales, when her breath caught in her throat. A wild-looking black stallion stared out at her from the cover of a book about Welsh folklore. The teacup rattled when she set it down on the saucer, but she hardly noticed. Lithesome, winged fairies and other imaginary folk adorned the cover too, but it was the stallion, with its mane flowing in the wind, that made her heart thud painfully against her chest.

Reaching out blindly for some support, she gripped the edge of the table and sank to her knees on the carpet. And stared, mesmerized by the sight of the horse that haunted her nightmares glaring back at her from something as mundane as a cover of a book. She reached out her hand, only to stop inches away. A picture of a horse couldn't hurt her, not that her dream one ever had. It had simply terrified her as a child and continued to haunt her.

She grabbed the slim volume off the rack and turned to the Table of Contents before she could talk herself out of investigating. There was a long, alphabetical list of folk legends. Right near the bottom, she found what she was looking for—the water horse.

She reread the information three times before she scrambled to her feet. Ignoring the unfinished cup of tea, she remembered to grab her purse and ran back up the stairs to her room and her computer.

Instead of checking her email, she logged onto the internet and did a search on the water horse folktale. Found throughout the United Kingdom under different names, the most familiar one being the Scottish Kelpie, there were many variations to the legend, but the basic facts were the same. Considered a malevolent water spirit, it was a shapeshifter who alternately appeared as a wild horse or a young man of about twenty-five. In horse form it lured unwary travelers to mount it and then it would plunge deep into the water, drowning its victims.

"I'm afraid of horses."

"I know, sweetheart."

"I'm afraid of horses."

"I know, sweetheart."

"I'm afraid of horses."

"I know, sweetheart."

"I've only ever been able to visit you in your dreams."

Megan slammed down the lid of the laptop and shoved her chair away from the desk.

No.

No way.

What she was thinking was certifiable, crazy. In a word, ludicrous. The fantastic creatures that inhabited fairy tales were mythical. Weren't they?

But, try as she might, once she remembered Owain's response when she'd told him about her fear of horses, she couldn't get it out of her mind. Or the confession he'd made the first night they'd met in the pub.

"I know, sweetheart. I've only ever been able to visit you in your dreams."

Put side by side with what she'd just read—

No.

No way. And yet she couldn't ignore the evidence or her dreams.

Snatching the folktale book off the desk, she stuffed it into the largest pouch in her purse and headed back out the door, determined to confront Owain and get some answers.

Chapter Seven

Megan was halfway along the main road heading north, when she realized she hadn't chanted her mantra, yet had ended up driving on the left. Sobered by the thought that she hadn't given a second thought to what she was doing, she slowed the car to a more sedate pace.

She rolled her shoulders a little, trying to ease the tension in them. She stifled a yawn, shook her head to clear it and concentrated on the road ahead. Operating on automatic pilot, her mind played and replayed every word she and Owain had exchanged since they'd met. In her usual, practical way, she hoped to remember some bit of conversation where she'd mentioned her nightmares before the horse had intruded on their picnic. Rationally there had to be some logical explanation for how he'd known, but the only one that made any sense, and no sense at all, was totally fantastic.

A few minutes later she passed the spa. No other vehicles were driving along the road in either direction, so she slowed the car to a crawl so she wouldn't miss the turnoff. She found it and followed the lane around a winding curve a fair distance before she spotted the farm up ahead.

A low wall enclosed the property, but the gate was open for her. She drove in and parked the car out of the way along the side of what appeared to be a shed. Cursing the effects of jet lag, she yawned again. Before she could open her door and get out of the car, Owain stepped out of the house. Resolutely, she grabbed her purse, shut the car door, and headed toward him.

He'd changed. He was now dressed in a fresh pair of jeans and a shirt, tails hanging out and only half buttoned, but the sleeves were rolled up, revealing the dusting of hair on his forearms. He looked downright delicious and totally human.

"Hello, sweetheart."

She ignored the hint of bare skin peeking through the placket of his shirt, his welcoming smile that held a blatant invitation in it, and the greeting. When she got close enough he held out his arms, as if anticipating she'd step into them for a hug. Hesitating mid-step she detoured around him and marched into his house.

Actually, to call it a house was to flatter it. From all appearances it was a Spartan, two-room cottage. A solitary, brownish-beige couch was tucked into one corner of the room. A rectangular table and a couple of chairs stood against the opposite wall. A familiar-looking picnic basket sat on the table next to an oil lamp.

She glanced over to where the kitchen should be. A single counter ran the length of the short wall with cupboards beneath. She couldn't detect a single electric appliance, let alone running water. Neat, clean, and utilitarian in the extreme, the room was further evidence that only confirmed, rather than denied her bizarre theory.

The door creaked behind her, warning her that Owain had followed her into the room. Clutching the straps of her purse a little tighter, she walked over to the table. She put the purse down, but didn't let go. A sudden wave of fatigue washed over her and she clutched the edge of the table. The rational side of her brain wondered, fleetingly, if she was about to make a fool of herself, but she had not come all this way to wimp out. She forced herself to stand a little straighter. Opening one of the zippered pouches on her purse, she pulled out the locket. She was fairly certain she should have produced it and asked her questions the first time she'd seen Owain at the pub.

Whirling to face him, she ignored the frown forming across his brow and reached out for the edge of the table again to prevent any temptation she might have to move closer. Holding out the locket she pressed the catch releasing the lid to reveal the portrait inside. Her hand shook, but she ignored that too.

"Is this a picture of you?" she asked.

Her question stopped him in his tracks. She watched his face very carefully, but it remained maddeningly impassive.

"Where did you get that locket?"

His question, in lieu of an answer, sank like a stone in her stomach. He might just as well have admitted he recognized it.

"Answer the question." She thrust the locket forward. "Is this a picture of you?"

"Megan." He ran his fingers through the longer locks of hair on the top of his head. The feral glint in his eye suggested it would be wise for her to drop the subject.

She didn't.

"Yes," he finally admitted, trapping her with his gaze, which had turned a cold arctic blue. "That locket—"

"Belonged to my Aunt Margaret who lived in the early eighteen hundreds. Care to explain how your picture got into a locket that's about one hundred and seventy years old and how you knew about this?" Releasing her grip on the table, she reached behind her and pulled the Welsh folklore book from her bag and held it up.

"Know about what, the Fairy Realm?" There was a hard edge to his deceptively casual tone.

"The horse. The black stallion that haunts my nightmares the same way you haunt my dreams."

"Visit. I visit you in your dreams."

She pushed herself away from the table and flung the book at his arrogant face. Lifting his arm, he easily deflected the paperback, which fell onto the floor by his feet.

"That depends, doesn't it?" she asked, forcing herself not to finger the heavy gold chain to which the locket was attached. "On who—or should I say what—you come as."

"Megan, don't." His voice was low and deadly with a hint of discomfort.

She gulped in a breath of air amazed at how far she'd pushed him already. Wondered how far she could push him for the truth before he pushed back. Wondered if she would even believe the truth, should she drag it out of him.

"Don't what? Don't wonder how it's possible that you were alive one hundred and seventy years ago and yet you don't look a day over twenty-five. Don't put two and two together and realize that you do haunt both my dreams and my nightmares. Which, according to the book and the articles on the net, makes you a malevolent water spirit who drowns—"

He lunged so fast, she barely saw him move. When he reached her, he swung her around and shoved her against the wall.

"Stop it, damn you."

His fingers slid through her hair, holding her fast seconds before his mouth descended onto hers. The kiss was brutally hard, but she welcomed the roughness, opening to him when he stabbed his tongue inside her mouth. He smelled of fresh male and tasted of sin. No matter how they came, his touch, his kisses, the taste of him were so much better than anything they shared in her dreams.

When they broke apart he kept his arms on either side of her face, penning her in. Okay, he'd pushed back. Instead of feeling pleased, she was scared. Scared about what she might learn, but now more afraid of not pursuing the answers she'd traveled across the Atlantic to discover.

"I do not drown people." He sounded belligerent.

Oh my God. She pressed her back against the wall and prayed her wobbly legs would hold her up. Not even daring to blink, she held his stare. He'd all but admitted—

"What do you do, then?"

His body trembled so close to her own, she felt the fear coating his skin. He closed his eyes.

"I am compelled to carry them to the Fairy Realm."

Oh my God. She swallowed and wished her heart wouldn't act as if she were running in a marathon. Loosening her grip on the wood-plank wall, she lifted one hand and lightly settled it over his heart. He flinched and his eyes opened, but she refused to pull back.

"Then it's true. You're a—"

Without warning he grabbed her arms and pulled her hard against him. The heat of his body seared through her thin blouse.

"Stop it, damn you," he yelled. He shook her, as if he intended to knock some sense into her. "Don't you understand? I'm trying to protect you."

Aside from rattling her brain, at the moment he seemed intent on intimidating her. She yanked her arms out of his grasp. He released her immediately and clenched his hands, giving her time to step back. Trapped between him and the wall, she didn't get far. His revelations made her more determined than ever to face the truth and she jabbed a finger into his ribs.

"Protect me. Protect me from what? You? You didn't even have the guts to tell me the truth about who you are."

He swore in crude if intelligible English and raked his hands through his hair.

"What truth, Megan?" His voice was savage and she had to force herself not to flinch or shy away. "That I'm seven hundred years old. That I'm a banished member of the Tylwyth Teg—what you mortals would call the 'fair folk'."

He looked up at her, a bleakness clouding his eyes. "That I'll regret to the end of my existence that the first time we met when you were but five years old, I terrified you. I couldn't risk you finding out what I am."

Megan's heart hammered in her chest. Mere mortal women such as her didn't generally believe in seven-hundred-year-old mythical beings who assumed the form of a gorgeous man. She glanced up at his hair. It didn't appear seaweedy—a dead giveaway, according to the folklore that a young man was really a shapeshifting water horse. But then, as he'd already established, the lore wasn't always accurate. Besides, did she really need more proof? Mere mortal women didn't generally have the dreams she'd lived with nearly all her life.

"So you lied to me instead."

His eyes had turned a flinty blue and he waved his hand in the air. "You lied to Mrs. Smith about how we met."

The air around her seemed to thicken and she felt stifled in the small space. Why was he fighting her—because she'd learned the truth?

"That's not the same thing at all. I made up a plausible story to pacify a nosy stranger. I would never lie to the man I—"

Before she said too much, she shoved him away and ran into the middle of the room. Furiously, she gulped in a load of air and blinked back the tears threatening the corners of her eyes. Pressing the heel of her hand against her eye, she dried the sheen that clouded her vision. She was not going to let him see her cry.

Except her vision didn't entirely clear and the adrenaline that had been pumping through her since his admission, whooshed out of her. Overwhelmed by fatigue, she staggered forward. Strong hands caught her and pulled her to safety against a sturdy body.

"Owain."

"Megan, sweetheart, what's wrong?"

It felt really, really good to lean against him.

"I don't know, I... It must be jet lag. I feel so tired." She closed her eyes.

"Megan. Sweetheart."

Owain was shaking her again. She blinked and looked up at him and smiled.

"Seven hundred years, huh. No wonder you're so arrogant."

He scowled at her. "Megan, listen to me. Did something happen after I left Mrs. Smith's house this morning?"

"Highhanded too. You thought you were so smart keeping your secret, but you're not."

"Think, woman. Did something happen?"

Why was he so concerned about what had happened to her? She'd discovered his secret.

"Ummm..." she frowned and tried to concentrate, "...I found the book. The one I threw at you. While I was drinking tea. Mrs. Smith insisted. On the tea, not the book." She smiled up at him. "I found that all on my own."

Without warning, he scooped her into his arms.

"Damn Rhiannon for interfering."

Her frown deepened as she tried to puzzle out what he'd said. "Who's Rhiannon?"

He started carrying her somewhere.

"The Fairy Queen who saw fit to curse me for loving a mortal woman. 'Twas her that tried to frighten you with the horse yesterday. I believe she drugged your tea."

She tried to shake her head. Mrs. Smith had given her the tea. When she couldn't, she jabbed him with her finger again. "Do you know why I believe you're a hundred-and-seventy-year-old horse?"

"Why, sweetheart?" He sounded tender, not angry.

"Because of my dreams," she announced triumphantly.

He lay her down on what she assumed was his bed. When he pulled away, she grabbed the front of his shirt. Warmth from his body seeped through her hand and up her arm straight to her head, clearing it a little. Still, she yawned. God, she was tired.

"Don't you see? It's a relief to know why the stallion keeps appearing in my dreams. To know it's you."

"*Sweetheart.*"

At the sound of Owain's voice calling to her, Megan surfaced out of a thick, black fog. She blinked, not immediately recognizing her surroundings. She appeared to be standing in some sort of wood. She looked around, totally lost. Where was she?

"*The farm is over yonder.*"

She whirled around to see Owain standing in front of a tree, pointing to his right. With a cry, she ran to him. He caught her in a fierce embrace. Only she discovered rather quickly how insubstantial Owain's shadow-self was. She felt his arms around her, but none of the warmth or the strength she'd come to crave.

"*'Tis all right. We are safe enough here, sweetheart.*"

She buried her face in his shirt, but his scent was so faint she could hardly catch it. Not the way she had back at his farm. She looked up at him. This didn't feel right.

"*Where's here, Owain?*"

"*In one of your dreams, sweetheart.*"

Wildly, she tried to pull away. "*No! I don't want to see you here. I want you.*"

He let her struggle against him for a moment and then he pulled her close to him once again.

"*Hush. Let me hold you. I haven't much time.*"

His hand made circles around her back. She melted against him, her arms stealing around his waist. There was so little of him to hold on to.

"*I hate my dreams. They're not enough.*" *Not nearly enough.*

"*Hush, sweetheart. I know. Let me make you feel better.*"

In an instant their clothing disappeared. Even the sensation of his bare skin against hers lacked the intensity of the real man. Who wasn't a man but some sort of mythical creature.

"*Don't worry about that now, Megan.*"

His hands continued to gently massage her back, lulling her into a sense of peace, however fragile. Amazingly, she relaxed and slowly the heat built between them. A case of simple friction despite the insubstantial nature of their shadow forms. The sensations were achingly familiar and for a moment she could almost believe they'd only ever known each other this way and that the reality had been the dream.

He lowered her to the soft green carpet of grass and she welcomed him inside of her. A faint sensation of warmth stole through her, but it wasn't enough to truly heat her heart. Her vaginal muscles tightened around him and he groaned. The sound was soft and low yet carried none of the fierce passion she'd come to expect.

And then it was over before it had really begun. Ephemeral desire spent like the wind going out of a sail. She buried her face against his shoulder seeking what little comfort she could.

He tilted her head back and settled his mouth on hers. Now that she'd felt and tasted the real thing, this kiss was flat. She wanted to wake up so she could experience zings zagging down her spine when the real Owain kissed her.

She looked up at him.

"Always remember, sweetheart. I love you."

Chapter Eight

Megan woke slowly, hardly aware of her surroundings until she rolled over and a shaft of sunlight slashed across her face. Squinting, she adjusted her position and looked around her. She was in a bedroom that defined basic—it contained the bed she was laying on, a chair near the door, and a wardrobe. There were no window treatments on the single window, which explained why the sun could stream in.

Given what she'd seen of the rest of his house, this must be Owain's bedroom. Without Owain in it. In fact the entire house felt quiet, which didn't make sense because she'd been arguing with him only moments before. Except the bedroom window faced west and she had definitely arrived at the farm before noon, so it must be much later than she thought.

She glanced down at her left wrist, only to realize she'd never put on her watch. How had she lost so much time? Her memory of her confrontation with Owain was vivid right up until the end. That's when things started to get fuzzy because she'd been so tired.

No. That wasn't right, either. But she couldn't exactly remember why.

Then, Megan remembered her dream. In which, it seemed to her, Owain had been saying goodbye.

She scrambled into a sitting position. She was still fully dressed. Owain hadn't even taken off her shoes. She called out his name.

Silence.

She shifted to the edge of the bed and realized she was still clutching the locket in her hand. Her thumb traced the etching on the lid. What had happened between Margaret and Owain that they'd lost each other? Whatever it was, she couldn't be too sorry because her dreams and the locket had led her straight to a man she'd grown to care about deeply. Meeting him again in her dream had only proven to her how much she wanted him in her life. Slipping the necklace over her head, she tucked the locket under her blouse and stood up.

Rather rumpled from sleeping in her clothes, she straightened her outfit and finger-combed her hair before leaving the bedroom. At first the room had the same stark appearance she remembered from earlier. Until she realized that the walls, the floor and the roof were all in disrepair. Anxiety knotted her gut and she hurried outside. The roof on the shed had fallen in and huge chunks of the wall that surrounded the property were missing. Seeing the dilapidated state of Owain's property, her sense of urgency grew.

What had happened between the time of her arrival and now to effect such a drastic change? The sun sank lower behind the trees, casting long shadows across the farm. She'd been asleep for most of the day and Owain was gone.

A bad feeling punched a hole in Megan's gut. She had to find him. But where?

She walked to the gate, which was hanging by a hinge and stared down the lane toward the river. The river. She broke into a dead run, barely stopping to check for traffic before dashing across the road and into the trees beyond. While she worked out regularly, she wasn't a runner. By the time she reached the field, she was forced to slow to a jog. The shadows around her lengthened and her stomach clenched from dread.

The fresh air and exercise were clearing her brain and she didn't like what she was remembering. Uppermost was the fact that Owain had told her that the Fairy Queen had cursed him. In every fairy tale she'd ever read, curses were very bad things.

Up ahead she saw the trees where they'd had their picnic lunch the day before. Had it only been yesterday? And then, there was Owain, standing with his back to her, gazing out at the river. She put on a burst of speed.

"Owain."

He turned. His eyes widened in surprise, but he didn't smile in welcome. She came to a stop just past the trees and bent double to catch her breath. She kept her eyes on him, though.

"What did you mean when you said you were cursed?"

"You were right," he said. "I am arrogant. I'm sorry I lied to you, Megan."

"You're also pretty lousy at answering direct questions. I want to know about the curse." She had not come this far looking for answers not to get them now.

Instead of responding, he pulled his shirt over his head and tossed it onto the grass. Despite the fact that the last two times he'd done exactly the same thing, they'd ended up making love, from the somber look on his face, she somehow doubted that was his intent this time.

"It doesn't matter now, sweetheart." He toed off his boots and began to unbutton his pants.

What was he doing stripping naked? She wasn't going to ask. This time she was going to stay focused on her goal.

"If it didn't matter you wouldn't have appeared in my dream just so you could tell me you love me."

That stopped him, for about half a second, and then he shucked his pants.

"You should go now," he said.

Considering his usual take charge attitude, he was being far too calm and remote.

She fell onto her knees on the grass. "Just when it's getting interesting?"

She'd pushed earlier and forced some answers from him. Maybe the same technique would work again.

At his side, his hands curled into fists. "Megan, please. I haven't done a good job up to now, but I do want to—"

"Protect me? Good, then you can start by telling me about the cur—"

Oh my God!

As the final rays of sunlight disappeared behind them, Owain's body shimmered. The edges of his skin blurred and refocused like a pulsing beacon. He stood rigid, a grimace of pain etched across his face. With each new surge, the air around him grew brighter and his body grew more and more indistinct. And then his limbs started lengthening, his entire body realigning itself with the new, four-footed shape emerging from what had once been a human form. Even his hair grew longer, forming a mane.

Within the space of a few minutes, Owain the man had transformed into a black stallion with a brilliant white blaze between his eyes. Intellectually, she'd convinced herself she believed he was a creature out of myth because it made sense within the context of her dream world. Instead of dreaming about a stallion and a lover, she'd been dreaming about the same person who'd assumed two different forms.

But it was a whole other part of her brain that had nothing to do with intellect or common sense that had to cope with and process what she'd just seen happen. What she was looking at—the wild stallion of her nightmares, except that he stood rather docilely gazing at the grass as though contemplating his next meal.

"You're beautiful," she said, not at all sure whether the horse could understand what she said.

The horse—Owain, shook his head.

Megan scrambled to her feet. The horse backed away.

She glanced around her. If the horse was here, that meant the Conwy must be the same river as the one in her dreams, only she hadn't recognized it because she and the horse met at a different spot.

"This is the Fairy Queen's curse, isn't it?" she asked. "That some of the time you have to exist as a horse."

The horse nodded and then shook its head.

Stupid horse. What did yes, no mean?

Well, yes had to mean the Fairy Queen since... She paused. Owain had called the Fairy Queen Rhiannon and had said she'd interfered. She'd purposely ridden the horse Peaseblossom to scare Megan and then she'd drugged Megan's tea.

Megan reached up and circled her hand around the locket. As Mrs. Smith, the Fairy Queen had also led her straight to the folklore on water horses. At every turn she'd tried to expose Owain's secret. So why had she drugged Megan's tea?

The bad feeling inside Megan got worse.

In every fairy tale she'd ever read, there was a way to break the curse.

The solution had to hinge on the fact that the Fairy Queen had cursed Owain for loving a mortal woman. In her groggy state, she'd assumed he'd meant he'd been turned into a water horse because he loved Margaret. But, while that might be true, in her dream he'd told Megan he loved her. She was a mortal woman and now Owain was a horse.

And the Fairy Queen had drugged her tea so that time would run out.

With that realization, Megan knew she'd blown it.

From the moment she'd seen Owain sitting in the pub, she'd been offered a once in a lifetime chance. And what had she done? She'd squandered it.

She'd convinced herself he was his own ancestor. She'd postponed showing him the locket and asking her questions. She'd reveled in spending time with him, thinking she had all the time in the world. Worst of all, while she'd been confronting Owain about hiding his true identity from her, she'd kept her own big, fat secret locked inside her heart.

She was in love with Owain Deverell. And she didn't give a damn who or what he was. Who he was was totally irrelevant to what kind of person or entity he was. Or the fact that he loved her.

But she hadn't once spoken the words and now it was too late.

She looked at the horse—at Owain.

Or was it too late?

Did a curse count if the Fairy Queen stacked the odds in her favor?

Surely there had to be some sort of rules governing curses and how they could be broken. Unfortunately, Megan could think of only one way to find out. She had to confront the Fairy Queen. And in order to do that she had to mount a honking, huge black stallion because then he would be compelled to take her to the Fairy Realm.

Slowly, cautiously, Megan walked toward the horse. With each step, she silently chanted the mantra, "This is Owain. This is Owain."

The horse watched her.

The closer she came, the more unnerved she became. It was one thing to tell herself that the horse was Owain and therefore wouldn't hurt her. Not that the wild stallion had ever hurt her. It was quite another to overcome a lifetime of equinophobia in a few brief minutes.

She stopped short of the horse. Its nostrils flared, but it didn't retreat.

Sensible, practical Megan Jones did not talk to horses or plan trips to alleged mythical kingdoms. Only she hadn't imagined the last three days. And love was definitely not a rational emotion. People did crazy things for love all the time.

"I don't want an argument. I don't want some highhanded excuse that you can't because you need to protect me. I need to mount you. I need you to take me to the Fairy Realm."

The horse blinked and then bent its forelegs until his body was low enough to the ground that she could climb on.

The longer she waited the worse it would be. The more she talked to herself, the easier it would be to talk herself out of what she had to do. And she had to do this otherwise the Fairy Queen would win.

Ordering her mind to shut up, she walked over to the horse.

It wasn't easy climbing on. Twice she slipped off its back until she discovered that if she gripped the sides of the horse with her legs she could retain her position. Her palms were sweaty from nerves, making it difficult to hang on to the horse's neck. And while she knew it was Owain, bent low over its back her arms wrapped as far as they could around its neck, the horse smelled of horse.

She shut her eyes tightly and swallowed the bile that rose from her rebellious stomach when the horse stood up. She did not want to see how far off the ground she was. Or see the horse walking toward the river—she could feel the ungainly sway of its body under her, thank you. And she especially did not want to see the water close around her, cutting off her precious supply of oxygen. All she had to do was to hang on and trust Owain.

The jolt as the horse landed on some hard surface and the sound of its clattering hooves jarred Megan out of her misery. It also loosened her tenuous grip on the animal under her and with a sharp cry she fell off, landing in an ignominious heap on the said hard surface.

She blinked and then blinked again at the sight of the silver tiled floor beneath her, the gold columns holding up the roof where walls should be and the silver, gold, and jewel-toned furnishings that adorned the massive room. An incessant buzzing sound, like that of insects investigating flowers on a lazy summer day caught her attention.

She looked up and into the faces of lithesome blue-eyed, blonde and black-haired fairies, almost identical to the ones shown on the cover of the book. Their fluttering wings were making the humming noise. To a fairy, they were dressed in see-through garments that appeared to be woven from silver, gold, and jewel-colored threads. They were also staring at her with wide-eyed curiosity. Or perhaps they were looking at the horse. She could sense him standing like a wall at her back.

Megan scrambled to her feet, feeling decidedly frumpy and fat. At least, through some bit of magic, she wasn't soaking wet.

"Welcome, mortal, to the court of the Tylwyth Teg."

Chapter Nine

At the sound of the lilting voice, Megan turned and came face-to-face with the Fairy Queen.

Wearing a silver-colored midi-sheath, a gold-toned ankle-length coat and calf-length silver-white boots, Rhiannon, Queen of the Fairies, looked like a refugee from a nineteen sixties go-go club. Of course the diamond-encrusted diadem atop her waist-length, gold hair did add a regal note to the outfit.

Megan nodded, not wanting to seem discourteous, but not exactly in a friendly mood. She also stepped closer to the horse, deciding it was best to make her alliance clear up front.

The Fairy Queen arched one pencil-thin eyebrow and smiled with seeming graciousness. "A bargain was struck. It cannot be renegotiated."

Rhiannon, it seemed, didn't believe in beating around the bush. Megan glanced at the horse who, surprise, surprise, was watching her. Its big, blue eyes reminded her sharply of Owain and they seemed to say, "Go for it." She supposed she might as well. Neither of them had anything to lose.

"You cheated. I demand a rematch."

Gasps and titters of shock broke out among the fairy ranks. Even the Queen stiffened, the smile leaving her face to be replaced by a hardened glint. Megan reached out and rested her hand on the horse's flank. Maybe a little back-up protection wouldn't be such a bad idea right about now seeing as how she'd just challenged a magical being who had a lot more power than she did. The horse snorted and shook its head—in warning.

Fairy folk scattered in all directions as a huge burst of red and black smoke billowed up from the floor. Except for the colors, it reminded Megan of the appearance of the Wicked Witch of the West in *The Wizard of Oz*—hardly an auspicious thought. The smoke dissipated rapidly leaving a very tall man who was way better looking than the Wicked Witch standing in its place. Elegantly dressed in black boots and breeches and a white shirt open to the navel, his silver hair tied back in a queue, he could have stepped off the cover of an historical romance.

"Who has issued the challenge?" The boom of the man's deep baritone reverberated throughout the room.

"I have." Megan hoped she sounded more confident than she felt at the moment. Obviously her choice of language had summoned this guy. As the only mortal in the room she was beginning to wonder if she was seriously outranked.

"What is the basis for this challenge?"

Once again his voice was loud enough to be heard by everyone and Megan understood, although she'd only been in the Fairy Realm for no more than ten minutes—and really *believed* in it for twenty—that she'd gotten herself involved in something very serious. Recalling Owain's phraseology, this time she modified her word choice.

"The Fairy Queen interfered in Owain's attempt to break his curse."

At her words the silver-haired man turned his gaze on her. She was a little unnerved to find herself staring into milky-whiteness.

"Do I have your permission to probe your mind to ascertain the truth of this charge?"

Her fingers dug into horseflesh but she nodded her agreement. It didn't even cross her mind that a man with his obvious magical powers couldn't see. All she felt was a swift, sharp pain between her eyes and then the sensation was gone.

He bowed his head slightly, as if in thanks. "You speak the truth."

His gaze now turned to Rhiannon. For a woman who'd been caught cheating, she didn't look too worried.

"The bargain is renegotiated," he said in a voice that sent a shiver up Megan's spine.

At his pronouncement many of the fairies retreated even further into the corners of the room. The Fairy Queen, however, stood her ground and gave him a curt nod, a small smile playing across her lips.

His focus swung back toward her. "Do you agree?"

Megan thought he was talking to her again but then the horse whinnied. Apparently satisfied the man lifted his hand and, seemingly out of thin air, a large hourglass appeared.

"Once you have crossed the threshold of your house, Owain, you will revert to your true form. You have 'til dawn."

"Wait," Megan cried out when he started to lift his hand. "We have until dawn to do what, exactly?"

The silver-haired man actually smiled and tilted his head, silently acknowledging her choice of pronoun. "To break the curse, of course."

Swiftly, no doubt so she wouldn't interrupt him again, he swept his hand in a circle. Megan swore she didn't move. That everyone else in the room and the room itself grew smaller, until she and the horse appeared on a street in front of a cottage. Unlike the court, this building actually had walls and a front door all made of wood, and what she took for glass in the windows. The house itself sat on a small lawn that was surrounded by trees. In fact they seemed to be in a forest. It was a scene straight from many a fairy tale.

Megan tried not to think of the implications as she walked behind the horse up a stone-paved walkway to the front door. The door opened of its own accord. The horse hesitated briefly and then clopped across the threshold. Megan followed her eyes on Owain.

The instant the horse's tail flicked past the doorframe a familiar glow shimmered around it. Megan watched in fascination as the four-legged animal transformed into the two-legged variety, but with a difference. While this creature retained the overall musculature that characterized the Owain she knew, a pair of butterfly-like wings sprouted and unfurled from his back and the top of his ears ended in points. And, naturally, he was naked.

Even though he'd told her he was a member of the Tylwyth Teg, Megan had somehow expected the horse to turn into the Owain she'd met three days ago at the pub. Instead she realized she was finally seeing the real Owain, free of disguises.

Awed she stepped forward. His wings fluttered a bit and she had the impression he was testing them. This close she could see the membranes projecting from his spine covered by a layer of gossamer-like scales, white with black tips. Tentatively she reached out and ever so lightly stroked. They were soft to the touch. His wing twitched and she instantly drew back.

"Does it hurt when I touch them?"

He didn't turn around and it took him some time to answer. "No. It's just been a while."

Since he'd had wings, he meant and Megan realized how strange this must seem to him too. As he hadn't objected she reached out again and lightly traced the membranous edge of one wing. He seemed to find that stimulating because his feathers rippled under her touch and he bit back a groan. Intrigued she continued to touch and explore, slowly making her way around his body until she faced him.

He was a truly beautiful, imposing creature. Unlike the fairies she'd seen at court, his skin was almost the color of burnished gold, which she took to be the effects of his long exposure to the sun. His hair was still an unruly black and his eyes were the same intense blue. They held her gaze steadily, waiting.

Reaching up on tiptoe she kissed the edge of his jaw. His exhale sounded rough and a smile courted her lips. She moved to his collarbone and kissed it. By the time her lips brushed against his nipple it was diamond hard. She licked. A sweet taste exploded on her tongue, promising a delicious treat if she cared for more.

She definitely wanted more. When she looked up Owain's eyes blazed with hunger and an odd wariness as if he thought she might stop.

She didn't stop.

She cupped his erection, eliciting another harsh groan from his lips.

"I have magical powers of my own," she whispered. "See what the sight of me does to you."

His laugh was guttural and he bent his head and nuzzled her hair. Much as she wanted to kiss him, she wanted something else more. Kneeling on the floor, she cupped his scrotum with her free hand and gently massaged it while her other hand pumped his steel-hard shaft. His hands clenched and unclenched beside his body and his wings slowly beat in time with each of her strokes. Finally, when she could wait no longer, she bent her head and took him into her mouth. A spurt of precome coated her tongue and she drank the sweet treat greedily.

She sank down on him, gently scraping the edge of her teeth along the sensitive veins in his shaft until he cried out. Vaguely she heard a flutter nearby and then the tip of one wing stroked her shoulder, sending a tremor of longing through her. His sac tightened in her hand, signaling his impending release. He thrust his hips forward, begging her to take him as deep as possible. She obliged as best she could, conscious of both of his wings enfolded around her head. His shaft pulsed inside her mouth and he shouted her name as his come shot down her throat.

She'd barely pulled back when she found herself being lifted off the floor and shoved against a wall. A hard mouth covered hers. She opened to the thrust of his tongue and shared the taste of him. Far from being sated, his penis was still erect and pressed firmly against her abdomen. Her naked abdomen. Somewhere between the wall and the floor her clothes had vanished. She couldn't help but laugh at his over-eagerness.

He broke the kiss as abruptly as he'd initiated it and his hand slid down her body to cover her stomach.

"May I?" His eyes searched hers, seeking permission.

For what, she wasn't sure, but she nodded. Heat immediately radiated from his palm warming her.

"It's not your time, sweetheart."

Time for— "Oh, you mean I won't get pregnant if we don't use a condom."

He nodded, but still didn't make his move.

My God, the man's protective streak was something else. And at that moment, Megan realized that wasn't a bad thing at all. Her fingertips caressed his face and she kissed him lightly on the lips.

"Then I guess we don't use a condom."

Hitching her leg over his hip, he rammed into her with the force of a man possessed. His thrusts were wickedly slow, his thick cock teasing the sensitive walls of her pussy until she thought she'd die from pleasure. This time the sensations were strong, vibrant—very real. He murmured hot words in her ear and she crooned his name over and over again.

Colored lights burst in front of her eyes and her body

answered as her orgasm overtook her. He stiffened and his wings flared out, arching high above them. He brushed his cheek against hers and his harsh breath fanned her ear. His burnished skin glowed a little brighter and at that instant his hot seed flooded her womb.

"Owain." She brushed her hands across the shoulders she'd been clinging to only moments earlier.

He lifted his head. Tears tracked down his face. "I'm so sorry, Megan. You shouldn't have had to face Arawn alone."

"I wasn't alone," she whispered. "You were with me."

Shifting his position, he lifted her into his arms and carried her over to a green and blue jewel-toned futon covered in pillows of different hues that reminded her of her bedroom at home. Within seconds she lay snuggled on his lap, her head resting against his broad shoulder. His wings were wrapped protectively around them, cocooning them from the rest of the world.

"I take it Arawn is an important guy," she said.

Owain nodded. "He is the Overlord of the Fairy Realms and the King of the Underworld. 'Twill be his word that decides our fate."

"I've already decided. I'm only sorry I didn't tell you I love you sooner."

Fresh tears spilled down his cheeks. "I knew. I knew even before you proved it by facing down a horse and Rhiannon."

"She didn't look too worried about being caught cheating."

"No doubt because she achieved her aim. Though she agreed to the bargain, she did not approve of my hiding my identity from you."

Megan sat up a little straighter. "Do you think that's why she interfered?"

"'Twould be her way, though for good or ill I cannot say. Nor do I care." He reached up and lifted up the locket that still hung by its chain around her neck. "I need to tell you about Margaret, though, so you understand why I struck the bargain I did."

"All right."

"She was fair and charming and caught my eye the minute I spied her walking by the river's edge one spring afternoon. Her hands held her skirt above her ankles because she thought no one was around to see her." He smiled at the memory and then, rather absently, he reached up and fingered a length of Megan's hair. "You share the same color of hair, though she wore hers in a knot atop her head."

"What happened?" Megan prompted.

"'Tis not an offense among the Tylwyth Teg to pursue a mortal for a dalliance, but I have never been interested in playing those kinds of games. The mortal realm has always fascinated me and I think it poor sport to treat its people so poorly."

"Very high minded of you," Megan said with a smile.

Owain gave her a stern look. "I pursued her. Courted her. In short I set out to win her. And yes, before you ask, she did know what I was, though I rarely appeared before her in this form. I declared myself—"

He stopped speaking abruptly. His thumb, she noticed, rubbed against the etching on the locket lid.

"Did she turn you down?"

He refocused his gaze on her. "In a manner of speaking. You see, in order to claim her as mine she would have had to come and live in this realm. She refused. And, being the arrogant man I am—" He paused again and quirked his lips. "I refused to give Margaret up and presented her with this token."

"She wore it for the rest of her life. It and the little bit that's known about Margaret's side of the story have been passed down through the women in my mother's family for generations."

"Thank you," he said and released his hold on the locket.

"You really loved her that much?" She was curious—not jealous—she told herself. He'd been cursed because he'd refused to give Margaret up.

His wings flared and he gave her a sharp look. "I love you. I want to spend my life with you."

She stilled at his declaration. Those three little words carried a lot of meaning, but they also meant compromise.

"I love you too," she said. "And I came here to fight for you. But I...Owain, I can't live here. For one thing I don't think there's much call for website designers."

"Hush, sweetheart." He silenced her with a finger on her lips. "I have not explained this well. I believed I loved Margaret, but I realize now my emotions were shallow. Love is not uncommon among the Tylwyth Teg, but it usually takes a long time to find. Centuries.

"I did not love Margaret as I should, as she deserved, for she should not have spent her life alone. I do not expect you to give up the life you've built for yourself."

"Then how—"

"I'll live in the mortal realm with you."

"What, but how?" She shook her head. He was being absurd. Fanciful. There was no guarantee the curse could be broken and even if it could by living with her he'd be breaking the rules all over again. It wasn't fair. And whenever life wasn't fair she invariably went on the defensive.

"You'd need a job. I'm not supporting you."

He frowned, deeply. "I do not need your support, woman. I have a job."

He tilted his head and whispered in her ear. Her eyes widened in shock.

"You're the perfectionist client?" Who was also a very successful author of young adult fantasy books.

"How do you think I knew you were coming to Trefriw to find me?"

Inevitably dawn came—much swifter than Owain would have liked, accompanied by Megan's stubborn streak. 'Twas a certainty life would never be dull with her.

After his confession they had talked little. Fortunately, their bodies had had no trouble speaking volumes and they'd passed the hours well.

It still awed him what Megan had done, who she'd faced all because she loved him. He'd chosen well when he'd gambled his life on her and his only regret was that he'd squandered a bargain when there'd been no need.

She had trusted him far more than he'd trusted her. She'd shown that trust when she'd ordered him to take her to the Fairy Realm and then faced Rhiannon and Arawn. Whereas, even at the end, he'd tried to protect her when they'd faced each other on the bank of the river. He was, most assuredly, the fool

Rhys had called him. He'd struck the bargain to protect his heart. Afraid another woman would hurt him as much as Margaret had the afternoon she'd told him she wouldn't leave her family, her friends, and her life for him.

When the Fairy Queen had cast her curse upon him he'd considered it poetic justice. Neither realm had wanted him for himself so he had been content to shun them both. Until he'd found Megan.

He held out his hand. "It is time, sweetheart."

"And I told you. I'm not meeting the Overlord, or whatever you call him, dressed like this."

"You look fair beautiful."

He'd dressed her in a sheath of brown jewel-tones that shimmered and caught the light in her eyes, making them sparkle. 'Twas his opinion she'd never looked better and since he'd never have another chance to see her in the garb of the Tylwyth Teg, he'd indulged his fancy. His own leggings were black and he hadn't failed to notice her admiration.

"I look ridiculous. I want my clothes back."

'Twas a definite certainty life would never be dull with her. He waved his hand and gave her her clothes back.

Still mumbling, she put her hand in his and together they walked to the front door of his house. He hesitated before commanding it to open, uncertain what form he would take when he crossed over the threshold. He did not want to be a horse again for however long he might live.

Arawn stood in front of the door. This day the Overlord's eyes were black, rather than the opaque cloud of a seer. 'Twas a sign he came to pass a judgment that all had best heed. Beside Owain, Megan gasped and her grip tightened on his hand. He squeezed back attempting to reassure her, but the truth was his own heart pounded against his ribs and a band tightened painfully around his chest.

Ignoring him Arawn turned to Megan. "You are unwilling to remain in our realm."

The words were more statement than question, but Owain doubted Megan would notice the difference.

"I...I..." Megan tried to pull her hand away, but Owain hung on. "Yes." Her shoulders slumped in defeat and she refused to look at him.

Arawn lifted his right hand. "Then you no longer belong

here. I will return you to your time and the place where you left."

Knowing full well that Megan would not let the Overlord's words pass without an argument, Owain stepped forward, blocking her view. Arawn crossed his arms and stood there waiting. For him.

Now that the moment was upon him, Owain didn't hesitate. He was the one who'd been cursed. Not Margaret, though she had suffered for his foolishness and not Megan. Each woman had made her choice—difficult though that choice had been—to remain in the mortal realm. Despite, or maybe because of, their love, they'd also been honest with him.

Last night Megan's declaration of love might have ended his dual existence. But, for the curse to truly be broken, he had to make a choice. For once he had to be honest—with Megan and with himself.

"I will go with her," he said.

The Overlord's face remained impassive. "You would go as a mortal, full, never to be a member of the Tylwyth Teg again."

"No," Megan shouted from behind him. "Owain you can't—"

He rounded on his stubborn sweetheart. "I can and I will. Did I not tell you I would live in the mortal realm with you?"

She nodded, her eyes still wide with shock at his announcement.

"I love you, Megan Jones. What is all of this—" he swept his hand to encompass the room, "—if I cannot share my life with you?"

Owain swore he heard a gruff laugh behind him and the words "So be it," but in the end he couldn't be sure. He was too busy fighting a raging current that tumbled him left and right. He'd long since lost hold of Megan and his worry over her made him fight all the harder. But 'twas useless for the current battered against him all the more.

And then it was over as swiftly as it had started and he fell, headlong, onto the grassy bank of the Conwy. He knew immediately that was where he was because he spied the trees, his pile of clothes, and the curve in the river's bend.

As a water horse his journeys between the mortal and fairy realms had been swift and sure. He lifted a hand and gazed on it. He felt no power coursing through his veins simply the none-too-steady beat of his heart. He pushed himself to a sitting position and saw Megan lying beside him. Her eyes were open and she was watching him. He rolled, covering her with his body and kissed her soundly on the lips.

"I am a mortal."

Her eyes shone with tears, telling him she knew what he was really saying. The enchantment was over—he no longer had to live in her dreams. She reached up and brushed her hand through his hair.

"You are also naked, again," she said, attempting to hide the start of a smile.

"Get used to it, sweetheart."

About the Author

Award winning author Robie Madison loves visiting mystical places and learning about other cultures and people. She's spent several years living abroad, allowing her to study human nature in a variety of settings and circumstances. These years also included a few wild exploits of her own. Multi-published, she uses her knowledge to enhance her stories. When not traveling or planning her next trip, Robie creates characters that can do the adventuring for her. She can also be found teaching writing courses online.

Please visit Robie Madison at www.robiemadison.com or send her an email at robiemadison@rogers.com.

Serengeti Heat

Vivi Andrews

Dedication

For Kristan Andrews, aunt extraordinaire, who keeps me in a never-ending supply of books during my starving artist phase. Thank you for sharing your love of romance with me.

Chapter One

Ava Minor was looking for trouble and, from the look of the Bar Nothing, trouble was exactly what she was going to get.

She stood alone in the dusty parking lot of the rundown honky-tonk, listening to the gravel spray as the taxi driver who'd dumped her there took his slimy leer and his smelly cab off to greener pastures. She'd asked to be taken to the most notorious pick-up bar in town. Now she stood in the parking lot, paralyzed by an attack of be-careful-what-you-wish-for jitters. Ava Minor, the cowardly lioness.

Friday night. Even in this rural backwater, the bar would be filled with human men on a Friday night. Men who wouldn't see the smallest, weakest lioness of her pride when they looked at her. They'd see a petite, sexy woman whose grace was just a little too feline, but they'd never suspect she was anything more than human.

More than human. That's what she wanted to be tonight. For once more than human, instead of *less* than all the other shifters in her pride. Less strong. Less fast. Less worthy.

Now or never.

Ava tossed her head, flipping her long, white-blonde hair over her shoulder. Her hair brushed her bare shoulder blades, teasing at her sensitized skin. Anticipation ran through her like electricity, charging every more-than-human sense.

She wasn't in the habit of making dramatic entrances, but when the heavy door slammed shut behind her and every alcohol-blurred gaze in the place rolled over her in blatant assessment, Ava struck a pose, planting a hand on one hip and arching her back.

The heat and smell hit her simultaneously. Clearly

ventilation was not a top priority in the establishment she'd selected for her first foray into the dark side. The stench of stale beer and sweat assaulted her nostrils, but beneath it all, almost completely masked by the eau-du-honky-tonk, was a subtle, tantalizingly masculine aroma that had her shivering in her high heels in spite of the smothering heat. Her inner lioness rolled over and purred.

Ava smoothed her hands over the denim hugging her hips. She resisted the urge to cross her arms in front of her bare stomach or tug at her shirt. She didn't know if she would have tugged it up or down; the crimson tube top stretched tight over her breasts didn't have much room for maneuvering in either direction.

Her audience appeared to appreciate her costume. Not a single gaze had veered away from her since the door slammed shut behind her.

A drink, she thought, eyeing the sparsely populated stools lined up against the chipped imitation mahogany bar. A beer or twelve would calm her jumpy nerves.

Ava strutted toward the bar, swiveling her hips in what she hoped was a decent parody of Marilyn Monroe. She felt the weight of a dozen pairs of eyes tracking her as she crossed the room, but being the timid good girl was too deeply ingrained and she couldn't bring herself to look around to bask in the attention. She kept her eyes locked on her destination, hoping her nerves came across as haughty sex appeal.

The man at the end of the bar leered at her as she approached. A regular Romeo with three missing teeth. Ava kept walking, ignoring the kissy noise he made in the direction of her ass as she passed.

Three empty stools down, Bachelor Number Two gave her a thorough once over from her tits to her toes and back again before making it all the way up to her face and giving her a lazy, you-know-you-want-it smile. It wasn't a bad smile. Cocky as all hell, but Ava was used to cocky men. She could handle this asshole. And he had all his teeth. *We have a winner, ladies and gentlemen.*

Ava hitched herself up onto the barstool next to her lucky bachelor—the man didn't know how lucky he was about to get. She resisted the urge to yank on her shirt when her Casanova's eyes locked on her braless breasts to enjoy the show as she bounced up onto the stool.

"Buy a girl a drink?"

Casanova's eyes dilated until they were all pupil and Ava smiled, her confidence getting a healthy boost. She may be a good girl, but that didn't mean she didn't have a voice like a phone sex operator. Smoky, husky and low, her voice was one of the many reasons her overbearing brothers insisted she remain silent as often as possible around the other men at the ranch.

But she wasn't on the ranch now...

Casanova waved the bartender over, never taking his eyes off her. "What's your name, darlin'?"

He had a smooth Texas drawl and Ava's back arched a little at the sound of it. The idea of hauling him outside and having her way with him was starting to gain momentum in her mind. She could do this. She could really be the bad girl for a change.

"Ava. Yours?"

She didn't care what his name was one little bit. Her nerves felt electrified, like she was a car someone was trying to hotwire. When the bartender plunked a beer in front of her, Ava sprang off the stool. She leaned against the chipped wood of the bar like a life raft as she downed half the bottle in one long swallow.

"Chance."

Chance? Oh, right. His name. Yippee. Ava took another drink. Her hips pushed back of their own according, sticking her ass out, almost as if her body expected the mate it craved to rip off her jeans and shove into her from behind at any second.

Ava slammed the beer back onto the bar. The alcohol was *not* helping.

She tossed her hair again and, again, the slide against her sweat-slick skin had her shivering. Hopefully, Chance wasn't looking for a long heart-to-heart before she climbed on top of him and took what she needed. She didn't think she could wait much longer.

"So..." Chance drawled, clearly intent on starting a conversation she didn't want to have.

Ava wondered how he would react if she put her tongue down his throat. He'd probably stop talking pretty damn quick.

She started to turn toward her lucky cowboy, when a distinctive scent hit her nostrils, dark and hot, like midnight on the savannah. Her body reacted to the presence behind her with a rush of moisture between her legs even before her mind registered he was there. A heavy hand landed on the back of her neck, not shaking her by the scruff like the errant child he probably thought she was, but pressing warm and steady and firm into her flesh like he could brand her with his palm.

Landon.

Ava didn't need to look to know who would be standing behind her, no doubt glaring at her and her Cowboy Casanova equally. She'd never reacted to another man the way she did to Landon King, simultaneously melting and tensing.

She pressed her thighs together to hold back the flood of heat, praying he wouldn't smell her arousal, but knowing he would. Why did it have to be him? Anyone else would have been preferable. She would have rather been caught shaking her ass at strangers by one of her over-protective brothers than the man who loomed behind her, the Alpha of her damn pride.

She'd been so careful to stay clear of him. So careful to ensure he would never know of her stupid infatuation, the mindless lust he inspired in her. Landon would never want her, that much was a given, so she preserved her dignity by making sure he would never know how badly she wanted him. Now all of that effort was about to go up in smoke. He stood less than three feet behind her. He was just as much of an animal as she was. He would be able to smell it on her. He would *know*.

Unless she could convince him that the thick heat of her desire wasn't for him.

Ava's eyes locked desperately on her Cowboy Casanova as he frowned up at the big blond god who had come to fetch her home.

"Can I help you with something, mister?"

"Sure you can," Landon growled. "You can get lost."

His growl hit her in the base of her spine, streaking upward, arching her back. She nearly came at just the sound of his voice. *Yeah, way to be calm, Ava.*

The Cowboy Casanova glanced at Ava, but she was too busy trying to get a hold of her lust to send him covert signals with her eyes. She wasn't even sure what signal she would have sent. If he ran off and left her alone with Landon, well, then she was alone with Landon. But if Casanova didn't vamoose, Landon sounded like he would happily remove the cowboy's arms from his body, and Ava was afraid he just might do it.

The Alpha of her pride ripping the arms off a cowboy in a local watering hole had lynch mob written all over it. She needed to get Landon out of here before his temper exploded.

"I don't think I can do that, friend," the cowboy said, making "friend" sound a lot like "asshole". He straightened, rising off his stool. He was a tall man, but Landon still had a few inches on him. And probably fifty pounds of solid muscle. The cowboy was lean. Landon was a tank. In any form.

"You don't look like her daddy and she ain't wearing a wedding ring, so until this little lady asks me to go, I'm staying right where I am."

Landon growled. Her Alpha still hadn't moved into her line of sight, but she could feel his unnatural body heat radiating against her back. She didn't have to look at him to know he was spoiling for a fight. In her experience alphas of both genders tended to be stupidly aggressive and *the* Alpha was worse than most. Of course, as one of the smallest betas in the pride, aggression of any sort was stupidity itself for Ava.

It was past time to diffuse the situation.

"I think you should go, Chance," she said.

Landon's hand tightened fractionally on the back of her neck before easing and stroking downward. *Was he actually petting her?* A tremor rippled down Ava's spine. She knew it was too much to ask that he not suspect what had caused it.

Chance eyed her. And the hand gripping the back of her neck. "Now, see," the cowboy drawled, "I'm not sure I can just walk away without some sort of assurance that the little lady is okay. You aren't scared of this bully, are you, Ava?"

Ava blinked in surprise. Either Chance still thought he had a shot of getting laid tonight, or he was a better man than she had given him credit for after his tits-to-toes inspection.

"I'm fine," she assured him. "Landon would never hurt me." He was sworn to protect her and the rest of his pride, but Chance didn't need to know that. Nor did she think it was wise to point out that if Landon decided to hurt her, there was nothing Chance could do about it. In a knock-down-drag-out, Chance wouldn't last five minutes against five-foot-nothing Ava, let alone the hulking Alpha.

"You sure, darlin'?"

Landon made a noise that had never come out of a human

throat, snarling wordlessly. He dropped his hand from her neck and took a threatening step toward Chance. His chest brushed against her shoulder and the contact jolted her. Ava looked down, fighting for control of her body, and saw his hand crooked into a claw, his fingernails extending and retracting, sharpening into claws and then flattening into healthy human nubs.

Landon was *way* too close to losing control completely.

"She's *sure*," he growled.

Ava turned toward Landon, putting her back against the bar, and raised her face to him. As always, the sight of him hit her low in her stomach, a blow to her equilibrium.

Tall and broad, every inch tanned and muscled, he could have stepped right off the set of a gladiator movie, thrown on a black knit shirt and jeans and wandered into the bar. A man so large should never seem graceful, but there was a sense of the feline in Landon, even in his human form. He kept his hair short enough that it just fell over his brow, but the mix of dark golds and browns still called to mind the heavy mane of an African lion. And his eyes, Ava always wondered how they could be mistaken for human. A bright feline gold with the slightest sheen of green, those eyes always seemed to see so much more than they should, piercing right through her.

"Landon," she said, her voice even smokier than usual. "Let's just go."

She reached across him to put her hand on his arm, so that her own arm stretched like a bar between him and his cowboy prey. Her arm wouldn't stop him, but she was counting on it to act as a psychological barrier more than a physical one. She gently squeezed his biceps and those green-golden eyes shifted away from Chance to lock on her.

Ava bit her lip. She'd never been so close to him before and the way he was looking at her...it was a miracle she didn't combust on the spot. But then his eyes flicked from Chance to her and back again, the martial gleam in them brightening.

"Landon," she said his name again, lowering her voice to little more than a purr. She shifted toward him. They weren't separated by much, so it didn't take much to press her front against his. His eyes slammed down on her, Chance forgotten. She had all of his attention now.

Now all she had to do was convince the big bad kitty that

he didn't want to kill the man who had threatened his territory.

Ava rubbed her body against his, a gesture that was more familiar in her other form, but she hoped would have a similarly calming effect. Her intention wasn't sexual. Social touching to soothe one another was common among the lions of the pride, but when Ava rubbed her cheek against his shoulder and tipped her face to scent his neck, she felt anything but soothed. Desire coursed through her in a shuddering wave, pooling in her stomach and releasing a flood of moisture and heat between her legs.

Landon inhaled sharply and coughed, a hard ridge against her stomach marking his body's reaction to her arousal. Ava knew better than to think his erection had anything to do with her personally. Any lion male scenting a female's lust would react the same way.

He closed one arm around her, pinning her to his front. "I'm taking you home." She felt more than heard his words vibrating through his chest.

Chance, wisely, didn't protest further as Landon ushered Ava out of the bar. Stepping out into the oppressive heat of the summer night, Ava scanned the parking lot until she saw Landon's jeep, starting toward it without being told. She'd caught a taxi to the bar, thinking her brothers would be less likely to track her down if they couldn't use the LoJack that was in all the ranch vehicles, but her carefully laid plan evidently hadn't slowed them down much.

"They sent you after me, didn't they?" Ava snapped, as Landon hustled her across the parking lot with an unyielding grip on her upper arm.

"Honey, no one sends me to do anything," he snarled. "I'm the boss."

An illicit thrill shot through her.

He'd come for her. Landon King, Alpha of the Three Rocks Pride, had come after lowly little beta Ava Minor. Which meant he actually knew who she was. Which meant she *wasn't* completely invisible to him.

It may not be a declaration of love, but life was looking a hell of a lot brighter than it had a few minutes ago.

"I was already in the bar when you showed up. A fact which you would have noticed if you hadn't been so busy shaking your ass at anything that would stand still long enough."

And, just like that, life was a dark and depressing place once again.

Of course he hadn't come for her. Why would he? As far as he was concerned, she barely even existed.

And as for her brothers...they probably hadn't even noticed she was gone. No one was out scouring the night for unimportant Ava Minor. Her little rebellion had been crushed without so much as a kiss from a stranger to make her feel like a woman.

Was that so much to ask? To feel different for a change? For once not the weakest member of the pride. For once not a protected little sister, a helpless little girl, a lioness so small she was never even included in the hunts. Tonight, for once in her life, she was going to be more. But it hadn't worked out that way. It never worked out that way.

Ava had never felt more invisible.

Chapter Two

Landon opened the driver's side door of the jeep and tossed her across the stick shift into the passenger seat. He'd all but thrown her into the car, but she didn't make a single sound of complaint. She curled into the far seat, more cat than woman, and he jumped in after her, slamming the door harder than necessary and barking, "Seatbelt."

What the hell had she been thinking walking into a place like that dressed the way she was? Acting like everything she had was up for grabs. Smelling like...*fuck*. The scent of her from half a room away had his cock standing up for duty. Sitting in the cab, the air around them smelled heavily of her. It was scrambling his brain. That was his only excuse for the fact that he had nearly shifted in the middle of the bar—in *public*—just for the satisfaction of ripping out that cowboy's innards.

Landon revved the engine to life and slammed it into gear. Gravel sprayed up, pinging against nearby cars, as he tore out of the parking lot. She clutched at the doorframe as he took the corner too fast. The jeep rocked, the left-side wheels nearly lifting off the ground, but instead of easing up, Landon's foot slammed down on the accelerator. Tires screeched and jolted as they found purchase on the asphalt of the county road and the jeep shot forward like a rocket, passing eighty miles per hour as the abused engine screamed.

She didn't make a sound.

Landon was still spoiling for a fight, his blood up higher than it had ever been outside of the challenge circle. His claws kept springing out, his usual, rigid control of the animal inside him beyond him in his current state. His body wanted to shift and go to battle, not to hunt but to fight for his territory, protect his pride. He needed the violence. And barring that, he needed to snarl at someone, verbally rip into someone until his claws no longer itched to fillet the cowboy who had stood too close to her.

Beside him in the passenger seat, Ava's calm mocked him. A silent challenge.

"What the *fuck* were you doing?"

She started at his tone, instinctively shying against the door. Her fear, subtle though it was, only served to enrage him further. Then she spoke and her words disabused him of the notion that she was afraid of him.

"I don't have to explain myself to you," she snapped, her voice brittle as she stared straight ahead out the window.

"Think again, sweetheart. As far as you're concerned, I'm judge, jury and executioner. So start talking."

She shifted against the door again and Landon took a deep breath, thinking to reassure himself that there was no tang of fear in her scent, but instead his head was swamped by a rush of heat. His hands tightened convulsively on the steering wheel. There was no fear in her scent. Only lust, thick and heady. He'd thought it would diminish once he got her away from her cowboy toy, but the close proximity inside the jeep made her scent even stronger. He was drowning in it. And hard enough to pound spikes.

"You're not talking..." he growled, the promise of a threat creeping into his voice.

"I could declare myself a nomad," she said defiantly. "Then you wouldn't have any rights over me."

Landon laughed sharply, incapable of actual humor in his current state, but bitterly amused. "Shall I call your brothers or would you rather tell them you've decided to go off the reservation yourself?"

She hissed a curse under her breath.

"I don't hear an explanation, Ava."

She turned to him sharply, blinking in surprise. "You know my name?"

"Of course I know your name," he snapped, made defensive by the fact that he *wouldn't* have known it if the cowboy hadn't said it in front of him. He'd known she was one of his pride by the scent of her and a vague sense of familiarity, but twenty minutes ago he wouldn't have known her from Eve among the lionesses in his pride.

He'd only known to dangle her brothers over her as a threat because he'd heard those brothers, four of his most effective enforcers, talking about their kid sister more than once. "Little Ava" was nothing like her hulking brothers. She was tiny, almost frail for a lioness. She couldn't possibly be fully grown, could she? Though in that outfit, she looked plenty grown-up.

"Your brothers are going to have kittens when they see you dressed like that."

"I just wanted to have a good time. Is that against the law?"

"Yes." The answer shot out of his mouth before his brain caught up. Technically, fun was not illegal either among the humans or the pride, but Landon would happily fabricate a law if it kept her ass out of that bar for the rest of her natural life.

She snorted, unimpressed by his heavy-handed answer. "My, my. Aren't we king of the double standard?" she purred, the sarcasm coating her words like molasses. "And what were you doing at such a notorious meat market, my liege?"

Landon hissed, spinning the wheel to take the turn onto the ranch road and nearly throwing the jeep into the ditch in the process. He got a little yelp of surprise out of her this time, but she quickly contained herself, silent and stoic as the jeep bounced painfully along the rutted dirt track.

She was right. He had gone to the Bar Nothing to find a nice, malleable human piece of ass and get laid. Ever since he'd won the challenge to take over the Alpha position in the pride three months ago, every lioness on the ranch had been waving her tail under his nose, angling to get her paws on the position of his mate. The female he picked would lead the Hunt. She would rule the pack in his absence and preside over the other females. She would be the strongest, the fastest. The best genetic material to pass on to his cubs.

He knew he needed to pick soon. The pride was unstable without an Alpha female in place as his mate. But he wasn't ready to choose just yet. He and his sister had been nomads before he had challenged for control of the Three Rocks Pride. He didn't know the pack and its social undercurrents as well as he needed to before he elevated one of the lionesses to be his mate.

He'd slept with a few of them—he was a cat, after all, and there was only so much teasing he could take—but he'd been careful not to lead any of them to believe that their efforts in his bed had pushed them to the front of the line for his consort. Tonight, he'd just wanted to relax. A simple, easy romp with a woman who didn't have political gain on her mind. Just sex. No obeisance to the big strong Alpha, and no machinations to become his queen.

Ava had shot his plans for the evening straight to hell.

"No response?" the assassin in question purred acidly. "Afraid you'll have to apologize for dragging me out of there?"

"I'm not the one who's going to be sorry if you don't stop baiting me, little girl."

She didn't back down from the threat. Her body angled toward him on the seat and she snarled, "If you can go out looking for a piece of ass whenever you feel like it, then so can I."

Landon slammed his foot down on the brake pedal. The jeep fishtailed and the brakes shrieked, bouncing and jolting them to a sudden stop. He cut the engine and crawled across the stick shift, caging her between his arms and the door. He loomed over her, his animal nature lapping up the flash of wariness in her pale gray eyes.

"Did you honestly think some human would be able to satisfy you?" he growled low, pressing in on her with his heat.

Her eyes widened, the expression in them suddenly raw and vulnerable, exposed.

"You should have just come to me if you needed to be fucked."

Anger burned away the vulnerability in her eyes. "Fuck you, you arrogant prick."

Landon laughed darkly. "All you had to do was ask."

Chapter Three

He slammed his mouth down on hers, ready to force her lips apart, but she opened for him willingly, hungrily. He jerked her hips across the seat toward him and her legs fell open. Landon fitted his hips into the invitation of her wide spread thighs and ground his aching cock against her clit, the friction making them both growl.

He plunged his tongue into her mouth, driven by lust and lust-fogged purpose. He needed to intimidate her into retracting, apologizing, *something*. The drive to make her submit was overpowering, but not as strong as his other motive. He would make her forget the puny human. He would drive every other man from her thoughts, banishing them with his body, claiming her wholly as his own.

Ava arched beneath him, her small hands fisting in his shirt and ripping it cleanly down the center. She hummed her pleasure into his mouth and her back bowed again, rubbing her breasts against his now-naked chest, her nipples hard little points through the thin fabric of her top. Landon yanked her shirt down to her waist and took one perfectly formed breast in his hand.

She was small, so much smaller than the other lionesses, but her breast filled his hand perfectly, the hard nub of the nipple teasing at his palm as he plumped the warm flesh. When he lightly pinched her nipple, she broke away from his mouth with a hiss, her hips pressing up, grinding against him mindlessly.

Landon gently scraped teeth too sharp to be human down the side of her neck, nibbling down across her chest and drawing the peak of one small breast into his mouth, careful not to pierce her soft skin. Ava moaned, her hands tangling in his hair, gripping so tight it hurt, but he didn't spare a thought for the slight pain. His attention remained fixed on her delicate, perfectly formed body, laid out before him like a feast.

He sucked and licked at one breast, the wet warmth and sandpaper roughness of his tongue wringing short piercing cries from her lips and spasmodic thrusts of her hips against his. He turned his attention to her other breast, to begin the process all over again. Her cries became his name and something in the tone of her voice cranked up the dial on his need for her. His control became a memory.

Landon growled, his claws tearing at her jeans. He needed her naked. *Now.* But though the denim shredded, it didn't melt away and the tattered ribbons of her clothing still bound her. She made an alarmed noise in her throat and Landon's head snapped up to meet her eyes. He was too desperate to be ashamed of his frenzy, but he managed to grunt, "Did I hurt you?"

Ava blinked at him, her clear gray eyes fogged over with want. "No...yes..." She shook her head as if trying to clear it and reached out a hand to him, almost as if she would stroke his face, but instead she ran a fingernail across his nipple. "You startled me."

Landon blinked at her uncomprehendingly. There was not enough blood flowing to his brain to work out what she wanted him to do. "Stop?"

She laughed and his cock jumped like a puppet on a string. "No. *More.*"

Thank you, God. Crying defeat for the moment on the wreck he'd made of her jeans, Landon attacked the fastenings on his own. He struggled with them, his hands refusing to stay in full-human form long enough to work the button fly.

Ava brushed his hands away. "Let me." The backs of her fingers rubbing against his shaft as she slowly, carefully worked the buttons was a new kind of torture in itself. Landon braced his hands on the seat and closed his eyes, determined to let her work and not fall on her like a ravening beast until she had freed his cock. *Then* he could be an animal. He just had to hang onto humanity for a few more seconds.

She shoved his jeans and underwear down over his hips. As soon as it was free, his cock sprang up, pointing due north like a fucking compass. Landon hissed as Ava wrapped her small soft hand around it.

Lights exploded in his brain. Landon wondered idly if he was having a seizure as Ava's hand worked slowly down to the base of his shaft, giving him a little squeeze and then a slow, tugging pull up his shaft to the head. He was going to die. That much was clear. But what a way to go.

He let her have two more torturous strokes before closing his hand around her wrist and squeezing gently. "Enough." His voice didn't sound human, which was fine by him. He didn't feel particularly human.

She released his cock, but he didn't release her wrist. He pulled her hand away from him, pinning it against the seat near her head. He lowered himself to take her mouth again as his free hand probed between the shredded remains of her jeans, seeking the source of the musky moisture between her thighs. He brushed one spot and her entire body jolted. *Bingo.*

Landon eased her—amazingly still intact—panties aside and pushed one finger inside her slick heat. Her hips pushed up against his hand and moisture swamped his finger. He worked his mouth against hers as he worked a second finger inside her, stretching her. She was so tight. Her pussy was going to feel like a goddamn vise on his cock.

Landon released her mouth as he removed his fingers, pressing his face against her neck to breathe in the intoxicating scent of her as he positioned himself between her legs.

"What's that sound?" Her voice was breathless.

Landon stiffened, trying to hear beyond the blood rushing in his ears. It took him a moment to identify the tinny ring-tone rendition of "The Lion Sleeps Tonight", his sister's idea of a great joke. "Shit. It's Zoe. She wouldn't call unless it's an emergency."

She'd better not have. He was about fifteen seconds away from the fucking promised land. If someone wasn't dying, someone was about to be.

He found his cell phone in the pocket of his jeans, tangled near his knees. "What?"

"Ava's missing!"

Landon blinked, startled by the depth of panic in Zoe's voice. He wasn't aware his sister had formed any strong attachments since their arrival in the pride three months ago, but her concern for Ava was unfeigned.

"I've got her." At least, he'd been *about* to have her, a few seconds before Zoe had decided she needed rescuing. "I'm bringing her back to the ranch now."

"Oh thank God," Zoe whispered. "I'll tell her brothers we can call off the search. Where was she? Is she okay?"

The mention of Ava's brothers searching—Jesus, they wouldn't search the ranch road, would they?—not to mention his sister's barrage of questions, had the effect of a bucket of cold water. Landon shifted off Ava, ignoring the small sound of protest she made, and retreated back to his own seat. He braced himself against the door, as far away from her as he could get, and tried to tug up his jeans one-handed without much success.

"We'll be back at the ranch in—" he glanced around, looking for a landmark through the darkness outside the jeep, "—five minutes. You can ask her all the questions you want, then."

Ava groaned from the passenger seat, pulling herself into a more traditional seated position, rather than her I'm-about-to-have-my-brains-fucked-out-on-a-bucket-seat sprawl.

"But she's okay?" Zoe pressed.

Landon looked at Ava out of the corner of his eye. She was a sight. Rumpled, sweaty, trying to get her top back into place over her breasts with her jeans in useless tatters from her upper-thighs to her waist. She looked gorgeous. Fan-fucking-tastic. "She's fine. See you in five."

He disconnected before Zoe could lob another question at him, mentally crossing his fingers that his ornery sister didn't keep calling him back every five seconds until they arrived at the ranch. Although, given his current control—or lack thereof—that might not be a bad idea.

Dropping the phone, he yanked his jeans back up over his hips and tried to shove his uncooperative cock back inside. He winced as each button closed, but managed to keep his hands from half-morphing into claws long enough to get his jeans fastened. Thank God. If Ava laid one finger on his fly, he was a goner.

Shit, if her brothers ever found out he'd come about five seconds away from fucking their baby sister in the front seat of a jeep, he'd be lucky to see his next birthday.

Landon started the jeep and punched the gas pedal. The vehicle jumped forward obediently, punishing them with a rough ride the last three miles to the ranch.

They were closer to the main compound than Landon had thought—though, to be honest, he hadn't been doing much thinking. Anyone out for a run tonight could have seen them, groping in the car like teenagers.

How had he let things get so far out of control? He'd never even noticed Ava Minor before tonight, but the second she'd walked into the bar, he'd wanted her. The scent of her, the way she pushed her ass back at him as she stood at the bar, the reckless challenge in her voice as she argued with him in the jeep, all of it seemed calculated to drive him wild.

The truth smacked him between the eyes, making him feel like a prize idiot for not realizing earlier. He should have realized it as soon as she walked into the bar, but his hormones had short-circuited his brain. It was so damn obvious.

Ava was in heat.

Chapter Four

She needed to say something. They couldn't have been driving for more than a few seconds, but the oppressive silence coming from the driver's seat made it feel like a millennia. He wouldn't even look at her.

"I take it they discovered my absence," Ava said, her tone a pathetic attempt at lightness.

Landon sounded about as light as a midnight hunt on the Serengeti. "Didn't you even leave a fucking note so your brothers wouldn't panic?"

Ava snorted. "Saying what exactly? 'Gone to get some nookie. Back by noon.' That'd go over real well."

"Better than not saying anything at all," he snapped. "They're searching the ranch for you, Ava."

Ava looked out the window, realizing they were on ranch land and had been for a while. In fact, they'd been on ranch land when they'd... "Oh."

"Yeah. *Oh.*"

Ava tipped her chin defiantly. She wasn't going to cower. She didn't have anything to be ashamed of, dammit. "So what? I deserve to get out just as much as the next girl."

"*Ava.*" Her name sound like a curse on his lips. "There are reasons why we do things the way we do," he said as if explaining the facts of life to a simpleton and hanging onto this patience by the thinnest of threads.

"Yeah, well, maybe your reasons are stupid." Keeping a healthy, attractive young woman with the libido of a cat cooped up on a secluded ranch with a bunch of men she couldn't have was downright cruel and unusual. Ava had seen Lifetime movies about religious cults that did the same and things always ended badly for the misogynistic pigs running the show.

"Valuing human life is stupid, now?"

They hit a particularly nasty bump and Landon was forced to slow to a reasonable speed.

Ava frowned. "What does human life have to with a—"

"*Ava*," Landon interrupted, her name sharp this time. "You're in heat."

"No, I'm no..." Her denial was automatic, but her voice trailed off as she mentally did the math. "Shit."

The shape-shifters who traded shapes between human and lion form didn't possess the exact physiological traits of either. A shifter lioness would go into heat only three times a year, lasting anywhere from a few hours to several days. And like their feline cousins, they wanted sex almost constantly during that period. Even the birth control shots she received to suppress ovulation couldn't combat the hormonal demands her body made during her heat.

"I don't see what that has to do with anything." Ava folded her arms across her still-sensitive breasts, knowing she looked like a petulant child, but feeling like one giant exposed nerve.

"You don't s—" Landon cut himself off, his hands fisting on the steering wheel. He bit out his next words with careful precision. "Have you ever had sex while you were in heat?"

A blush rose up her already warm face until she felt like her cheeks were on fire. "No." She left her answer at that. He didn't need to know that her entire sexual history consisted of a few bumbling encounters in dorm rooms the one semester of college when her family had eased up on the reins enough to allow her to live on campus.

She'd been embarrassingly celibate ever since she'd moved back to the ranch. As if it wasn't bad enough having four ridiculously over-protective older brothers lurking around every corner, the lionesses who weren't old enough or genetically desirable enough to mate were cloistered while they were in heat to avoid unwanted pregnancies. So her opportunities for sex in heat were severely limited.

"When a shifter is in heat, everything is amplified," Landon explained, his tone carefully blank. "Many females, particularly the younger, less experienced ones, will shift uncontrollably when they climax. *That* is why we have rules against seducing humans during heat. It isn't safe to be with someone who can't defend himself, or understand what the fuck just happened when he finds himself in bed with a several-hundred-pound lioness."

Ava's blush was getting downright uncomfortable. "I'm sorry," she muttered in the direction of her lap. "I didn't realize." But then her remorse faded and she frowned at the Roman gladiator driving the jeep. "It still doesn't seem fair. You guys get to go around screwing anything that moves and we have to be virgin priestesses."

"I'm not telling you not to get fucked," Landon snapped. "I'm telling you not to fuck a human."

Ava bit her lip on the complaint that was poised to jump out of her mouth and mortify her—that the only lion she had ever wanted was *him*. She was afraid he already knew. The way she had reacted to him, wordlessly begging him to take her, had made her feelings for him pathetically clear.

She had wanted him since the second she saw him walking through the compound the first day he arrived, wary and worn from his travels. Even before he was Alpha. She had felt desire tightening her body when he was just another reckless nomad, a lion without a pride. She'd had more of a shot with him then. The second he became Alpha was the instant he rose out of her reach.

To a nomad, any lioness was a prize, even a small, abnormal one. But the Alpha? He would mate with the strongest and fastest among them, and Ava would never even come close.

So why had he leapt on her in the jeep? Was it possible he could really want her? Or was the truth much more awful than that? Could he have somehow learned of her infatuation? Was he taunting her? Playing some horrible game? Was that why he had stopped just short of taking her?

Ava glanced over, her eyes locking hungrily on the impressive bulge beneath his fly. No, he wanted her all right. There was no doubt about that.

Landon looked over at her—just in time to see her staring at his crotch. Ava's blush reached terminal levels as he shifted uncomfortably in the seat. "That's another reason unsuitable females are sequestered when in heat."

Ava flinched back from the words like he'd slapped her. *Unsuitable?*

As they pulled into the compound, he went on relentlessly. "Any male coming into contact with you, looking and smelling and acting the way you did tonight would have lost control and climbed all over you. That's why there are *rules*, Ava."

She averted her face as he slowed the jeep, rolling slowly between the low-lying bungalows that made up the ranch compound where the pride lived. She was *not* going to cry in front of him. Even if he was telling her that the electric, soul-searing almost-tryst they had shared not ten minutes ago was nothing more than a forced chemical reaction.

Ava felt an ominous tightness behind her eyes and swallowed thickly, fighting to keep it together. So what if he didn't want her? So what if he was saying he never would have touched her if not for the hormones messing with his impulses? He was just the only lion she had ever wanted. What was so special about that?

Landon parked the jeep in front of a small cluster of bungalows. Hers wasn't one of them and his was on the opposite end of the ranch, but she wasn't about to argue the point with him. At the moment, she needed to get away from him. Fast. Before she started blubbering all over his upholstery.

Ava threw open the door and launched herself out into the night, running toward the nearest familiar bungalow, Zoe's. She managed to get the door firmly closed behind her before she collapsed to the floor in an undignified heap and burst into tears.

Chapter Five

In retrospect, bursting into Zoe's one room home with her clothing in shreds and collapsing into hysterics was not the best course of action. After Ava brought herself under control, it took a long and embarrassingly detailed explanation to calm Zoe enough that she stopped threatening to bring in Ava's brothers. Or worse, her own.

Ava sprawled on the one item of furniture in Zoe's place, a low, sturdy, king-sized bed, and watched her friend prowl the floor. Ava didn't know why Zoe's five-ten Viking goddess appearance didn't intimidate her, but for some reason the former-nomad was the only lioness in the pride she felt completely comfortable with.

Too alphic for Ava's preferred method of strategic retreat, Zoe stalked across the room attacking the problem head on. "He said you were unsuitable? That was the word he used?" Zoe questioned, no shock or outrage in her tone, just a need to get the facts straight.

"Unsuitable," Ava repeated, trying to distance herself from the pain of the word. It hadn't been said to her, she told herself. She was just recounting the experiences of some unknown third-party, talking about last night's TV drama. It wasn't *real*, this hurt she was feeling.

Zoe shook her head, frowning in confusion. "That doesn't sound like him. He's always said that cloistering the women who weren't 'pure' enough to breed was barbaric. Just like tossing perfectly strong males out of a pride when they matured because of the threat they posed to the Alpha."

"He tossed out Leonus and Kato," Ava reminded her.

"Who ran this pride like their own private harem before

Landon challenged them for control. Half of the lionesses hated them. Those two were not the type to take their defeat lightly. If he hadn't banished them, they would have ripped the pride apart. But he didn't throw your brothers out, did he?"

"Neither did Leonus and Kato when they took over. Too afraid of them."

"Which is why the Bastard Coalition never bothered you, but that isn't why Landon keeps them around. He likes your brothers." Zoe tipped her head to the side, pausing in her pacing to consider some new angle. "Which might explain why Landon felt so guilty for jumping on you in the jeep."

"Fear of my brothers?"

"No, respect for them. And exposure to their idea of you. They talk about you like you're fifteen, Ava. And while you may look like a mature young woman, you're small enough that Landon probably thought he had come this close to raping a baby."

"I clearly wanted him," Ava protested.

"You're in heat. He thinks you don't know what you want, that you can't control your body."

"I'm not howling and scratching the walls yet," Ava snapped.

"Of course you aren't, and I'm not suggesting you will. It's my brother who had a hormonal lobotomy tonight, not me." Zoe began pacing again, her long-legged stride eating up the room. "What did he say exactly?"

"I don't know," Ava hedged, as though the words had not been seared into her mind, leaving a ragged scar in their shape. "Something like 'There's a reason *unsuitable* females are sequestered. *Any* male who smelled you would have lost control.'"

Zoe turned toward her sharply, tossing the hip-length mass of her dark golden hair over her shoulder. "He said he lost control?" she asked eagerly.

"He said anyone would have," Ava corrected.

Zoe waved away the clarification, smiling smugly. "You made him lose control!" she crowed. "Of course, you did, he destroyed your jeans. Oh, this is *good*. Big, bad Alpha can't keep it zipped around sweet little Ava. I love it."

"I'm glad one of us does," Ava grumbled, hugging her knees to her chest.

"Don't you see, Ava? This is fantastic."

Ava grunted, not sharing Zoe's enthusiasm.

"Landon *never* loses control. He's too busy playing master of the universe. But, *you*, Ava. You wrangled an alpha in a rage out of a bar fight, no mean feat. And then you incited him to jump you, without even trying. You *ruled* him tonight."

"Then why did he stop?" Ava blurted, blushing furiously when Zoe laughed throatily.

"Kitten, if you want a spot in my brother's bed, that isn't a problem. But if you want to be his mate, his partner, the love of his life, rule the pride and breed little Landons off him, then you're going to have to grow a spine and get ready to fight tooth and nail, fang and claw, for him, because no matter how much he wants you, he isn't going to make you his one and only unless you can prove that you aren't a submissive little doormat."

"Little being the operative word," Ava snapped. "I can't just run around challenging the female alphas, Zoe. Some of them have a hundred pounds on me in their human form. I wouldn't last five seconds."

Zoe smiled, a purely feline curve of her lips. "There's more than one way to skin a cat, Ava-dear. Just because you can't take them in a fight, doesn't mean you can't dominate them."

"I don't think—"

"Then I guess you don't want Landon," Zoe cut her off brutally, frustrated by her prevarications. "Because until you stop meekly obeying every order, bowing down to your bullying brothers and the bullying cats angling to be Landon's mate, you will never be strong enough to deserve him. If you want to mate the Alpha, you need to be the biggest, baddest kitty in the pride."

"But I am the smallest," Ava wailed.

"Physical size doesn't mean shit," Zoe snapped. "Size is a state of mind, kitten. And yours is only microscopic because you are too damn scared to go after what you want."

"I can't—"

"I don't, I can't, I won't." Zoe threw her hands up in the air and stalked to the opposite end of the bungalow. "I wash my hands of you. You need to change your attitude, but if you don't want it for yourself, let alone for darling Landon, there is nothing I can do."

"Zoe..."

"I'm done," she said, her voice sharp and dismissive. Then she turned and her face softened at Ava's stricken expression. "I'm glad you're home safe," she said, much more gently. "It just drives me crazy when people are too frightened to go after the things they want. You play it safe and all you end up with is a lifetime of should-have-beens."

Zoe turned to look out the window, once again dismissing her.

Ava climbed off the bed, tugging at the wraparound skirt she had borrowed to replace her massacred jeans. "I'll return this tomorrow."

Zoe waved away the comment without turning from the view. "Keep it. It's too short on me anyway."

"Zoe..."

"I'm not mad at you, Ava," Zoe said, still without looking at her.

Ava knew Zoe couldn't stand indecision. Everything was black or white to her, but Ava couldn't seem to stop seeing the grays in every situation. She waited for Zoe to go on, but the silence stretched. "'kay," she said finally. "Good night."

"Night, kitten," Zoe said, her tone affectionate even though she continued to gaze out the window. "Bite those bed bugs back."

Ava laughed softly and slipped out into the darkness outside. There were no floodlights in the compound and the moon had long since set, but Ava could easily pick out the shadowy shapes of the bungalows from the dim, distant light of the stars.

She set off across the ranch toward her own little one room house, stepping silently so as not to alert the sensitive ears of her pride members. The midsummer heat was still stifling, even so long after sunset, but Ava didn't mind the weight of it on her skin. Lions were often nocturnal hunters, active in the coolest part of the night, but the itch along Ava's spine was not the urge to shift and run after game. She had prey of a different sort on her mind.

Landon's jeep had disappeared, presumably back to his own bungalow, but for all she knew he was off sating himself with some "suitable" female. Ava clenched her teeth against the flood of angry jealous that welled up at the thought.

Who he slept with was none of her business. He didn't belong to her. He never would. In fact, in days, weeks at most, he would select his mate and then he would belong heart, body, and soul to someone else. Someone big and strong who Ava would be afraid to go up against. If she even stared at him too long, his mate would be within her rights to take her down a peg.

She sighed. Even her fantasies had an expiration date.

Ava stalked through the night, her skin slick from the heat, both external and internal. She'd been in heat before, but it had never felt quite like this. Landon's presence, in the jeep, in the bar, over the last few weeks around the ranch, had amplified everything.

Her skin felt two sizes too tight. She walked fast because if she slowed, even for a moment, the slow, writhing pressure would take over her limbs. Her breasts were heavy and tender, the flesh between her legs swollen and wet. She'd had precious little satisfaction in the jeep. Just enough to drive her even further into this madness without providing any relief.

Ava rubbed at the tension in her neck, the touch transforming into a caress sliding down her throat, the softness of her own skin teasing her fingers. She flung her hands out, fighting the temptation to touch herself, and stopped on the darkened path in front of a bungalow, breathing too quickly after her walk.

She looked up, confused to find that her feet had not carried her home. That instinct had been overridden by the clamoring of her body. The shadow of a figure within stalked past the lit window.

Landon.

Ava shuddered at the sight of him. She could never be his mate, that much was clear, but Zoe's challenge to go after what she wanted still rang in her mind. She might not be able to have him forever, but she could have him tonight. This may very well be her one chance to be with Landon before he irrevocably belonged to another.

Her skin was about to crawl away without her and only Landon would do to scratch her itch. No other male, man or lion, had ever made her feel this spiraling insanity of lust.

Any male would lose control if she went to him, in heat, and waved her tail in his face. *He* would lose control. And if he didn't...did it even matter? She'd already embarrassed herself—ripping his clothing off him, begging for more. Why not go for full-fledged humiliation?

She shook away the thought. She wouldn't be humiliated. Tonight she wasn't weak, passive Ava. Tonight she was a feline goddess, hopped up on hormones and irresistible to men.

Ava tipped back her chin, feeling purpose blazing through her. Tomorrow, she would be invisible Ava again, but tonight, she was *his*.

Chapter Six

Landon prowled across his room, the spacious bungalow feeling like a cage, as thoughts of Ava chased him. The memory of her fleeing from him, sprinting into the safety of Zoe's bungalow, burned in his mind.

He didn't blame her for her fear. He'd been a beast, feral and uncontrolled, attacking her like that in the jeep. Was it possible she really hadn't realized she was in heat? How could she not have known what her scent was doing to him?

Landon growled low in his throat as he stalked the room, the blind need she had ignited in him still burning in his gut. He should have dropped in on another lioness or two before coming back to his own place. Shana had made it clear on numerous occasions that she was always available to him, more than willing to crawl into his bed whenever he would allow her there. She was an ambitious minx, but he knew exactly what he was getting with her. She would never make him feel unhinged and out of balance the way Ava did.

Shana was strong and fast, aggressive and manipulative. She would make an excellent consort, but Landon hadn't been able to bring himself to declare her so. Some instinct had always held him back. But at the moment, those same instincts were screaming for him to track Ava and brand her as his own, body and soul. So perhaps his instincts with the females of this pride were not to be trusted.

Landon turned and paced. Paced and turned. The bungalow in the ranch compound designated for the Alpha's use was second in size only to the Great Hall where the pride gathered for ceremonies, but it felt microscopic tonight. The high ceilings with rough, exposed wood beams seemed to press down on him. And even the natural wood floors, nicked and scarred by the claws of his predecessors, taunted him with everything he could not allow himself to do.

He couldn't shift. Not tonight. When he took his other form, the animal in him had too much control. He would not be able to stop himself from hunting Ava down and proving his ownership of her in the most primitive way. He couldn't risk running on all fours through the acres of private land belonging to the ranch. Even that freedom was denied to him tonight.

The creak of the step outside his door sounded unnaturally loud to his heightened senses. Landon spun to face the door, falling into a crouch, his lips pulling back in a snarl. He knew better than to expect Ava to come to him, but second to her presence, the one he wanted the most was that of a threat. Someone he could decimate. His heated blood would eagerly boil over into violence.

The step creaked again. The intruder didn't knock. Landon's eyes locked on the door, watching the knob as it turned, inch by inch, waiting, ready to spring.

"Landon?"

Her voice, husky and scratched, was a blow to his composure, cracking the façade of his inhuman control. She already sounded as hoarse as if she'd been screaming his name all night.

Ava pushed the door open a few inches and peered inside. When she saw him there, crouched for attack, she froze with her hand on the knob.

Ava eyed him hungrily. He was barefoot and bare-chested, wearing only the snug blue jeans he'd had on earlier, the partially buttoned fly straining over his erection. She dimly recalled ripping his shirt off earlier and silently thanked herself for her foresight. The muscles across his chest and shoulders stood out prominently in his tense stance, his tan skin gleaming in the golden light of the lamp.

His appearance stole her breath, primitive and wild. She knew the feral gleam in his eyes should have frightened her, but instead she licked her lips, her own excitement ratcheting up to a frenzied pitch in instantaneous response.

Ava forced air into lungs that felt suddenly tight and refused to expand all the way. She tossed her head, defiant of the threat implied in his stance, his eyes. Her hair flicked around her shoulders and his nostrils flared as if reacting to the scent of her shampoo.

Feeling daring and far too excited to be touched by fear, Ava shoved open the door all the way and stepped into the predator's lair. The door fell shut behind her with an audible click through the humid silence.

"What are you doing here?"

His voice was more beast than man, but the shiver that shot down Ava's spine had nothing to do with fear.

"You told me to come."

Landon straightened, as though suddenly recalling his less than human posture, but his new stance was no less threatening. He took a step toward her then stopped, feet braced, glowering down at her. "I don't remember telling you anything like that."

Ava wet her lips and his eyes tracked the movement. "You did," she insisted.

There was no question that she was in heat. The feline had taken over entirely or she would never be able to say what she was about to say without stammering, blushing and collapsing in a mortified heap. Ava cleared her throat. She wasn't going to say this twice. She tipped back her chin, looking straight into his eyes.

"You told me to come to you if I needed to be fucked."

He didn't react beyond the almost imperceptible stiffening of the muscles across his shoulders. For what felt like an eternity, he gave no response, watching her with heated green-gold eyes that revealed nothing.

Ava held herself perfectly still under his gaze, afraid if she moved the moment would shatter and he would toss her out on her ass. She flinched when he took a step toward her, startled to have the statue resolve itself once more into a man. Another step and he stood directly in front of her, separated by mere inches but careful not to touch.

"I did say that, didn't I?" he mused, husky and low.

Ava caught her breath and held it, her eyes falling closed as he leaned in until his face hovered over the curve of her neck. He inhaled deeply and Ava felt herself mimic the action without conscious direction from her brain. The scent of him hit her nostrils and shot straight to her clit. A gush of fluid drenched her thong and Ava gasped, breathless again, sucking in another lungful of him.

"Do you know what you're doing?"

She couldn't answer. Did she? How would she even know? She'd forfeited brain function in favor of sensation the second she walked in the room and now he wanted her to contemplate the repercussions of her actions? Impossible.

Ava nodded, eyes still closed, praying that was the right answer, the answer that would make him touch her.

"Good."

When he did touch her, it wasn't where she wanted it. Where she needed it. His hand closed like a shackle around her wrist. He touched her only there, and with the cool brush of his breath blowing against the side of her neck. His thumb rubbed a small, rhythmic circle against the pulse-point on her inner wrist and Ava felt her entire being narrow to that point.

She wanted to leap on him, tearing both of their remaining clothes off. Knock his feet out from under him and beat him to the ground. She wanted him fast and rough and hot, but she stood motionless, hypnotized by his stillness, captivated by his unyielding control. Helpless to hurry him, she let herself feel.

The hand circling her wrist was impossibly warm, the air he blew against her skin icy cool. He was firm but gentle. The patience of his current stillness refuted the frenzied wildness that had been in his eyes when she walked in, but she knew it was still there, lurking just below the surface, waiting for him to lose the battle with the beast. Ava couldn't wait.

She opened her eyes. He was still bent over her, inhaling her scent, his muscular chest right in front of her face.

Ava leaned forward and bit him right above his nipple. Her human teeth sank into his skin, hard enough to leave a mark, but not hard enough to make him bleed. Landon hissed and snarled, spinning her away from him to break her hold. Ava released him with a wicked little laugh. He jerked her back against him, her back to his front, one arm a tight band across her bare stomach as the other still caged her wrist. The stiff fabric covering his erection pressed into the small of her back. Ava leaned back against him, rubbing sinuously.

"You're a feisty one, aren't you?" he growled, his breath stirring her hair.

"What are you waiting for?" She bumped her hips back against him. "You're obviously up for it."

He whipped her away from him again, this time to tow her across the room toward the wide, sturdy bed. Ava started to climb on the mattress, but Landon grabbed her and spun her until her hips were pressed up against the footboard, facing the bed. A hand on the center of her back pressed her forward until she was bent over the rail of the footboard, her hands braced on the mattress, her ass presented to him like a present.

He wasted no time unwrapping her. "You're going to be sorry you taunted me," he growled, stripping her borrowed skirt so quickly she barely had time to gasp before he was pulling down her tube top. The stretchy fabric caught on her hips, but that didn't slow him down. Landon grabbed the shirt and her thong, yanking them together down her legs.

Completely naked and totally exposed, Ava had never felt more powerful. She fought the urge to writhe with sheer pleasure, then gave into it when his palms slid up the backs of her bare legs, cupping her ass almost reverently. Dipping his fingers between her legs, he found the juices dripping down her thighs and hissed something that might have been a prayer or a curse. "*God.* I'm sorry, baby, I can't wait."

The sudden loss of his hands and the heat of his body behind her had Ava turning. Landon stood a few feet back, wrestling with the buttons on his fly, though the difficulty this time was not his hands, but the heavy erection pressing against the seam. Ava reached out a hand to help.

"No."

Ava snatched back her hand, startled by the abrasive command. Landon, his hands now folded almost protectively over his cock, closed his eyes and took a deep breath.

"I can't have you touching me right now, Ava," he said, his voice strained. "I won't last."

Ava was tempted to test his control, but she didn't think her own need would wait for him to recover if he was right. She resumed the position he had put her in, watching him over her shoulder. "Well, come on then," she urged, when he didn't immediately drop his pants and dive at her.

Landon opened his eyes, saw her position and groaned, closing them again. But his motivation was apparent. His claws sprang out and he slashed down the outer seams of the jeans, whipping his pants and boxers off like a Chippendale's dancer. His cock sprang up, thicker than she remembered from the jeep and already glistening with the first drops of pre-come.

Ava squirmed, her body screaming for him. What was he waiting for? An engraved invitation?

Landon moved up behind her, the heat of his body enveloping her. She dropped her head forward onto her arms, bracing her feet and arching her back to give him easier access as he shifted behind her, making accommodation for the drastic differences in their heights.

When she felt his head at her entrance, Ava moaned. Landon froze at the sound.

She wondered if there was anything within reach she could throw at his head. What the hell was he *waiting* for? Her insides were coiling, twisting, every nerve on high alert, waiting for his possession.

Right when she was about to scream her frustration, he moved, sliding the head in, then working another inch deeper. Oh, *yes*. He was bigger than anyone in her limited experience and she was naturally tight, but she stretched to take him in another inch, then another. He filled her so perfectly, but she needed him deeper. She needed him faster and harder, but he just eased forward, controlled and smooth.

Then he stopped. Again. Ava hissed.

"Landon." His name was a plea. Hard. Deep. *Please, please, please.*

She saw his hand gripping the footboard, the knuckles white with strain. "I'm sorry, Ava," he groaned, easing back.

She stiffened in alarm. If he backed out on her now she was so going Lorena Bobbitt on his ass.

"You're so fucking tight," he bit out, sounding like he was on the verge of asphyxiating. He slid out until just the tip was still inside her. "Am I hurting you?"

Men were such fucking morons. "I have never felt anything so fucking fantastic in my entire fucking life, you fucking idiot," Ava snapped, her tone far from loverly as she swore more in that one sentence than she ever had in her life. "Now would you please just *fuck me already*?"

Landon made a choked sound that might have been a laugh. "Yes, ma'am."

He gripped her hips between his hands and slammed into her so high and hard that her toes lifted off the ground entirely. Ava screamed. Half a second later, she came screaming. Every cell in her body felt like it expanded and exploded, shattering her into a thousand tiny pieces. Landon rammed into her two more times before he fell over the edge after her, roaring, his body stiffening and jerking against her back.

Chapter Seven

That wasn't enough.

Ava's first conscious thought after her brain put itself back together was the realization that the Hiroshima sex she and Landon had just had was barely enough to take the edge off. She needed more and she needed it *soon*. Fuck, being in heat sucked. She couldn't even enjoy a good afterglow. Although, she did get the kind of sex that people wrote sonnets about, so she probably shouldn't complain.

Her second conscious thought was that footboards were not meant for lying over.

"Landon."

He grunted, his weight still pressing her down onto the wooden rail.

"Landon. As much as I love *this*..." she tightened her inner muscles where he was still lodged and her lover groaned appreciatively, "...this isn't the most comfortable of positions for me."

He swore with feeling and shifted his weight off her, his cock slipping wetly out of her body. He gently turned her and lifted her into his arms, carrying her not around to the side of the bed as she had expected, but across the room to the only other room in the bungalow, the bathroom.

He perched her on the edge of the sink and wet a washcloth with cool water. Standing between her knees, the big bad lion looked tentative, his movements cautious, as if she were as fragile as porcelain.

The chill of the washcloth pressing against the hot flesh between her legs had her gasping at the surprising pleasure of the contrast. Landon brushed her hair back away from her face with his free hand, still wielding the delicious washcloth with the other.

"Are you sore?" he asked gently, not meeting her eyes. "I know I was too rough. I couldn't control myself."

Ava snorted. When Landon's eyes snapped up to inspect hers, she rolled them at him. "You are such a baby," she scolded. "This—" she wrapped her hand around his cock, which was already stiffening even so soon after their first bout, "—is not the terrifying monster you seem to think it is."

He snorted and she grinned.

"I liked it," she promised, then shook her head sharply. "No. I *loved* it." Ava leaned forward, the high counter putting her face on a level with his. She gave his cock another friendly stroke and gently scraped her teeth along the side of his neck before whispering directly into his ear, "I wanted it harder, Landon. Deeper. Rougher." His cock jumped a little in her hand at every word. She laughed darkly. "This was fabulous. But next time..." She sucked his earlobe into her mouth, giving it a gentle nip. "Next time, I expect you to ruin me for all other men."

"Done." Landon lunged forward and caught her mouth, his tongue plunging inside and tangling with hers.

Apparently next time was starting right now.

Ava linked her legs loosely around Landon's waist and draped her arms across his shoulders. Their first bout had taken the edge off enough that she could enjoy the kiss for the moment without feeling like she needed to crawl inside his skin. Her lover was not so patient.

His hands skimmed lightly over her arms. They framed her collarbone, his thumbs brushing the pulse points in her neck before he turned his hands, tracing the outer edge of her breasts and across her stomach with the backs of his fingers, all without releasing her mouth.

Then suddenly he slowed the kiss until it was languid and drugging, pulling at her soul through her mouth. Ava hummed her pleasure against his lips.

She didn't know if it was different because she was in heat, different because she'd never been with another shifter, or different because it was Landon, but every sensation seemed magnified a thousand times beyond her previous experience. It was a miracle she hadn't shifted at the climax as Landon had predicted.

Ava turned her head, breaking her mouth free. Landon didn't stop kissing her. He just moved his kisses along her jaw, nibbling down the column of her throat.

"I didn't shift," she bragged, proud of her superlative control. Even the puniest lioness had some positive attributes. Unsuitable. Ha!

"Mm." Landon took his nibbling southward, reaching the upper curve of her breasts.

She smacked him lightly on the shoulder to get his attention. He needed to be appreciating what a paragon of self-control she was, here. "When I came. I didn't shift. Like you said I would. I can control it."

"Mm-hm." His tongue flicked across her nipple.

She gave him another smack, not quite so gentle this time. "Landon!"

He groaned and looked up, his hands quickly taking up where his mouth had left off. "What? I'm doing good work here."

Yes, he was. "I didn't shift," she pointed out. Again.

He shrugged. "Doesn't happen every time. I didn't shift either, but it was a near thing. I think I left some claw marks in the footboard."

It doesn't happen every time? That was it? No recognition of her superhuman control? No acknowledgement that she wasn't useless and *unsuitable* and totally unworthy of his attention?

Ava shoved at his shoulder. "Let me down."

Landon frowned, visibly perplexed, but he didn't budge. "You're mad."

"Well spotted, Sherlock. You figure that one out all by yourself?" Big dumb alpha.

"How did we get from foreplay to mad? I'm confused."

Ava resisted the urge to tell him for the thousandth time that she had not shifted. Didn't he understand the significance? Did she have to spell everything out for him? "I'm not unsuitable."

Landon blinked uncomprehendingly. "What?"

"I'm not unsuitable." This repetition thing was really starting to get annoying. One would think the leader of the pride would need to be able to listen a little more closely.

He frowned. "I never said you were."

Vivi Andrews

This time when she smacked him, she put her weight behind it, really giving it all she had. "Yes, you *did*."

"Ava." He ducked, though she was hardly capable of bruising the big hulk, let alone doing real damage. "I would never say that about you."

"You did!" she insisted. "In the jeep. You said I was unsuitable and should be kept away from the other lions when I'm in heat. You said the only reason you jumped me was because I broke the rules and wasn't cloistered off like I'm supposed to be."

Ava winced internally. She hadn't meant to say quite so much. She didn't really want to be reminding Landon that the only reason he was with her right now was the potent hormone cocktail they were both swilling. And she certainly didn't want him to hear the disappointment in her voice that he only wanted her because she was in heat. The last thing she needed was him wondering why else *she* would want *him*. How mortifying if he suddenly realized she'd been secretly in love with him for months.

Fortunately, Landon was a masculine member of the species, and therefore incapable of deducing the origin of her emotional meltdown. Instead, he focused on her attack on his integrity.

"I didn't say that!" His hands had long since dropped from her breasts to brace on the counter on either side of her. He loomed over her, his own temper snapping at its leash. "I was trying to explain why I attacked you that way in the jeep," he protested. "I wasn't talking about you being unsuitable. I completely lost control, Ava. I couldn't even maintain my human form. You make me so crazy. All I can think about is getting inside you. I shouldn't be allowed to want you like this. Your brothers have been among my few allies since I arrived here and how do I repay them? By banging their little sister." The fight went out of him and he dropped his forehead down to rest on her shoulder. "God, what am I doing?"

Ava ran her hands from the base of his neck across the sculpted muscles of his back. "You told me I was unsuitable because I make you crazy?"

Landon groaned. "I didn't say you were unsuitable, Ava. And if I did, it wasn't what I was trying to say. I thought you wanted that fucking cowboy, that I was smelling your attraction

128

to him and reacting to it. I was so sure you didn't even *want* me and then I practically fucked you right there in the front seat. I needed there to be some reason for it. Some way to explain it. I've never reacted to another female's heat the way I have to yours tonight. The scent is intoxicating, yes, but never so irresistible. But when you walked in here, I *couldn't* let you leave. I think I would have broken down and sought you out even if you hadn't come. I had to have you, Ava."

He whispered this entire speech against her shoulder. Ava held herself perfectly still, afraid if she moved that he would remember she wasn't the irresistible goddess his body had tricked him into believing she was.

"You drive me crazy too," she confessed, resting her head against his shoulder as she continued to trace the lines of his back. "I wanted you. In the jeep. In the bar."

He lifted his head, but Ava kept hers hidden. "You ran to Zoe's."

"I thought you didn't want me."

His fingers traced a trail from the base of her spine around her ribcage, reminding her that she was naked and wrapped around him. Her pulse kicked into high gear as he bent to press his face against her neck, inhaling deeply. His hands closed over her breasts. "Me not wanting you was never an option."

The reprieve her body had granted her was over, all of the symptoms of her heat returning in a thundering rush at the touch of his hands. She writhed on the counter, her hips slipping off the cool surface, but Landon's body was there to catch her, firm and immovable. He caught her against him, chuckling low at her lack of feline grace, and kicked the bathroom door shut. He spun to pin her against it, their entwined bodies hitting the door hard enough to rattle the frame.

Ava purred in her throat, locking her ankles more snugly at his back and bracing herself with a hand on the towel rod. Clearly Landon was taking her request that he not hold back this time very seriously. She loved a man who could take direction.

As Landon occupied her mouth, she ran her hands over every inch of him she could reach, basking in the breadth of his shoulders, the warmth of his skin, the firmness of his muscles against her fingers. He was a specimen in his prime and he was all hers. Ava ignored the niggling whisper in the back of her mind that tried to remind her that he was hers for a limited time only. Once he took a mate…

The thought spurred an aggressive jealous streak she didn't know she had. Ava bracketed his head in her hands, holding him captive as she increased the pressure and urgency in the kiss. In this moment, he was *hers* and no one else's.

Landon responded readily to her spike of need. His fingers, which had certainly not been idle, found their way to her wet, heated core and he speared one long digit high into her pussy. Ava jolted at the impact. Her head smacked back against the door, but she was mindless of the insubstantial blow, her entire being focused on his finger working inside her. She snagged his lower lip between her teeth, urging him on, inciting him to a frenzy. Landon growled against her mouth.

He hitched her higher against the door, and then guided the heavy arousal that had been wedged between them unerringly to her tight sheath. Ava grabbed for the towel bar again, her other arm locked around his shoulder as she braced for his delicious invasion.

"Make it hard." She panted the reminder against his skin.

Landon bared his teeth in a silent snarl, locked his fingers on her hips and slammed her down onto his shaft, half-seating her in a single stroke. Before she could adjust to his sudden presence, he pulled out and drove home again, deeper, higher. It took three more strokes before her tight pussy could accommodate his full length. When he hilted against her, they moaned in unison. He held for a moment and Ava clenched her inner muscles around him to keep him there, drowning in the perfect sensation, the exquisite relief of his body thick and hard inside her.

"Oh God, it feels…" There were no words to describe the soul-searing perfection of the feeling. Landon didn't wait for her vocabulary to return. Instead, he set a pace that quickly deprived her of her powers of speech. Ava was reduced to panting, gasping moans as Landon made good on his promise for a hard, rough ride. Attentive to the tenor of her cries, he adjusted his angle until each sure stroke was another stab of ecstasy.

Ava heard a high-pitched noise twining around the pounding against the door and realized it was her own high-pitched keening. The sounds Landon made were feral music to her ears. He drove into her until she was clinging to the precipice, so close to tumbling over the edge, holding desperately to her sanity, knowing that each second she held off her climax it grew in intensity. Landon shifted, his own face straining against the inevitable, shifted his hold on her, lifting her legs higher, changing the angle of her hips subtly before ramming home one last time.

Ava screamed, her back arching like a bow as white light exploded behind her eyes. Landon gave a ferocious roar and slammed her into the door. The sound of splintering wood was completely lost beneath their orgasmic cries as the door gave way, tumbling them back into the bedroom.

Landon landed hard on top of Ava, still seated deep within her, and his weight sent her off again, shooting toward the stars. Still caught in his own orgasm, his hips flexed hard into hers, pressing her down into the remains of the door.

She was still shuddering from aftershocks when he rolled off her, hauling her with him and draping her across his chest. Ava focused on the little things—breathing, the gradually steadying drumming of Landon's heart against her ear—until she could make her eyes focus enough to realize she was gazing at the shrapnel of their lovemaking.

She snickered.

"What?" Landon grunted.

She laughed harder, tucking her face against his chest. Her hormones must be working overtime because he still smelled fantastic to her, even reeking of sweat and sex, man and beast.

He swatted her backside half-heartedly. "What are you laughing at?"

"I probably have splinters in unmentionable places." She giggled, perversely delighted by the destruction they had wrought on his bathroom.

"Hm, we'd better check."

Landon deftly flipped her over and began a *very* thorough investigation. Ava moaned through her laughter. She could definitely get used to this.

Chapter Eight

"How is it you managed to hide from me for the last three months?" Landon mumbled the question against her breast. They had finally made it to the bed after thoroughly christening the floor and her heat had subsided to a soft thrumming at the base of her spine, screwed into abeyance by Landon's superhuman efforts. But he still couldn't seem to stop touching her.

They curled around one another in a knot at the center of the bed, forming a private cocoon where the realities that kept them apart outside this room didn't exist. Ava winced internally as his question threatened her ability to ignore those realities.

"I'm hardly the kind of girl to come to the Alpha's notice."

He frowned against her skin, even that subtle movement a caress. "What does that mean?"

"Landon," she sighed. "You've seen my lion form—"

"I told you I could make you shift." He chuckled smugly, the vibration carrying through her body.

She swatted him, unwilling to be distracted now that he had brought it up. "You know how small I am. I'm hardly the type of girl to attract the attention of the Alpha."

"I like how small you are." One long finger plunged inside her, leaving her no doubt as to his meaning.

Ava caught her breath and closed her eyes, letting sensation wash over her. "How can I still need you like this?" she gasped as he shifted his body over hers.

This time their mating was slow and sensual, each deliberate movement of his body wrenching at her heart. When he eased off her onto his side several minutes later, Ava twisted to fit her back against his front, tucking her chin to hide her face. Her emotions were too close to the surface, filling her eyes to glistening and threatening to betray her.

Landon threw a leg across hers and wrapped one heavy arm around her waist, holding her snug against him. His mouth traced patterns on the back of her neck, never still.

She needed distance. She needed to remind her heart that it could not get too attached to this passionate, surprisingly playful, intelligent, dynamic, honorable man. With her face still hidden, Ava made herself say the words that needed to be said.

"You'll be taking a mate soon, I expect." Her throat threatened to close off, but she choked out the next few words. "It will need to be someone strong. Someone who can lead the Hunt." Even if they were only hunting the domesticated cattle on their own ranch, the ritual of it was essential to their culture.

Landon stilled at her first words, but then he made an agreeable noise and began kissing a line across her shoulder again.

Ava made herself go on. She needed to be clear. She would not be pitied. She wanted him to know she had no expectations to be his partner, no matter how much her heart might ache at the idea of anyone else taking her place in his arms. "Have you given any thought to which of them you will choose?"

This conversation was agony, but she *would* have it.

His mouth stopped against her shoulder blade. "I've wanted to learn a bit more about the pride before making an irrevocable decision," he said, his voice frustratingly devoid of inflection. "Who would you have me choose, Ava?"

Now he wanted her to pick her own rival? "I couldn't make such a choice for you. She must be strong and fast—"

"Tolerant, progressive in her way of thinking..." His mouth glided back to the nape of her neck.

Ava gritted her teeth. He was taunting her now. She knew as well as he what was required of the Alpha's mate. "Firm enough to rule in your stead."

"Wise enough to rule without violence..."

"Large enough that none of the other lionesses could physically threaten her to get their way..."

Landon suddenly grew very alert at her back. "Has someone been threatening you, Ava?"

She rolled her eyes, not caring that he couldn't see the gesture. "I'm the runt of the pride, Landon. Everyone bullies me. It's practically the national pastime."

His arm tightened almost immeasurably against her stomach, the muscles suddenly iron hard. "Your brothers allow this?" he growled.

"My brothers can't be everywhere and even if they could, a lioness should fight her own battles." Ava smiled wryly. "Or be smart enough to give in when a battle with someone twice her size is imminent."

"That isn't how I want my pride to be." Landon's body was impossibly tense. It was like being in bed with a marble statue.

"We can't always get what we want, Landon. Shifter prides have been a hierarchy of strength for as long as anyone can remember. I don't think they're going to suddenly start changing now."

"We *will* change," he vowed. "We may be animals, but that doesn't mean we have to abandon all reason. The weaker ones should not be punished. No one should be allowed to decide who is eligible to breed and who isn't."

"It keeps the gene pool strong," Ava countered, having memorized all of the arguments that were supposed to comfort her in the knowledge that she would never be allowed cubs of her own. As a tiny, albino lioness, she was practically considered deformed.

"Survival of the fittest does not include breeding restrictions," Landon snapped. "And a select coalition of males being allowed to breed with the females is just as ridiculous."

"Even if, as the Alpha, you decide the coalition?"

"There are no conditions on decency, Ava."

She twisted around in his arms until they faced one another. His expression was fierce, determined. Ava smiled a little at his idealistic resolve. "Zoe said you wouldn't force the strong young males to become nomads as you were forced out of your pride. Don't you fear that one of them will overpower you and toss you out of your home?"

"If we didn't micromanage every aspect of their lives and forbid them from ever having sex with the females, then I imagine the young, strong males would be much less likely to want to rip my head off."

Ava gently stroked a finger across his cheek. "It is a lovely idea, Landon. Justice and equality for all often is. But do you really think you can accomplish all that? Change our wild and savage ways?"

His green-gold eyes held hers steadily. "Not alone."

Ava tucked her chin and snuggled close to him, burying her face against his chest to avoid his penetrating stare. He would need a true queen as his consort if he was going to accomplish his dreams for the pride. "Then you had better choose wisely," she murmured, closing her eyes against the painful knowledge that she could never be that choice. Not for him. Not for the pride.

Chapter Nine

Landon's first sensation upon waking was hunger, and not the hunger that had consumed him during the hours of the night before and well past dawn. His stomach felt like it was wrapped around his spine, consuming itself in a futile quest for sustenance.

He realized he hadn't eaten since before seeing Ava in the bar last night. Lion shifters had naturally high metabolisms and between the sexual marathon and the extra energy expended from the one time they'd shifted, he felt like he'd been starved for a week, rather than fasting for a matter of hours.

His stomach growled ferociously, but Landon didn't move. He held himself perfectly still as Ava sighed and rubbed against him in her sleep. She was half sprawled across his chest, her long white-blonde hair blanketing them both. He ran his fingers through the soft strands. Often a shifter's human mane would resemble the pelt of their other form—in his travels, Landon had once met a tiger with gold hair and black stripes at his temples—but he had still been surprised by the pale luminescence of Ava's coat when she shifted the night before.

White lions were rare in their feline counterparts, perhaps one in a thousand born with the anomaly, but they were practically unheard of among the shifter culture where any hint of the unusual was brutally bred out. Landon had never seen a white lioness before last night, which made him wonder where Ava had been hiding during all of the gatherings over the last three months. He was sure the unusually bright sheen of her fur would have caught his eye in any form.

She curled toward him instinctively in her sleep and Landon smiled. She was so skittish when she was awake, always holding part of herself away from him, hidden behind her enigmatic pale gray eyes. For all that she gave of herself generously, as purely uninhibited a lover as he'd ever had, she always kept that part of her safe. Separate.

Except when she slept. At least her subconscious was willing to acknowledge that she belonged with him.

Landon didn't know when the decision had been made, but sometime between that first teasing taste of her scent in the bar and their lazy post-coital chats as dawn broke, he had made his choice. Ava was the only lioness he could imagine taking as his mate. She would not cling to outdated traditions, but would help him bring a sense of humanity into their less than human world. She would support him, argue with him when he needed it, and was brave enough to step between him and his prey when his ire was up, strong enough to face down his misdirected anger. She was ideal.

Now all he had to do was convince her of that fact.

She was so eager to run from him, his little mate. So ready to hand him off to someone she had decided was more *suitable* to rule beside him.

Landon tightened his arms around her sleeping form. His stomach grumbled again and again he ignored it. There was no food inside his bungalow. None of the sleeping quarters on the compound were set up with kitchens. In the communal living environment of the pride, all meals were taken at the mess hall. It had taken Landon some time to accustom himself to eating with his pride, after the years he and his sister had spent fending for themselves, but he had found, much to his surprise, that he enjoyed the familial feeling the large community meals inspired.

Attendance at mealtimes was not required, even the pride-first oriented lions had too much feline independence for that. Snacks were always on hand in the kitchen for those who chose not to dine with the group, for whatever reason. So his and Ava's absence at breakfast, which they had long since slept through, at least wouldn't be noted.

If they were still missing at dinner, it might raise some alarms—and Landon might die of hunger, if the ache in his stomach was any indication—but he was hopeful he would be able to convince Ava to become his consort before then. His plan consisted largely of keeping her trapped in bed until she said yes. Not terribly sophisticated, but hopefully all the coercion she would require.

He stroked her hair away from her face and she hummed and sighed against him as she slept. He had worn her out, poor thing, but it seemed her heat had finally subsided. The scent of her no longer demanded that he wake her just so he could make love to her again. Their libidos were finally allowing them some rest.

He wondered how the rest of the pride would react to their pairing. She wasn't who they would have picked for him, if he'd put it to a vote, which he had actually considered doing at one point, when all of the candidates had seemed identical in ambition and appeal.

Landon was still trying to find his way in the pride, for all that he was their leader now. He'd been a nomad for so long, responsible for only himself and Zoe, who was entirely capable of taking care of herself. Without the protection of the pride, they'd had to be constantly on alert, never knowing when it was safe to shift or hunt, always wary of exposure, being caught and turned into a science experiment.

He had been constantly tense, waiting for the ax to fall, always on edge, but life here in the pride was one hundred and eighty degrees different.

The pride owned all of the land for miles in every direction around the ranch. Security measures to keep out prying eyes— even some that distorted satellite photos that might compromise them from space—were in place all around the compound. Every member of the community contributed, some within the ranch, those who chose working in nearby towns, but the rhythm of life here was slow and easy. Hammocks were strung between the bungalows for long afternoon naps in the sun.

The shifters were deliberate in their actions, productive when they needed to be, enjoying a lazy reprieve when they didn't. The pace of life here was a replica of their Serengeti cousins rather than the frenzied, worker-bee mentality of the average American human.

It had taken some getting used to for Landon, but he had come to love it, though he'd never felt that he truly belonged. Until last night. Until Ava.

Somehow she had made him feel like one of them. He had

been searching for an in, trying to earn the acceptance that he'd already been granted, and then last night, between one heartbeat and the next, Ava had brought him home. He didn't want to lose that feeling any more than he wanted to lose her. Though, now that he felt like a true member of the pride, he knew he would not lose that sense.

Losing Ava was a much more real danger.

How was it that the woman he'd been seeking, the one he knew instinctively was meant to be his mate, didn't want the position? Could she have so little awareness of her own value?

She was extraordinary, and it fell to him to convince her of that. If he didn't die of starvation first.

She was soundly asleep. Maybe if he slipped out quickly to grab them some food, he could be back before she—

His thoughts broke off as the door to the bungalow slammed open, ricocheting off the wall with a deafening *bang.*

Ava sat up, abruptly awake. Landon shoved her behind him, already crouched to protect her, as Caleb, the second oldest, and largest, of Ava's four brothers burst into the room.

"Ava's missing!" he shouted then stumbled to a halt when he recognized his sister's pale eyes peering at him over Landon's shoulder.

Michael, the youngest of the four, plowed into Caleb's back as he stormed into the room behind him. Then he looked up and saw what had shocked his brother into immobility.

Michael reacted first. He shifted instantaneously, one moment a large, heavily muscled young man, the next a massive, dark golden lion with a jet black mane that had still not grown to full maturity. Caleb shifted a fraction of a second later. Larger than his brother, with streaks of reds and browns in his dark mane, he was fully grown and a much more formidable opponent.

Caleb snarled and instinct consumed Landon. Something threatened his mate.

He launched himself off the bed, shifting in mid leap to land in front of them on all fours, roaring his rage, his hackles high beneath his own golden mane.

Caleb matched his height at the shoulder, but his body was heavier. Landon knew his superior speed and maneuverability would be little advantage with Michael there, younger but still dangerous in his own right, to even out the fight. In the blind rage filling his mind, there was no question as to whether he would fight them. He would protect his mate.

Caleb shifted his weight on his haunches. Landon braced to receive the attack, when suddenly a small white lioness leapt between them, hissing at the dark pair and batting a paw at Caleb's muzzle. Her claws were not extended, but the big lion jerked his head back and coughed in surprise and anger.

Landon snarled to hear the aggressive sound directed at his mate, but Ava's small, lithe form crowded him back, pressing him away from her brothers. She rubbed her head beneath his chin and leaned her slight body against his, maintaining herself as a barrier between him and the other lions. Landon let her herd him away, reason slowly returning as he realized her brothers would never hurt her, no matter how his instincts might scream otherwise.

Ava purred loudly, the vibration soothing him. She shoved against his body until he lay down, separated by the length of the room from her brothers. She then turned and hissed angrily in their direction. Both of the lions took a step back, their taken-aback reactions oddly human.

Caleb shifted back first, hastily reaching for the clothing that had been all but destroyed by his rapid shift. Nudity was not scandalous among the pride where they all walked in two skins, but apparently finding his little sister naked in bed with his Alpha had given Caleb a newfound respect for modesty.

Michael remained in lion form, as Landon suspected he would until he himself shifted back.

Caleb wrapped the remains of his shirt around his waist like a loincloth and extended a hand to the white lioness. "Come with us, Ava."

Landon couldn't contain the low growl that rumbled in his throat. They would not take his mate.

Chapter Ten

Ava gazed back and forth between her brothers and her lover. This was not how she had imagined her night with Landon ending. Though, to be truthful, she hadn't envisioned it ending at all. Knowing a fairy tale has to end and picturing herself actually walking out the door were two very different things.

And she had known. She did know. It was time for her to leave. But that didn't make walking away any easier.

Ava took a step toward Caleb's outstretched hand. Landon lunged to his feet, growling, but Ava knew better than to think his possessive posturing was anything more than instinctual reflex. It wasn't like his emotions were involved, after all.

Ava hissed at him over her shoulder, urging him to back down, not to make a fuss. Across the room, Michael growled low. Landon couldn't stop her, not with her brothers here. Perhaps their presence, mortifying as it was, was for the best.

Ava continued across the room. Landon didn't make another sound, though she could feel his green-gold eyes tracking every twitch of her tail. She padded past her brothers without pausing and out into the late morning sunlight. She didn't stop to await the scolding she knew was coming, instead breaking into an easy lope, heading toward the tiny bungalow she'd claimed for her own.

Michael followed, all but stepping on her tail, until she spun and swiped at him, snarling irritably. The youngest and most impulsive of her brothers backed off a few steps, but continued to dog her steps until she leapt up onto the small porch in front of her place and whipped around to hiss at him. Caleb was beside him, once again in his lion form, and they easily could have bullied their way into the bungalow after her and demanded answers she was in no mood to give, but instead they surprised her by darting off to the other end of the complex. Doubtless to round up her other brothers to present her with the full force of their anger. Ava shuddered, her fur rippling over her body. What a lovely thing to look forward to. Being taken to task for finally doing something for herself. Finally stepping out of the protective bubble her brothers had built for her at birth.

Ava turned and smacked the door open with her paw, pleased for once that the doors on her house never latched properly. She started to pad toward her closet, but whipped around with a snarl, sensing another presence in her small sanctuary.

Her place wasn't large or luxurious, as all of the premiere accommodations belonged to the strongest members of the pride. Ava had intentionally chosen the smallest, most squalid shack in the complex, the one that no one would bother to steal from her, and turned it into something remarkably cozy. Cozy, but still barely large enough to turn around in, and certainly not large enough for anyone to hide from her.

Shana wasn't trying to hide though. She very much wanted her presence to be known.

One of the few lions Ava had ever seen whose hair didn't match her pelt, the tall, muscular redhead stood in front of Ava's vanity. Gilded by the sunlight streaming through the window, Shana was breathtaking, statuesque and completely self-assured. She toyed with a piece of jewelry, unconcerned by the threat of the white lioness crouched only a few feet away.

"Oh, don't stop on my account," Shana said, waving a hand magnanimously. "By all means, change."

As Shana did not seem inclined to give her privacy, Ava didn't see much of an alternative. She shifted into her human form, straightening the kinks out of her spine that always seemed to accompany the shift, and turned to pull a sundress out of the closet and over her head. She turned back to Shana, clothed, but by no means comfortable.

"What do you want?" she asked bluntly.

She realized her error as soon as Shana's eyes flared with surprise. "My, my, look who's finally grown some teeth." Shana let the pendant in her hands drop to spin at the end of the chain. "Are you so certain your lover will protect you, little Ava? He isn't known for being steadfast. Trust me."

Ava fought not to wince visibly. It had been foolish to hope no one would know about her night with Landon and downright idiocy to think the other females vying for position with him wouldn't respond to her implied threat to their aspirations. She should have known that Shana would come to take her down a peg. She just hadn't expected the reminder that Landon had slept with the gorgeous redhead to sting quite so viciously.

"No comment? Don't tell me you've lost your courage already? Poor little Ava."

She continued to spin the pendant and Ava's eyes flicked down, attracted by the movement, then held by recognition. It was hers. Ava had bought the green-gold stone in town less than a month ago on impulse. The setting was simple, the stone itself not particularly valuable, but Ava hadn't been able to put it down.

It was the exact shade of Landon's eyes.

Apparently, Shana had recognized the color as well, rifling through Ava's meager jewelry box as she waited for her to return.

"Quite pretty, this," she remarked, too casually for Ava's comfort. "I think I might borrow it. It would flatter me, don't you think? Maybe I'll wear it tonight."

"Tonight?"

Shana laughed, not kindly. "Little Ava, don't tell me you've forgotten. Tonight is the Midsummer Hunt." She gave a feline smile. "I know he hasn't said anything, but speculation has been going around that the Alpha will name his mate tonight." She held the pendant up against her throat. "I'll look fetching standing beside him wearing this, don't you think?"

Ava couldn't speak. She knew Landon hadn't given Shana any reason to think she would be his consort, but the larger lioness's acid-tipped words brought home the reality of the situation. She knew better than to stand up for herself and try to take back the pendant. Shana was bigger and stronger and never turned down a fight, no matter how petty.

A wave of defeat swamped her. Ava couldn't even keep possession of one worthless little pendant. How was she supposed to keep order in the tribe as the Alpha's consort?

Landon would choose another. And apparently, he would

do it tonight. In time for his new mate to lead the Hunt.

"Well, I'll be off then," Shana said brightly. "You don't mind if I borrow this, do you."

It was not a question. Ava kept her head down, as the larger, notoriously temperamental and aggressive redhead stalked out of her home, spinning the "borrowed" stone pendant in her hands.

After the fantasy of last night, reality's brutality stung. Ava curled up on the floor beside her twin bed, determined not to cry.

It was galling enough when Landon realized he didn't know where the woman he wanted to make his mate lived. Doubly so when he had to go knocking on his little sister's door to get directions.

Zoe opened the door on the first knock and leaned against the frame, scraps of shredded denim dangling from one finger. "Missing something?"

Landon felt an unfamiliar heat rushing to his face when he recognized Ava's mangled jeans. He snatched them out of Zoe's hand and shoved them behind his back, though that did nothing to lessen his sister's knowing smirk. "I need you to tell me which bungalow is Ava's."

Zoe shot him the look she had perfected as a toddler. The how-is-it-possible-I-share-a-genetic-code-with-this-moron look. "You don't know where she lives?" she asked incredulously.

He ignored the question, waiting and hoping she would give up the information without a hassle.

She folded her arms and frowned at him. "Why do you need to see her so badly? What did you say to her?"

So much for that hope. "I'm not in the mood for games, Zo. Just tell me where she is." He had to find Ava and convince her she belonged with him. Preferably before her brothers returned to rip his arms from their sockets.

Zoe glowered at him, unimpressed by his demand. "It's a game if I want to make sure you haven't hurt my friend before I sic you on her?"

"I would never hurt her. You know that."

"You wouldn't smack her around or anything, but you're still just a big dumb man and big dumb men say stupid, hurtful things all the time. Did you really tell her you thought she was unsuitable?"

Landon winced. "That was a misunderstanding."

"And why'd she run off without telling you where to find her? Was that a misunderstanding too?"

"Her brothers showed up," he gritted out.

Zoe's face tightened. "Meddlesome punks. Trust them to ruin everything." She shoved herself away from the doorframe and sent an acid glare in the general direction of the Minor brothers' bungalows. "Ava's place is on the south edge of the ranch. It's that little cabin. You know, the one that looks like a stiff wind would blow it right over."

Landon knew the place, but it had never occurred to him that anyone might actually live in the shack. Let alone Ava.

He made his way to the southern edge of the compound, giving the Minor brothers' turf a wide berth. He drew up short when he saw Ava's cabin—and the hot-tempered lion standing guard on her rickety front porch.

Ava's youngest brother, Michael, snapped to attention and spun to face him when the breeze carrying his scent alerted him to Landon's presence.

"Get away from here!" Michael roared. His hands broke out into claws as his temper called up his most predatory form.

Landon shoved the wadded up remains of Ava's jeans behind his back and raised his other hand in classic surrender. He approached slowly. "I just need to talk to her."

"I said get away!" Michael's spine bowed as his lion form struggled to break free.

Landon's own lion instincts rose in response, the urge to shift and fight nearly overwhelming. "Don't think you can keep me from her, cub," he heard himself growl.

Michael bared his teeth in a snarl. He tensed to spring and Landon braced himself to take the impact.

"Stop it, both of you!"

Ava appeared on the porch behind her brother, her pale gray eyes flashing.

"Go back inside, Ava," Michael ordered without turning. "This doesn't concern you."

Bad call, buddy.

All of Ava's ire honed in on her brother. "It doesn't *concern* me? I'm the *only* one this concerns. Get off my porch, Michael."

Michael appeared to realize—much too late—that he had erred. "I didn't mean—"

"I said get away," she snapped. "I can talk to whoever I want."

"But Tyler said..."

"Leave!"

Michael left, but not before he cast one last threatening glare at Landon.

When he was gone, Landon came forward, drawn toward Ava, until the look she shot him froze him in place.

"Just because I don't want him around, it doesn't mean I want you here."

Landon thought wistfully of the woman who had curled around him so warm and accepting in her sleep. There was no trace of her in the forbidding glower of the woman on the porch.

"I come in peace," he offered lightly, extending the tattered denim toward her.

A flicker of a smile tried to break through Ava's glare and failed. "That's a pretty pathetic peace offering."

Levity hadn't worked, so he tried a more serious tack. He met her wary eyes directly, urging her to see his determination. "We have more to say to one another, Ava."

The expression that tried to break through her anger this time was heartbreakingly sad and utterly resigned. "I've said all I have to say."

"I haven't."

For a second that seemed to drag on forever, he thought she would turn him away. Then she shrugged and stepped aside, nodding toward the narrow doorway. "Come in then."

He had to duck to cross the threshold and, once inside, he couldn't straighten fully without knocking his head on the exposed beams of the ceiling. He felt like a bull in a china shop, his shoulder nearly knocking a small framed photo of Ava and her brothers off the wall when he turned to study the space she had made her home. In spite of the shabby exterior, Ava's cabin had a cozy, if unimpressive, charm. An unassuming hominess.

She stepped into the tiny room behind him and closed the

door. As soon as it clicked shut, the memory of the last time they'd been alone together rose in his mind. The room was saturated in her scent and his body reacted to it, his instincts screaming that she was *his*.

Now all he had to do was convince her of that fact. The confident temptress who had seduced him last night was gone. In her place was a meek waif who refused to meet his eyes.

She leaned against the door and fidgeted with the knick-knacks on the window ledge to her right. "So, this is the reality," she said, waving a carved lion figurine at the room at large. "Small."

"It suits you." He saw her face close off and internally winced. Evidently not the right thing to say. As she continued to fidget and glance around the room, blushing and squirming, he realized with a jolt she was ashamed of her home, even though it seemed homey and somehow perfectly *her* to him. "I like it. It's cozy."

The look she shot him was saturated with disbelief, but she didn't come right out and call him a liar. He wasn't sure if that was progress or not.

"When Zoe and I lived without a pride, we didn't have much of anything. You learn to appreciate the things that make a place a home." He carefully straightened the photo he'd knocked askew.

She continued to fidget and he reached out to rescue the lion carving she was twisting to death. She snatched her hands behind her back when he brushed her fingers, relinquishing the carving without a fight.

The wooden figure was small enough fit in the palm of his hand, but the details were so intricate and the artisan so skilled, he could immediately identify the form. It was a miniature replica of her brother Tyler as a crouching lion.

"Amazing," he murmured to himself. He noted a dozen similar figures, each readily identifiable, scattered on ledges around the room. "You like carvings?"

She flushed and squirmed, but this time there was a quiet pride beneath her nervous fidgeting.

Landon smiled broadly. "You made this? It's beautiful." He stepped toward her, brushing his thumb across her cheek. "My little Ava has a hidden talent."

Her pleasure at his praise visibly evaporated and she

flinched away from his touch. "I'm not your little Ava."

That remained to be determined.

"Fantasy time is over, Landon," she went on coldly. "We're back in the real world now and in the real world I live in the smallest cabin on the ranch. Not because it's *cozy*. Because I am the smallest, weakest, most pathetic lioness around and I can't fight for a better one."

She waved one arm, the gesture taking in all the little possessions that made the place her own. "These things are only mine because no one else wants them enough to bother to take them from me. And you think, what? That I'm your *queen*? Wake up, Landon."

He caught her waving hand and linked their fingers, holding tight when she tried to yank free. "I think you're my mate. *You* are what I need. You're right for me and right for the pride."

He tipped her face back with the hand that still held her carving, staring into her eyes, searching their depths for the secret key that would unlock her doubts. He wanted nothing more than to kiss away her fears, but the wildness in her eyes held him at bay. He may be the Alpha now, but he knew fear.

"I've lived wild, Ava, without the protection of the pride. I understand picking your battles."

"I don't pick my battles." She knocked his hand away from her face and jerked her fingers from his hold. "I *fear* battles. Your mate can't be a coward, Landon. And that's all I'll ever be."

"Ava, I don't—"

"Why are you doing this, Land—?" Her voice broke on his name. She shoved away from him and moved as far away from him as she could in the cramped space. "You can't actually want me. Is this some kind of game to you?"

Tears trembled on her lashes. All her barriers were down. She gazed at him with a vulnerability that made his heart ache in his chest. He reached toward her, aching to pull her into his arms and protect her from everything that could ever hurt her. Even himself.

"Ava, no. Of course n—"

"*Landon!*"

The roar came from Ava's porch, giving Landon just enough time to jump out of the way before the door exploded inward, flying off its hinges as the Minor brothers stormed into the already crowded cabin.

Michael was back. And he'd brought reinforcements.

There was no more terrifying sight, objectively speaking, than the four behemoth older brothers of the woman one had recently screwed in every way physically imaginable coming at you with murder in their eyes. Unless it was the sight of the woman you love in tears.

Landon braced himself for the beating he so richly deserved.

He was mildly surprised when fists didn't immediately start flying toward his face.

"Outside! No brawling in my house!"

They all turned to look at her. The tears were a memory and in their place was the icy, distant mask that had greeted him this morning.

Landon vaguely noted that Ava hadn't said no brawling at all. Apparently, she thought kicking his ass was okay, so long as they didn't wreck her house to do it.

Her brothers filed out, silent and grave, but Landon hesitated, his heart tight. He couldn't leave her like this. Ava watched him steadily, her face closed to him again, any ground he had gained in the last few minutes erased. The cool strength in her gaze only convinced him further that he had made the right choice, but she clearly didn't agree. He'd had his shot to convince her she was his, and obviously he'd fucked it up.

Outside, Tyler barked his name. "I'm leaving," he shouted back, reluctantly putting action to the words and mentally adding, *for now.* He hadn't given up yet.

Landon stepped out onto the porch to face the firing squad and quickly moved to the open area in front of Ava's cabin where he'd have the best maneuverability if they suddenly decided to jump him. Not that he didn't deserve a few good licks. He'd known he was betraying their trust, but that hadn't stopped him. Landon wondered idly if anything could have stopped him from claiming Ava. Frankly, he doubted it.

The Minor brothers ranged around him, taking position at compass points to box him in, but staying out of his reach.

Tyler, the oldest and apparent designated spokesman of the group, grunted. "Will you go quietly or do you want to do this in front of the entire pride?"

Landon glanced around. It was early afternoon, a popular

siesta time among the cats, and there were few bystanders to qualify as "the whole pride", but he stepped out of his defensive stance, opting for a strategic retreat. Tyler fell into step beside him as he forced himself to walk away from Ava, her other brothers ranging behind.

"Did you know who she was?"

Landon almost wished he could say he hadn't. Ava's only resemblance to her large, dark brothers, was a slight similarity in the shape of her eyes. It would be so easy to claim ignorance and escape the blame.

"I knew."

Directly behind him, Michael growled. Tyler shot him a quelling look and returned his gimlet stare to Landon. "Would you care to explain how she ended up naked in your room?"

Another opportunity to deny his culpability. All he had to do was say Ava had walked into his room and asked to be fucked. It was truth, but it wasn't the whole story. And Ava being held responsible for their night together didn't sit well with him.

"I found her in the Bar Nothing in town last night. Brought her back here."

"That pick-up bar?" Michael yelped. "Ava wouldn't be caught dead in there!"

"Mike, shut up," Tyler said calmly, his attention never wavering from Landon. "You brought her back to your place," he repeated. "And you knew who she was."

Landon swallowed. He wasn't afraid of the brothers, but he did dread their reaction. Even more than the fist he was sure he was about to get in his face, he dreaded the loss of their trust. "I did."

Tyler nodded slowly, his face revealing nothing. "Is there anything you'd like to add?"

Landon considered mentioning she was going to be his mate, that this was not the one night stand they assumed it to be, but Ava was so stubbornly against the idea. She thought she didn't want the position and no one was going to bully her into taking it but him. Her brothers would just have to wait, and think the worst of him, until he could convince her to see reason.

Landon stopped, facing Tyler squarely. "No."

"I see."

Landon was willing to bet Tyler didn't see, but he maintained his silence, meeting his stare head-on.

At length, Tyler nodded to his brothers. "We're done here."

Caleb and Kane peeled off without comment, but Michael snarled at Landon, jostling his shoulder as he brushed past. Tyler waited until his three younger brothers were out of earshot before turning back to Landon.

He didn't see it coming. One second he was on his feet, the next he was sprawled out on the ground, holding his aching jaw. Tyler loomed over him, his face still dangerously expressionless.

"You so much as look her way again and I'll kill you," he said with icy calm.

"You're staying?" Landon hadn't realized until that moment how much the idea of them leaving, and taking Ava with them, terrified him.

"We're still discussing it," Tyler said flatly. "You'll have your answer tomorrow if we decide to leave the pride. See you at the Hunt."

Ava's oldest brother walked away without another word.

One day to convince Ava to become his mate and if he even looked in her direction, her brothers would tear him apart. Landon sat up, cradling his jaw, and swore with feeling.

Chapter Eleven

Ava normally hated the Hunts—the last thing she needed was a quarterly gathering of the pride to remind her how inadequate she was—but tonight she was actually looking forward to it. It was masochistic in the extreme, but she needed to be there when Landon selected his mate. Her heart needed to see him do it, officially give himself to another woman, if it was to have any hope of letting him go.

He'd seemed to want her so much. He'd actually seemed to care. Seeing him in her home, her tiny pathetic *cozy* little home, had been both mortifying and thrilling. Mortifying because he had seen her as she really was, in her true environment, but thrilling for that same reason. He had seen the real her. And he had wanted her still.

Ava needed visual proof that it had all been a fantasy. She needed the vicious slap of reality to crush the hope in her heart that just wouldn't die.

Her brothers had been lurking nearby all day, ever since they'd run him off, but so far none of them had mentioned her nocturnal activities. She knew it was too much to hope that they never would, but she was hoping their surprising lack of curiosity lasted as long as possible.

Tonight, she took particular care with her appearance, even though the sarong she wore would only be discarded when they all shifted for the Hunt and all traces of make-up would be absorbed in the transformation. Ava wanted to look good when Landon saw her again, though she avoided analyzing *why* it was so important that she impress him with her sex appeal. An appeal she hadn't even known she had until last night.

When she stepped out onto the small front porch of her

cabin, Tyler straightened from his post, leaning against the rail. He fell into step beside her, a large, silent presence at her back, escorting her across the compound like she needed a bodyguard.

His overprotective posturing was oddly welcome. Ava was feeling a little too vulnerable, on her way to watch Landon choose her replacement in his bed, and her brother's presence was a comfort, even if his intention was to be her jailer rather than her buffer against the world.

The pride always gathered for the Hunt in the natural amphitheatre on the far side of the complex. The ranch had once been a summer camp and that amphitheatre was where campers showed off their amateur dramas on parents' day and gathered for weenie roasts and jamborees, but now the old pines encircling the space saw celebrations of a slightly more bacchanalian nature. Ava had often amused herself, as she sat in the darkness during pride gatherings, wondering how the founders of the original camp would have reacted if they could have spied on some of the "clothing optional" parties that were so common among the lions. The lack of clothing was more practical than puerile—the change destroyed any clothing not discarded before shifting—but somehow Ava suspected the old camp counselors wouldn't see it that way.

The amphitheatre was already filling when they came into the clearing. Tyler steered her to a spot near the raised platform where her other brothers had already gathered. She stopped next to them and they quickly formed a living wall around her.

Ava rolled her eyes. There was protection and then there was annoying, overbearing, bullying overkill. She could barely move and she certainly couldn't see a damn thing with their massive backs shoulder-to-shoulder blocking her view.

How was she supposed to get the catharsis of seeing Landon with another and releasing her love of him if all she could see was a row of bulging deltoids?

Ava twisted around, trying to get a better line of sight. There was a gap between Michael and Kane behind her, not wide enough for her to slip through, even if they hadn't been watching her like hawks, but big enough for her to see a slice of the rest of the audience.

The Three Rocks Pride, so named because of the three rocks that marked the boundaries of the original camp, was larger than the prides of African lions, with approximately fifty members at any given time. Most of those fifty were mingling behind her, some nude, some wearing easily disposed of wraps like her own loosely-tied sarong. In the shifting crowd, she spotted Shana, wearing only the "borrowed" pendant and a feline smile.

Ava forced back the surge of irritation—and bile—that rose up at the sight of that smile. Shana may very well be the Alpha's Consort by the end of the night and she would just have to get used to it. Tyler turned to frown down at her when she couldn't quite stifle a gagging noise.

Then he turned back toward the platform and Ava knew, without being able to see a thing, even before the restless crowd behind her began to quiet, that Landon had arrived. She could *feel* him.

Silence rippled out from the platform. When the only sound was the all-but-inaudible hum of excitement, anticipation of the Hunt firing in every shifter's blood, Landon spoke, not raising his voice, but somehow making himself heard to every corner of the clearing.

"Friends..."

Ava half expected him to call out to Romans and countrymen next, but he continued on a much less Shakespearean bent.

"This is our first opportunity to Hunt together since I arrived among you. I have had a few months to learn your ways and find my place among you. There is a great strength in our pride, but my rule is going to be a time of change and that change will begin tonight."

Some among the crowd shifted uneasily, but most of the pride hung on his words. He was a charismatic speaker, their Alpha. Even Ava, who could not see him through the wall of flesh around her, was drawn up in the power of his voice. He held the crowd in the palm of his hand, wrapped in the draw of his presence more than the words he said, but Ava heard every word.

"Our strongest young men will no longer be turned out of the pride when they reach maturity and no longer will the females be required to remain with the pride their entire lives. We will foster relationships with other prides to provide other opportunities for our young, rather than seeking isolation in a world that is steadily closing in around us. Like any species, we must adapt or face extinction. We are powerful predators, but our social evolution leaves much to be desired. We can learn much from our human neighbors in matters of tolerance and understanding."

Though many were still caught up in his words, the restless rumblings in the crowd were growing now.

"I do not threaten our traditions," he assured them. "The Hunts will continue, but instead of my mate leading the Hunt and selecting those who are allowed to participate, it will be thrown open to all who wish to participate, but required of none."

Ava felt a surge of relief at his words. The only thing worse than not being selected for the Hunt, in her opinion, was being selected and then struggling to keep up with the stronger, faster lionesses. She'd always thought it was horribly unfair that her slighter weight had not translated into superior speed. There ought to be *some* advantage to being the runt.

"My mate will be my voice in the pride when I am not here, but there will be no more ruling by force, no more bullying the weaker members."

Ava snorted to herself. How Landon expected to be able to enforce the no-bullying rule was beyond her. Changing the format of the Hunt was one thing, but he couldn't just wave a magic wand and eliminate the hierarchy of strength within the pride.

"We are both animal *and* man. We are capable of civilized—"

"Heresy!" A rough, sickeningly familiar voice cut across Landon's, shouting from the back of the amphitheatre.

Ava turned, along with most of the rest of the pride, and watched as Landon's banished predecessor, Leonus, stepped out of the shadows. She looked around for his enforcer and ever-present sidekick, Kato, but the hulking bully was nowhere to be seen.

"Lions rule by strength," he roared, approaching the platform as the pride members parted like the Red Sea to allow him to pass. "If they do not, then what right have you to rule over me, Landon King? Would you change our very nature, boy? Is this what has become of my pride in three short months? Anarchy over tradition? A destruction of the very values that make us what we are?"

Landon's voice rose, calm and confident, over Leonus's. "I do not demand that you change your values. I do not even demand that you live by my rules. Only that you do so if you continue to live here, at Three Rocks."

"Throwing others out of their homes now, boy?"

"We all have a choice. Live here honorably, or live elsewhere however you please."

"The only honor is in victory," Leonus shouted. "I have returned to challenge you to reclaim mine."

A collective gasp swept through the pride. It was not unheard of for supplanted lions to return to challenge those who had taken over their pride, but Landon's victory over Leonus had been almost laughably easy three months earlier when Landon had been half-starved from the uncertain life of a nomad and Leonus had been at full strength. Now that their positions were reversed, Leonus could not hope to succeed. Not fairly, at least.

Ava looked around again, wondering where Kato was hiding. She was not left to wonder for long.

A roar not heard in the pride for three months echoed across the amphitheatre from behind the platform. Leonus shifted right behind her and suddenly her brothers swept her away from the platform. Ava caught a glimpse of Landon, already in his lion form, being knocked from the platform by Leonus's huge enforcer. They landed in a tangle in the space Ava and her brothers had just vacated, and Leonus leapt forward to swipe at Landon, claws out.

Ava cried out in protest before her view was once again blocked by her brothers. She stared at their immobile backs in shock. Why weren't they helping Landon? This was no true challenge, no fair fight. How could they just stand by and let him be mauled?

She spun, scanning the crowd, looking for others springing to his aid. She saw Shana, standing back with her head tipped to one side as if watching a sporting match, with no real interest in who came out the victor. At the back of the crowd, she could see Zoe shoving her way to the front, but by the time she got there...

Whereas Ava was right next to the action, separated only by her brothers, standing with their legs planted wide.

She reached for the tie on her sarong, shifting and snaking between Caleb's legs before the fabric had time to flutter to the ground.

As she darted forward into the cleared area, Landon, his golden coat spotted with blood from the claw marks across his shoulder, shoved with his powerful hind legs, throwing Kato's bulk off him and rolling clear of Leonus's snapping jaws. He scrambled away from them, freezing in a defensive crouch when the small white lioness suddenly appeared at his side.

Leonus and Kato squared off against them, hesitating now that the odds had been leveled against them.

Ava snarled, trying to look formidable and less like a puny little weakling who had never fought for anything in her life, never dared dispute her place in the pride. Landon stepped forward, his body shielding hers from the aggressive males, but she would not let herself be protected. Not at his expense. She stepped forward with him, all but shaking with fear but determined to stand by him.

Then suddenly Caleb appeared at her other shoulder, shaking his red-black mane. Tyler roared from Landon's side as her other brothers prowled forward, aggressively circling Leonus and Kato. Zoe broke from the crowd in time to feint at the would-be usurpers, hissing and barking. With a ripple of movement, the rest of the pride quickly took their lion forms, crowding around with bared teeth and claws.

Landon drew himself up and roared, the fierce vocalization echoing in the amphitheatre. The shadows of that roar chased his attackers as they turned tail and fled. Zoe and Michael leapt after them, intent on driving them out of the Three Rocks territory. Half a dozen others quickly joined them, eager for a run.

In the chaos that followed their departure, as some shifted back to human form and others celebrated the pride's victory in lion form, Landon nipped Ava's ear to get her attention and herded her away from the roiling crowd to the relative privacy behind the platform.

He shifted back to human form and she followed suit, accepting the sarong he whipped off the shelf behind the platform and wrapped around her. Careless of his own nudity, his eyes raced over her as if to assure himself she was whole. Ava's did the same, her eyes drawn again and again to the gashes across his shoulder where Leonus's claws had gouged him.

"Those cuts look deep. You should—"

"It's nothing," he said roughly, brushing aside her concern. "What were you thinking?"

Ava blinked, startled by the abrupt question. "What?"

"You could have been hurt, Ava."

"You *were* being hurt, Landon. What did you expect me to do?"

His face twisted, his expression conflicted, as if he couldn't decide whether he ought to be angry or elated. "The lioness who is brave enough to fight at my side, throwing all concern for her own safety out the window, is my true mate, Ava."

His words were like treasures, but Ava knew better than to think she'd be allowed to keep them. "I'm not strong or fast..."

"No. You're smart and brave. And you tell me when you think I'm being a foolish idealist."

"You are," she insisted. "The pride won't accept me as your mate any more than they will accept all your other changes."

"They will accept you and you will help me show them how to accept the other changes."

"Landon," she sighed. It was a lovely dream, but one of them had to stay awake and face reality. "The consort is never someone like me."

"No, but maybe she should be."

"And if the pride won't accept me? What then?"

"Then we find another pride. It isn't so bad, you know, being a nomad. I would rather be an Alpha without a pride to rule than to rule this one without you." He cupped her face between his hands. "Be my mate, Ava. Be my love. Be all the things that only you can be. Please, just say yes."

He was a fool. It would never work, but staring into the gorgeous green-gold eyes of the man she loved, she couldn't think of a single reason why. All she could think was what a miracle it was that he wanted her, lowly little Ava. He saw her answer in the tiny feline smile curving her lips before she gave him the single word that would seal their fates.

"Yes."

Landon whooped and swept her up against his chest, spinning her around until she was laughing and dizzy. When he stopped spinning, he continue to hold her pressed tightly against him, her feet inches off the ground. His lips brushed across hers, a soft question. She tightened her arms around his neck and answered him the only way she knew how, with her mouth on his. Passion spiked instantly, sharp and hot between them, even though her heat had long since subsided.

When she pulled back, they were both breathless and the light in Landon's eyes promised that she would not be given a chance to catch her breath back.

"I suppose we'd better introduce you to the pride," he said, slowly easing her feet back down to solid ground.

Anxiety tangled in her stomach. That was the one hitch in her perfect dream. He had said he would be her mate without a pride, but he obviously did not believe they would repudiate her as his mate. What would he do when it came time to put actions to his words? Would he choose her? Or the pride he had fought for and won?

Landon leapt up onto the platform, tugging her behind him. As Landon raised his hands for silence, Ava looked out over the crowd. Those who had run off Leonus and Kato had returned. She saw Zoe looking unbearably smug and her brothers frowning up at her as Landon held her hand tightly in his own, preventing her retreat.

She didn't hear the words Landon called out over the crowd. Her nerves buzzed too loudly in her ears. She saw surprise on many faces, frowns on some—her brothers among them—and, amazingly, smiles on more than a few. The buzzing in her ears diminished when Landon raised their entwined fingers to his lips, brushing a kiss across her knuckles, and a rough cheer went up. Ava flinched a little at the sound, blinking owlishly. They were cheering her? Pathetic little Ava?

"Now, to the Hunt!" Landon shouted. A thousand golden hues of fur sprang out in the crowd as the pride shifted. Zoe was among the first to tear out of the clearing, leading the charge toward the poor cattle herd on the menu tonight.

As the amphitheatre emptied, Ava looked at Landon, still standing beside her, watching his pride depart with an easy smile on his lips and her hand clasped tightly in his.

"Wouldn't you like to join them?" she asked softly.

Her lover, her *mate*, turned to her and smiled wickedly. "I only have one kind of prey on my mind tonight."

Ava smiled, feeling a female, feline power she had never known before this man came into her life. "You'll have to catch me first."

She leapt from the platform, shifting in the air, and landed on all fours in a run. She heard a masculine chuckle transform into a distinctly leonine sound and the sounds of pursuit behind her, but she did not look back. She raced through the compound toward his bungalow, feeling him close on her heels, knowing he was letting her win, matching his pace to hers, but she didn't care. For once it wasn't about being the fastest or the strongest, just about running with her mate. Laughter she couldn't express in this form bubbled in her heart like champagne.

She bounded up onto the front step of his bungalow inches in front of Landon, shifting as he did. His arms wrapped around her and he pressed her against the door, his stunning heat and strength warming her to her core. His mouth closed over hers. Ava's dizzy happiness would not be contained and she laughed against his lips, coiling her arms around him.

She felt him fumbling for the doorknob. He drew back from the laughing kiss, a small frown pinching his eyebrows as he raised his hand between them. Dangling from his fingers was the green-gold pendant. Ava gasped and Landon arched his brow in question.

"What is it? Some kind of pride mating medallion?"

Ava laughed. "Something like that." She raised her hand and cupped the pendant in her hand, smiling to herself. Shana must have run here to leave it for her. Ava's eyes filled with tears and she blinked them back, surprising herself by how affected she was by Shana's small concession. Landon was still frowning, now with concern. She reassured him with a blinding smile. "You know, love, I think your idealistic fantasy might just have a chance of working."

His frown eased into a cocky grin. "I never doubted it for a second."

She held the pendant up next to her mate's eyes, comparing the color. She sighed, "Perfect."

He traced the curve of her face with one finger, his eyes trained steadily on hers. "My thoughts exactly."

She raised up on her tiptoes to meet his kiss, a wild dizzy heat spiraling through her body at the first brush of contact. He shoved the door open and swept her into his arms. Landon carried her across the threshold and kicked the door shut, all without lifting his mouth from hers. Ava curled into his arms, a feline smile curving the mouth he held captive, and purred.

He laid her on the bed, lowering himself beside her and she stretched like the cat she was, at home in her skin and in his arms.

"So there's only a risk of shifting at climax when I'm in heat?" she asked him as he nuzzled the side of her neck, inhaling deeply.

"No, anytime you lose control it could happen," he murmured, sliding down her body.

Ava arched against him and smiled. "Make me lose control, Landon."

Her lover laughed low against her skin and bent his head to do just that.

About the Author

To learn more about Vivi Andrews, please visit her website at www.viviandrews.com or stop by her blog at http://viviandrews.blogspot.com. Vivi loves to hear from readers. You can email her at vivi@viviandrews.com.

Look for these titles by
Vivi Andrews

Now Available:

The Ghost Shrink, the Accidental Gigolo
& the Poltergeist Accountant

Karmic Consultants Series
The Ghost Exterminator: A Love Story

Serengeti Storm

Print Anthology
Tickle My Fantasy

Kiss and Kin

Kinsey Holley

Dedication

I sat on the porch drinking champagne with my two sisters-in-law one night and said, "Y'know, I think I could write a paranormal romance." They said, "Of course you can."

I wouldn't have started, and I couldn't have finished, without them.

I had this fantasy that one day I'd get published, and we'd sit on the porch and drink champagne to celebrate, and when the book came out I'd dedicate it to them. We've done the champagne, so here's the dedication. To Vickie and Wendy.

Chapter One

Lark inspected her reflection in her antique full-length mirror. Applying final touches to her makeup, she pursed her lips and smudged her gloss just a bit. She pulled her auburn chestnut hair into a carefully messy chignon, touchable stray wisps framing her face the way Taran liked it.

Dressed in a purple lace bra, boyshorts and four-inch stilettos, she struck a little pose. Which dress to wear?

They both showed off her legs. The chic black cocktail number featured a fun little twirly skit, and she fancied herself a fun twirly kind of girl. On the other hand, she liked to look like a bad girl sometimes, which she did in the lavender sheath with the plunging neckline and the slit up to mid thigh.

She held up each dress beneath her chin, one at a time, and eyed herself critically. *Lavender, black. Lavender, black.*

She heard Taran getting ready in the bathroom, but when he suddenly appeared behind her—a werewolf could move so swiftly and silently it seemed he teleported—he wore nothing but skin. Taking a hanger in each hand, he tossed the dresses aside. He laid a large, warm hand on her stomach and pulled her tightly against him while his other hand cupped her breast. His thumb rubbed circles around her nipple through the thin lace.

"What are you doing here?" he growled softly. His stubble tickled her neck as he nuzzled. It made her laugh.

He rolled her nipple between two fingers and she sighed, reaching back to run her fingers through his dark gold hair. His other hand now cupped her mound, barely touching, and she ground her hips, silently urging him to press harder. He chuckled.

"I'm trying to choose a dress," she smiled. "Which do you like?"

"Neither," he replied. "I vote for naked." He nipped her shoulder and slid his hand inside the boyshorts.

Their gazes met in the mirror, the only way she could maintain eye contact with him. Lust glittered in his eyes, making them shine like emeralds. Her dark blue eyes melted in submission. In heels, she stood almost as tall as he did, but she looked petite against his much larger body.

"I can't go to dinner like this, and neither can you," she murmured.

"True." He ran his tongue lightly down the back of her neck. "Anthony's has a dress code. Reservations at eight, right?"

"Yes." She shivered.

She gasped as his middle finger sank into her folds and stroked.

"So..." he smiled against her neck, "...I've got ten minutes to make you come. I can do that with one arm tied behind your back."

He took his hand out of her panties, spun her around and pinned one of her arms behind her. She moaned in anticipation as his mouth came down on hers, and she woke up.

Damn it. Shit. Damn, damn, damn, shit.

Lark rolled over and slammed her head into the pillow.

She couldn't even manage a decent sex dream about him—she always woke up when it got to the good part. Her subconscious just rolled its eyes and said, "This is too farfetched for *me* to handle, kiddo. Dream about someone in your league—like George Clooney, maybe. He'll ask you out before Taran notices you're grown, much less shows any interest."

She showered, trying not to think about Taran as she did it.

Detective Taran Lloyd yawned with boredom as he stood by the bar and observed the patrons of Le Monde on a typical

Saturday night. A pricey club, it attracted an affluent crowd, and a mixed one: humans, werewolves and other shifters, people who looked a little more than a little fae. The only thing they had in common was a willingness to pay five bucks for a bottle of domestic beer and seven for well drinks—or the ability to find someone who would do it for them.

He grimaced. He'd like a drink himself, but regulations prohibited drinking on duty.

The intimate nightclub featured wood-paneled walls, polished hardwood floors and a lot of recessed lighting. Music loud enough to dance but not too loud to talk, waitresses pretty but not too sexy, bartenders fast but friendly—if not for the fact that three women reported missing this month were last seen here, it would've been a great place to bring a date.

He tried to remember the last time he'd gone on a date.

"Detective?" Daniel Denardo, the HPD Shifter Investigations Unit's rookie, interrupted Taran's musings.

"Yeah, Danny?"

"What are we supposed to look for here?"

Taran smiled wryly. "If we get lucky, some guy will pick up a chick, throw her over his shoulder and run out, and we'll arrest him. But I don't think we'll get lucky. So we hang around and watch, talk to people, ask if anyone saw the women, noticed unusual behavior, that sort of thing. I'd rather no one know we're cops yet."

As soon as he said it, he noticed Lark across the room at a banquette with another woman and four slimy-looking wolves in suits. Taran automatically considered any guy with Lark slimy-looking. These wolves looked like Eurotrash. Eastern European wolves ran drugs and weapons in and out of the country, and SIU suspected they'd expanded into the sex trade. Rich European werewolves frequented Le Monde. Apparently Lark did too.

She sauntered toward the bar.

"Shit," he muttered.

"What's the matter?"

"I'll be back in a second. Why don't you mingle."

"I can do that," Denardo replied cheerfully.

"What are you doing here?" he growled softly.

Those words, that voice, just hours after the dream, freaked Lark right the hell out. She started so violently her perfectly chilled Cosmopolitan sloshed the front of her dress. Her nipples stood at attention. He didn't even notice.

She grabbed a handful of napkins. "Damn it, Taran, what—"

"Quiet," he said fiercely as he stole her breath with a smile. He never smiled at her like that. He rarely smiled at her at all. She stared up at him, dumbfounded. He clamped a meaty paw on her elbow and dragged her away from the bar toward an empty table.

The dark blue pinstriped suit, a fitted European cut, and the custom-tailored, crisp white dress shirt looked great on his long, muscular frame. Taran didn't live on his detective salary alone.

"Act like we're having fun." Irritable as always, he still wore that stutter-inducing smile. It stopped short of his luminescent green eyes. "Why are you here, and who are those wolves?"

"None of your business..." she grinned gaily, "...and I don't know."

A few golden strands of hair drifted across his eyes. He wore it halfway to his shoulders; HPD grooming regulations exempted werewolves. She always itched to brush his hair aside. One day she'd do it, just to watch him react.

"I'm serious, Lark."

"You're hurting me, Taran."

He let go instantly but continued to stare at her, knowing she'd answer him.

She heaved a dramatic sigh. "I'm here with my friend Eloise, who's into some Eurowolf whose name I don't remember, and he's with his bros, and they're all creepy and boring, and one of them keeps trying to pick me up, and after you replace the Cosmo you made me spill, I'm going home. This just is not my night."

"Are you driving?"

"No, I'm talking to you. Why? Do I look like I'm driving?"

He didn't laugh. He never laughed.

"El drove. I'll take a cab home. Where's my cosmo?"

His sharp cheekbones and strong chin, and the pale, thin

scar scoring his left cheek from his ear almost to his mouth, gave him a look of menacing power. That disappearing smile, though, made him look like a fallen angel. A hulking, six-foot-six fallen angel who could change in five minutes in broad daylight—the mark of a powerful alpha werewolf.

"Don't tell anyone you know who I am," he ordered. "I'm working a case."

"What kind of case?"

No reply.

"Fine, whatever. I won't tell anyone I know you."

He nodded and turned to go.

"Um. Hello?"

He turned back. "What is it?"

"You owe me a drink."

He pulled a ten from his wallet and held it out, staring at her eyes as he did so. She snorted at the cheap shot power play, but it worked—a human couldn't maintain eye contact with an alpha.

She looked at the bill in his hand. She didn't take it. Instead, fueled with courage from her first cosmo, she put her hand on his outstretched arm and leaned in, her head grazing his cheek. Their bodies almost touched. A werewolf's normal body temperature was one hundred five point three; for the millionth time in ten years, she fantasized about snuggling up to his warmth.

Her pulse hammered in her throat as she whispered, "Taran? If you want people to think your cousin is a hooker, you could at least pretend I'd get more than ten bucks. Otherwise, go buy me a drink, you lazy bastard."

He growled low in his throat. She peeked up at him. Taran meant "thunder" in Welsh. It fit him when he looked like this.

"Wait here," he snarled before stalking off to the bar. The crowd parted for him by instinct, like zebras at a watering hole when the lion drops by for a drink. He returned with her cosmo.

"Thank you, cuz," she cooed sweetly to his shoulder. New drink in hand, she steeled herself for another excruciating twenty minutes with Eloise and the Euro cheese. Would he watch her walk away? As if.

Taran rarely saw Lark without friends or family around.

When he found an opportunity to watch her walk away, he took it and he savored it, because he liked the way it hurt.

The killer dress, long sleeved and stretchy, cut low in back, clung to every inch of her. It hugged her beautiful ass and stopped short of her knees, which meant twenty inches of leg still showed. His mate had legs like a fucking racehorse.

Did she know he hated the "cousin" crap? Sometimes he was tempted to think she did it to torment him, but he knew she didn't. Unlike many beautiful women, Lark didn't tease. If she knew how he felt, she'd react with disgust or pity. Disgust would make family functions uncomfortable, and alphas didn't tolerate pity.

Her scent, her laughter, the caress of her hair against his cheek would torture him for hours. He used to turn to other women whenever he needed to ease this blissful pain.

That didn't work anymore.

"Wow."

"Uh? Oh—I didn't see you come back," he said, turning to Danny. "Wow what?"

"The girl in the green dress. I mean, look at those legs."

"Those are my cousin's legs," Taran said dourly.

"Oh, um—sorry." The brunet beta instantly dropped his gaze.

"It's all right." Taran sighed. "I know she's hot."

"None of my cousins look like that, that's for damn sure."

Taran smiled tightly. "We're not actually blood. She's my brother's cousin."

"Oh, right. You and your brother have different fathers."

"Yeah. Myall's dad is human. Lark's his niece. My mom and stepdad raised her after her parents died. Myall thinks of her as a sister."

"So you think of her as family, too."

Taran nodded. "Yeah, a little."

No. Not at all.

"She play basketball?"

"Soccer and volleyball," replied Taran softly.

"Beach volleyball?" Denardo leered. The smile faded as he looked at Taran's face. "Just a joke," he muttered. "How tall is she, anyway?"

"Five ten." *Ask me anything. Her favorite color is purple, her favorite food is Mexican. She's scared of roaches but pretends she's not. Great dancer, lousy singer. She'll laugh at the dumbest movie and the stupidest joke. Likes kids and rain, hates cats and golf. She's twenty-six. Her shampoo smells like apples and she thinks I'm an asshole.*

"All right," he said. "Let's start mingling around here."

She returned to find El laughing uproariously with her new werewolf boyfriend and his pals. Lark suspected El wouldn't drive herself—or Lark—home tonight.

"There you are!" El shrieked. To the werewolves she said, "Y'all excuse us a minute. Come on, Lark."

Lark shrugged and belted half the cosmo before setting it down to follow a weaving El.

"What d'ya think?" El asked when they reached the bathroom. Lark noted the slurred speech and droopy eyelids. Definitely not driving.

"About who? Your Russian guy?" She stared at herself in the mirror as she waited for El to finish. *I should wear more makeup.* She liked her dark blue eyes and snub nose well enough. She considered her brown hair, with its auburn highlights, her best feature. Thick, straight and glossy, it fell to just below her shoulder blades. She wore long bangs in front, parted on the side. *It's an okay face. I need more makeup.*

"Dominik is Czech. He's loaded." El giggled. "I'll probably go home with him, if that's cool with you?"

"I only came out tonight because you didn't want to go out alone!" Lark said, exasperated. Dominik apparently didn't care enough to pick Eloise up and take her out.

"Please don't be mad, Lark." El pouted. "I really like him, and I don't want to be alone tonight."

Lark didn't blame El for being a ditzy narcissist—she couldn't help it, not with all that fae blood. It made her annoying but irresistible to all three species of sapients.

"Whatever, El. That's fine." She'd already planned to cab it.

As they walked back to the table, Eloise looked over to the bar. "That's your cousin the cop, isn't it?"

"He's not my cousin," Lark responded reflexively.

"He is so hot. I know that guy he's with."

"You do?" She wouldn't look in that direction; she didn't

want Taran to see her watching him.

"I don't know his name. He's a friend of Luc. You remember—the French wolf? We went to Vegas a lot."

"Luc with the Ducati?" Lark wasn't a fur chaser, but she loved fine motorcycles.

"Yeah, he took me out on it a few times. This one time we rode to Austin..."

El talked all the way back to the table, promptly ignoring Lark once they got there. Lark drank her cosmo and ignored the other werewolves. She people watched, trying to guess couples on first dates, couples just hooking up, couples breaking up. When she got bored, she Taran watched. He never glanced in her direction, so she felt free to spy until a flock of geeks descended on a table and blocked her view.

The werewolf who'd tried to buy her a drink— Sergei/Stefan/whoever—offered her a chair at one point. She declined. A little later, she thought maybe she'd reconsider.

The whole world listed to the left sharply and suddenly. She grabbed the edge of the table and swallowed hard. The music got both louder and harder to hear. The room began to spin very fast, like in a movie where the camera pans around and around until the viewer gets sick and dizzy.

She didn't see El and the Czech werewolf anywhere. Another guy, dark haired, joined the group now. Lark concentrated on staying upright while she tried to get the attention of the werewolf next to her. She labored to keep her eyes open.

"Hey," she said. It came out nearly inaudible. "Hey!" she tried more loudly, and took one hand off the table to put it on the shoulder of Stefan/Sergei/whomever. He finally looked up at her; she all but sagged on him at this point. He said something. It sounded all muffled and distorted, like it came from underwater.

He flashed her a smile—an insincere, predatory smile. Panic paralyzed her.

The other werewolves and the new guy looked straight at her. She suspected they recognized her distress, yet they just stood there and watched.

The werewolf stood and grabbed her upper arm. She tried to pull away and almost fell down. The other werewolves ignored her. Now she knew they did it deliberately. All around her people talked and danced and jostled. No one noticed her about to pass out while this scumbag clutched her arm and his buddies ignored her.

She grabbed a chair, trying to pull away. The werewolf put his arm around her waist as if to help her. He kissed her on the cheek. Helpless, more terrified than she'd ever been, she was about to be dragged away in the middle of a crowd.

She tried again to pull away, then pushed at him feebly—for God's sake, the guy stood four inches shorter than her. *I'm not drunk,* she raged helplessly, internally, *I'm just...dizzy, and sleepy and scared, and...*

Taran. Taran could help. But she couldn't see him—she couldn't see anything. She had double vision, maybe even triple, after only two cosmos.

Sobbing with fear, she began to scream. "Taran! Taran! Help me! Please! Tar—" No matter how hard she screamed, nothing came out but a thin wail no one would hear over the noise of the club.

She choked on her sobs and fell silent, but finally people noticed. The crowd in front of her seemed to ripple. A bunch of people screamed and fell down. The creepy werewolf let go. Someone caught her as she fell.

Please be Taran.

The scents and sounds of places like this played hell on a werewolf's senses. Alcohol and perfume, sweat and pheromones and fabric, all ran together in one meaningless smell. Music and voices, ice against glass against bottles, created a background roar through which he struggled to pick out words. He could hear better in here than any human, but nowhere near optimal.

It took a few minutes for the sound of someone calling his name to pierce the cacophony. A voluble blonde chatted him up; he'd dropped the name of a missing woman, she'd claimed to have known her slightly, but as they talked Taran realized the blonde didn't know anything useful.

That's when he heard it, faintly at first.

"Taran!"

Why would Lark call him from across the bar, when he'd just told her...

"Taran! Help me! Please! Tar—"

175

The cop heard the terror in her voice; the wolf responded. Taran shoved his drink at the startled blonde, who didn't take it. He ignored the dull thud of lead glass hitting hardwood. Soda splashed the blonde's legs as he closed the distance between him and Lark in seconds. Tables, chairs and patrons flew everywhere. Taran ignored it all, focused solely on the werewolf with his arm around a feebly struggling Lark. The werewolf let go of her abruptly and disappeared.

Taran caught her as she crumpled. Only then did he become aware of other people around them again.

He knelt with an unconscious Lark in his lap. Bouncers came running. He snarled, "Call 911, *now!*" and they ran to comply.

He smelled the earthy odor indicating incipient change; it came from him. He hadn't changed involuntarily since his teens; stress could make betas do it, but alphas only did it under extreme emotional duress. A mate's near abduction would qualify.

If he changed in the middle of a stirred-up crowd like this, humans and non-humans alike might panic. He lowered his head and closed his eyes so no one would see if they began to yellow. A minute later, he had it under control.

A guy identifying himself as a doctor checked Lark's pulse and pupils.

"I saw her thirty minutes ago. She didn't get passed out drunk that fast. She doesn't drink like that."

"No respiratory distress, heartbeat's good," replied the doctor. "If someone slipped her a mickey, it'll show up in a tox screen."

Denardo dispersed the crowd and leaned over Taran's shoulder.

"What do you want me do?"

Taran didn't take his eyes off Lark as he stroked her hair and face.

"You get a look at the wolves she was with?" he asked Denardo absently.

"No. I was over there." He gestured to the other side of the room. "I didn't notice anything wrong till I heard people screaming."

"I got a little rough with the crowd," Taran muttered.

"I talked to some people at the next table," the rookie continued. "They said it just looked like a wolf and a drunk girl. She didn't make any noise they could hear."

Drugs might have made her unable to scream. It would explain why none of the missing women created a scene before disappearing. Maybe they'd tried and couldn't.

"I thought she looked like she was in trouble, and when I got over here a wolf was dragging her out."

He didn't mention he'd heard her scream. He'd only heard because Lark was his mate. No one needed to know that.

"Well, now we know how those women went missing," he muttered. "It happened in the middle of a crowd. No one noticed a thing." A cold, heavy weight sat in his stomach and something squeezed his heart—probably stark terror, which, like involuntary change, he'd not experienced in fifteen or twenty years.

He didn't realize he held her tightly against his chest until an EMT tapped him on the shoulder and said deferentially, "Sir? We need to get the lady on the gurney."

He stood with Lark in his arms and laid her gently on the cart.

"I'm a cop," he informed the EMT. "I'm coming with you."

Chapter Two

Lark drifted below consciousness. Just as she felt herself surfacing, a wave of cozy warmth would crest, break and drag her back down. Voices rose, fell away and rose again. She rather enjoyed the sensation. Best of all were the dreams of Taran; not sex dreams, but she didn't mind. In the dreams, he stroked her hair, caressed her hand, talked to her gently. Only in her dreams did he do things like that.

Eventually, less pleasant sounds intruded—beeps, honks and hisses, several voices speaking at once. The snuggly warmth began to dissipate.

"I think she's waking up." She recognized her best friend's voice. "Lark? Sweetie? Can you open your—"

"Move." Taran, speaking in his real life voice—curt and grumpy.

"Hey, watch it, assho—did you see the way he just pushed me?"

"Give the wolf a break, TJ." Nick Wargman, the Houston Alpha and Taran's best friend, sounded amused. It took a few seconds' concentrated effort, but Lark opened her eyes to see Taran leaning over her, smoothing her hair with the back of his hand, his face very close to hers. She noted the dark circles beneath his sunken eyes. His customary stubble looked more like a beard.

"Hi," he said quietly. "How do you feel?"

She frowned, confused. Why was he here? She tried to think about what she last remembered. Her mind gaped open, vast and empty like after a big booze binge, only she couldn't remember going—wait. She did remember going out. Didn't she? She went out, she...couldn't remember. She gasped and tried to sit up, suddenly panicked and choked for air.

Taran gently pressed her shoulders back down. "Take it easy, Lark. You're okay, you're—"

"Hey, sweetie. It's okay, we're all here." TJ came around to the other side of the bed and took Lark's other hand, casting a "fuck you, too" look at Taran.

"What happened? Why I am in the hospital?" she asked hoarsely.

"You're—"

"Nick," Taran said loudly. "Would you please ask your *secretary* to back off? I need to ask Lark some questions, and your *secretary* is in my way."

"You son of a—"

"Minion, let's step outside for a minute," Nick said. "We need to tell a nurse she's awake anyway."

TJ started to argue, then looked at her boss's face and stopped. Standing on her tiptoes to kiss Lark on the cheek, she whispered "I'll be back," and walked out, but not before pausing at the door to toss an "asshole!" over her shoulder. Nick winked and smiled at Lark before he closed the door behind him.

Taran didn't watch them go. His gaze remained fixed on her, one of her hands firmly in his; with his other he began stroking her brow again.

Faded blue jeans and a long sleeved, fitted beige sweater had replaced last night's suit. He looked stale and disheveled and yummy. Maybe she didn't care what had happened to her, she thought, as long as he just touched her like this a little longer.

"Why were you such a jerk to TJ?"

"Never mind that," he replied impatiently. "Do you remember last night?"

She closed her eyes to think. "Yeah. Yeah, I do," she said slowly. "El picked me up, and we met some wolves she knew. I saw you. Didn't I?"

He nodded. "Yes. We talked."

"You spilled my drink on me."

He grinned at her. She wondered why the heart monitor didn't explode. "I startled you. You spilled your drink on yourself. I bought you another one."

"Okay. What happened after that?"

179

"I'm not sure. At some point, someone slipped some GHB in your drink. It's used as a date rape drug, like roofies."

"I know."

"I lost track of you until you screamed for me. I ran to where you were, and a werewolf had his arm around you, and..." He paused for a minute, frowning, and stared at the wall above her head. For a moment, his hand gripped hers so tightly it hurt.

"You looked like you were trying to get away from him," Taran continued. "When I showed up, he let you go. He and the other werewolves ran."

"I remember feeling sick," she said slowly. "And I tried to—I tried to tell one of the guys at the table, but—they just watched me. They wouldn't help, and no one..." She paused. She hadn't cried in front of him in years. "I screamed and screamed, but it felt like nothing came out."

"I heard you," he said quietly. "You called for me, I got to you, that's what matters. You may have actually helped us."

He told her about three women who'd disappeared, all of them last seen at Le Monde.

She sat up suddenly. They nearly bonked heads. "Eloise!" she gasped. "What happened to Eloise?"

Taran shook his head. "She wasn't there when I got to you. I looked her up on your cell phone. I started calling her last night, right after we got here, but she's never answered or returned the call."

"Last night? What day is it?" Daylight shone through the drawn blinds.

"Sunday." He glanced at his watch. "About ten."

"You think she's gone, don't you?"

He nodded. "You know anything about the werewolves she met there?"

"Just that they were European. One of them was Czech."

"Yeah, that's what I thought. We've been hearing about Eastern Europeans werewolves in town, running drugs and guns and women, and..."

He stopped as a nurse came in to check on her. After a brief, brisk exam, the nurse said the doctor would be by shortly and left.

"You want me to go get you something to eat?"

"No, I want you to finish telling me about the European werewolves. Drugs and guns and women and what, Taran?

"Just...some very bad things."

She thought of the stories she'd heard, of women kidnapped and sold into brothels catering to werewolves, including werewolves who liked to change during sex. She'd always assumed such tales were urban myth, especially as they started in Europe, which never accepted werewolves and shifters as readily as the U.S. and South America.

"I've heard they like women with fae blood," she whispered. "Because there's less chance of pregnancy."

"Do you know how to get in touch with her family?"

"No, but someone at work will. Why haven't I seen this in the news?"

He frowned and looked abashed. "We wanted to make sure Le Monde really figured in the women's disappearances. We couldn't alert whoever's doing this, because they'd just go to another city, and we didn't want to cause a panic, maybe start a wolf scare."

The doctor arrived. After a quick examination, he announced he wanted to keep her another night. Before she could protest, Taran cut in.

"Is that necessary? You said she seems okay. She hates hospitals."

"Most people do..." the doctor began.

"No, she really hates them," Taran said. "If I make sure someone stays with her, can she go home today?"

"Well...I guess so." The doctor sighed. "But I want someone with her the rest of the day, just to be sure. The effects of GHB can linger as long as twenty-four hours, so no driving till tonight at the earliest. I'll start the discharge." He left.

"You knew about my hospital thing?"

He shrugged and looked away. "Yeah. I guess Mom or Myall mentioned it once."

TJ had brought some clothes from Lark's apartment. Taran stepped out into the hallway so she could get dressed.

As soon as the door closed behind him, TJ jumped at him like a curvaceous little terrier. "Finally. You done? Is she okay? Did you yell at her? If you yelled at her, I swear..."

Nick slouched against the far wall, silently laughing.

Taran put an arm across the door to block TJ's access. "She's dressing."

"So? I've seen her naked a hundred times."

Momentarily distracted by the image that summoned, he didn't protest when TJ, all of five foot two, walked under his arm and through the door.

He went to join Nick against the wall.

"You okay, wolf?" asked his Alpha quietly.

"They almost got her. They almost took her, in the middle of a crowd."

Nick nodded. "You think they planned it in advance?"

"No." Taran shook his head. "Right now, I'm thinking this El chick was the target; they probably expected her to show up alone. Maybe she went willingly, maybe the other women did too. But when Lark showed up with El, and got a good look at them...I'll have to check my notes, but I think the other women also went there alone to meet someone."

"You think they recognized you? Pegged you for a cop?"

He shrugged. "Don't know. It's possible. If they did, and they saw her talking to me..." He put his hands on top of his head and leaned back against the wall.

"I keep thinking about her being dragged out of there, no one noticing, and she wakes up alone and terrified, and they..." He closed his eyes, unable to finish.

Nick crossed his arms and stared at the floor, ponytail dangling over his shoulder. "She's not your blood, Taran."

"No. She's not."

"So...feelings. You've got feelings."

"Yeah. She'd be shocked to hear it, but yeah," he said morosely, grateful he could trust his Alpha with this.

"As opposed to just wanting to fuck her."

"Right. Although I definitely want to do that, too."

"Are these feelings the biologically imperative, completely out of your control, last for a lifetime kind?"

"Yep," he said resignedly.

"Your mother's adopted daughter."

"Yep."

"Shit," said Nick. "I'm sorry. If it makes you feel any better, I know how—"

TJ emerged from the room.

"I'll drive her home," she announced.

"No," he said calmly. "I will."

"Why?"

"Because I said so."

"What if she doesn't want you to?" the tiny redhead said stubbornly, hands on her hips. "What if she—"

"TJ, we're leaving."

"Wait a minute, Nick, I want to know why—"

"TJ." Nick didn't raise his voice. But he said it with all the force of a Pack Alpha, and it worked on humans as it did on other werewolves.

"Fine." she said quietly. "I'll meet her at her house."

"Whenever I get her there."

"Asshole."

"Leaving, minion," said Nick. "Now."

She rolled her eyes. "Right behind you, master."

Lark looked so forlorn, so vulnerable as she sat the edge of the hospital bed, dressed in jeans and a sweater with her long legs stretched in front of her. Her glorious chestnut hair hung limp around her face. A raccoon mask of smeared mascara ringed her eyes.

She'd never looked lovelier to him. He'd do anything to protect her.

"Where's TJ?"

"Nick needed her to do some stuff for him," he lied without compunction.

"On a Sunday? When her best friend was almost kidnapped? That sucks."

He shrugged. "You're stuck with me." She just looked at him.

"Hey," he said softly. "I'm not that bad, am I?"

She jumped to her feet without a word and ran into the bathroom. He followed when he heard her vomiting.

"Lark—"

She waved a hand behind her back to shoo him away. He ignored her. He gathered her thick hair in his hands, making sure to get all the errant wisps out of her face. He held it for her and rubbed her back as she threw up.

Even as she puked, moaning wretchedly, he repressed a disgraceful shudder of pleasure at the feel of her hair in his hands. He'd wanted to run his fingers through it so many times, for so many years.

He remembered the hard-on he got when she spilled a drink on herself last night; today he couldn't keep his hands off her in the midst of her obvious misery. What would he do next, he mused—feel her up in her sleep? If he could get away with it, then yeah, probably so.

She stopped retching but remained on her knees, gulping air and resting her head in her hands, elbows propped on the bowl. He didn't let go of her hair.

"Okay," she eventually said in an unsteady voice. "I think I'm done."

He stood behind her while she brushed her teeth and splashed water on her face. Their eyes met in the mirror as she scrubbed at her mascara. A weird expression crossed her face.

"You okay?" he asked quietly.

She shrugged. "I will be. Thanks to you. I was so stupid. If you hadn't been there..." She dropped her head so he couldn't see her face.

With his hands on her shoulders, he drew her back against his chest. He closed his eyes, memorizing the feel of her body pressed against his. She didn't look up, but she didn't try to shrug him off.

"Silly brat," he grunted. "Why do you think you're stupid? You didn't do anything wrong."

She took a breath. He heard it catch. "I know better than to walk off and leave my drink, especially when I'm with a bunch of people I don't know. That's like rule number one for single girls in bars. I don't know why I did it."

"Because you're not perfect, and people forget to do things they should."

No answer. He dropped a quick kiss on top of her head. He'd never done anything like that before. She didn't react at all. That scared him.

"You want to stop at a drive through on the way home?" he asked again.

"I don't think so," she said softly. "I feel nasty. I want a shower."

"Yes, ma'am. Let's get you home."

She didn't speak as the orderly wheeled her out of the hospital, or while they waited for the valet to bring his Mercedes around. He tried to think of something comforting, or reassuring, or halfway witty to say, but he couldn't. He never could, he reflected bitterly. So he called the department to check in. He told Danny he was taking Lark home.

Once on the road, she startled him when she reached over to lay a hand on his arm.

"Taran?" she asked uncertainly.

"What?"

"I want you to be honest with me, okay? You can tell me. I need to know..."

"Know what?" he said, staring straight ahead and wondering wildly if she'd sensed something.

"Did something horrible happen to me, and you don't want to tell me?'

He turned to look at her in bewilderment. "No. What makes you think that?"

"Because," she said, dropping her hand, "you're acting so sweet and gentle, it kind of scared me, and I thought..."

"Shit, Lark!" He nearly plowed into an SUV stopped at a light. "Why can't I just be nice to you?"

"I don't know, Taran. I ask myself that all the time." She gave him a small smile, nothing like the smartass-brat grin he usually got.

He swore again under his breath. The light turned green.

"Maybe I'm being nice to you because someone drugged you and tried to kidnap you and you could've wound up dead. But hey, now that you're okay, I can just go back to being an asshole."

"Not necessarily. I mean, I could get hit by a bus tomorrow." She grinned wider that time.

"That's not funny, Lark."

"Sure. Like you'd know funny."

They got to Lark's apartment to find TJ waiting for them. When Lark asked her friend what Nick had needed, TJ just smiled at Taran and murmured, "Oh, you know how those alphas are."

Taran looked annoyed, which Lark found strangely comforting. After ordering TJ to stay with her at least another four hours—TJ cheerfully told him to bite her ("but if you do I'll tell your Alpha")—Taran left. He threatened to call and check on her later.

"So. The Great Werewolf Detective seemed kind of concerned about you, didn't he?"

"I don't want to talk about him, Teej. I just want a shower."

"Okay, but at least tell me what you think about the way he—"

"Hey, TJ? How's Nick? How many women has he fucked this month, and have you told him it kills you?"

She instantly regretted the horrible, nasty words, but after all the trauma, and in her state of nervous exhaustion, she didn't feel like dissecting her endless, hopeless, unrequited crush one more time. They'd been best friends for thirteen years. TJ would let this one slide.

Sure enough, after a minute of hurt silence she threw her arms around Lark and squeezed.

"Look, bitch," she said into the general vicinity of Lark's breasts, "that's just mean, but I'm sorry anyway. You've had an awful time, and you're right. No talk of asshole werewolves. How about midday margaritas? On second thought, no booze. Let's order Chinese and veg on the couch..."

She kicked TJ out around six. Her best friend hesitated to leave, asking over and over if she wanted her to spend the night, but Lark insisted she could stay by herself. She promised to call TJ if she changed her mind.

She briefly considered staying home from work on Monday, but she didn't want to talk about the ordeal and she didn't like to lie. Besides, comfy pajamas, fuzzy socks and a good night's sleep fixed almost everything. Tomorrow she'd feel normal again.

Once asleep, she found herself in another dream—a bad one this time, and not just because it featured no Taran. She dreamed she was asleep in her bed, warm and safe, when someone tried to bust down her front door. In her dream she laughed—the unknown assailant couldn't get in, because when she'd moved in here Taran and Myall had insisted on installing a steel door. She'd thought it excessive at the time, but she appreciated the hell out of it now, in her dream.

She heard a godawful fight—from the sound of it, right outside her door. The steel door finally gave way with a mighty crash. The godawful fight fell into her front room. She sat up in bed and screamed, because she realized she wasn't asleep after all.

The pitifully faint trail threatened to go cold if he didn't chase some leads. After he dropped Lark off, he went to meet with Le Monde management.

They didn't have much to tell. The mysterious European werewolves spent a lot of time and money—always cash—at Le Monde, and they attracted hordes of women. No one knew their names, and they never made trouble.

Le Monde managers knew of the three women's disappearances—four now, with Eloise—and the threat of publicity scared them enough that they agreed to let undercover officers pose as staff.

The DA had failed in his attempts to get search warrants for the homes and computers of the first three women—the judge didn't see enough evidence of foul play, even given all the women's fae ethnicity and the fact they'd all gone missing from Le Monde. Now, however, with Lark's drugging and near-abduction, and Eloise's disappearance, presumably with the same wolves who'd tried to take Lark, the DA tried again. When contacted on Sunday morning, the judge granted the warrant.

Either El made a lot more money than Lark, or she had someone helping to support her lifestyle. Her corner loft apartment was in one of downtown Houston's most exclusive buildings. Taran could see clear to Sugar Land from the living room's two picture windows.

He took a small phone book and some photos he found on the fridge and her bathroom mirror—a few pictures of Eloise and girlfriends, more of Eloise and different wolves. He'd ask Lark if she recognized anyone. Forensics would send someone to get Eloise's computer. Now that they had a warrant for her stuff, they'd apply for the other three women and see if any names, numbers or emails popped up more than once. When someone showed up to dust for fingerprints, he left.

Something still nagged at him from last night, apart from the lingering horror of nearly losing Lark. If the wolves had thought Lark enough of a threat to try to take her, would they just walk away now? Might they consider her a loose end? They could easily learn her identity; Eloise may have told them.

He couldn't ask the department for help. He was weaving this case together with gossamer threads to begin with, and concerns for Lark's safety wouldn't merit police protection.

He'd been awake for thirty-six hours; he figured he could go another twenty-four before he dropped. He almost called Denardo to tell him he was headed back to Lark's Museum District apartment, but didn't. No one but Nick needed to know about his feelings. He got to her apartment around six.

The older complex sat on a cul-de-sac, tucked away among million dollar homes and swank boutiques and restaurants. It backed up to a tall wooden fence. On the other side of the fence, traffic roared down Bissonnet Street day and night. Bad guys paying Lark a visit would likely do it from the cul-de-sac.

Taran couldn't say for sure they'd try to come after her; he thought he might be using that as an excuse to sit outside her apartment and whine with frustrated longing, but he decided to delay introspection for a while.

The complex didn't have guest parking on the grounds. He parked a block down the street. From here, he could see the walkway leading to Lark's unit four doors down from the front of the building. He put the top up for privacy; in this neighborhood, a Mercedes convertible wouldn't attract attention.

A car purred into the cul de sac around nine—another Mercedes, a blue SL-Class Coupe worth three times as much as Taran's Cabriolet. It passed him and pulled up directly in front of the complex. Four footed, the hair on his back would've stiffened; on two feet, his neck itched, his nostrils flared and his cop sense screamed for attention.

Two wolves got out—a tall, slender alpha with brown hair and a shorter, stockier, red headed beta, both dressed in jeans and black T-shirts. Taran got out of his car. They stopped and turned to look at him.

The three of them stood like that for perhaps five seconds before Taran threw himself at the alpha, who ran to intercept him while the beta sprinted for the apartment building. He had seconds before the beta got to Lark. Even exhausted and with nerves shot to hell, an alpha wolf with a mate in imminent danger could summon vast reserves of fighting strength.

The alpha ducked Taran's first punch. When he threw his own, Taran caught the fist in his hand and twisted, snapping the wrist. The alpha howled and stepped back before spinning to level a roundhouse kick that caught Taran on the side. Taran grabbed the leg before the alpha retracted it. He jerked, sending the other wolf crashing to the ground on his back. The alpha kicked. Taran jumped out of the way, landing beside the other wolf's head, which he kicked with his steel-toed cowboy boots. He heard a satisfying crunching sound, and the alpha stopped moving—not dead, but not going anywhere, either.

Taran raced for Lark's apartment.

He grinned with malicious glee as the beta attempted to kick the door down. That fucker was solid; he and Myall had made sure of it.

The beta didn't try to run, but just kicked the door harder. He stank of meth and whiskey, which explained why he didn't flee at the sight of Taran. Wolves involved in criminal enterprises, especially the drug trade or mob enforcement, got their betas stoked on speed and alcohol, which temporarily suppressed their instinctive submissiveness. A beta with a short-circuited flight response made for a dangerously unpredictable fighter.

The door finally gave way with a resounding crash just as Taran jumped the beta. Taran heard Lark scream as he and the beta went vaulting across the tiny den, crashing into the bar separating the den from the kitchen. The beta kicked hard and rolled away from Taran. He sprang to his feet and turned for Lark's room.

Taran shouted, "Lark! Stay in there!" as he dove into the beta's back and took him down face first. The beta squirmed and bucked, trying to throw him off. Taran grabbed a chunk of his hair and slammed his head into the hardwood floor. The fucked-up bastard barely paused before he started bucking again, arms flailing and legs kicking.

"Fuck!" shouted Taran as a searing pain shot through his leg. He looked down to see a knife protruding from his thigh. The beta had been walking around with a goddamned silver knife in his pocket.

Wolves who carried silver knives were pussies.

He yanked the six-inch blade out and plunged it into the

beta's back. The wolf howled in pain, joining his voice to the chorus of sirens Taran suddenly noticed. The howling stopped abruptly, and *then* the bastard sure as hell stopped moving. Blood ran out of his mouth and pooled on the floor beneath him.

Taran rolled off the dead wolf, groaning in pain and exhaustion as he lay on his back on the cold, hard floor. He heard the bedroom door creak. It flew open as Lark ran into the den.

"Taran! Taran—oh God, you're bleeding, honey, you're bleeding," she babbled, skidding to a stop and kneeling beside him. She kept babbling, but he didn't hear anything after she called him "honey".

She smelled fantastic, of apple shampoo and the girly stuff she put on her skin; even her fear smelled good to him. Her hands warmed him as she ran them over his face and his chest and down to his leg—the knife had gone in the outside of his left thigh, missing his femoral artery and his quad, and it hadn't been in there long enough for the silver to do much damage. The dark stain on his jeans stopped spreading.

He started to sit up.

"Don't move." She knelt over him, her long hair falling in his face. He decided he could stay like that for a bit longer.

"I called the cops," she said, stroking his face.

"Lark, I am the cops," he said with a tired smile.

Then he noticed her shaking hands, one on his face and one on his chest, and her pallid face and red, puffy eyes. He pushed her hands away and sat up.

"Hey," he said in surprise, "hey, come on, it's okay. I'm not that hurt." She started to cry and buried her face in his shoulder. He gathered her in his arms across his lap—avoiding the bleeding thigh—and shushed her, murmuring words of comfort. He ran his hands through her hair and stroked her back while she sobbed, and he lost himself for a few moments in the feel and the scent of her. If the only way he could hold her like this was on the floor with a knife wound in his thigh and a dead werewolf next to them, so be it. He wished the sirens weren't so close.

A sweet ache of pride and longing flooded him as he hugged her and rocked her back and forth. She'd been through one traumatic night already, only for someone to attack her again and invade her home, and she didn't go stark fucking hysterical. She stayed out of his way and called the cops, and now she worried about him, not about her busted door or the dead wolf.

He looked up to see a small knot of people in varying states of dress standing in the open doorway, staring at them. He started to say something to the neighbors when two uniformed wolves pushed their way into the crowd, followed by two EMTs with a stretcher.

"Coming through, let us through please," said the second officer through the door. "Please, folks, everyone go back to your apartments. We need to talk to the folks in here. Thank you," he finished as the neighbors drifted back to their own units, speculating on the cause and nature of the disturbance and the very large guy on the floor holding Lark in his lap.

He tuned the neighbors out and turned his attention to the officers, one of whom said, "Excuse me, ma'am? Detective?"

Lark mumbled something about washing her face and fled to her room.

Taran showed his badge to one of the officers, whose name was Hinojosa, and gave his statement. He recounted almost everything; he left out the part about sitting in the cul-de-sac for three hours, saying he'd arrived at the same time as the two wolves.

"He pulled a silver knife on you?" Officer Hinojosa asked with raised eyebrows.

"Yeah, that one there, sticking out his back," Taran replied.

"Pussy," the cop sneered.

The EMTs wanted him on the stretcher and into an ambulance, but since neither was a wolf and they didn't have a tranq gun, they couldn't make him do it. He let them help him stand up—he knew he couldn't do it alone—and he agreed to let them look at his thigh.

Lark came out of the bedroom with her hair pulled back in a ponytail. She flinched a little, uncertainly, when he put his hand out to—what? Hug her? Stroke her face? Kiss her in front of the cops and the EMTs? Their moment of intimacy had passed, and he would deal with it.

He hated dealing with it.

"I'm going to let these guys look at my leg," he told her quietly. "You talk to the officers. When you're done, pack enough clothes and stuff to be gone for a few days, maybe a week."

"Why? Where am I going?"

"My place." She started to argue. "Lark, I'm not discussing it with you. You can't stay here, they may try again. I need you where I can protect you and know you're safe."

"But I don't want to get in the way," she said fretfully, crossing her arms and hunching her shoulders, "or cramp your style or anything,"

"I don't have a style. Or anything. I have five bedrooms and I only use one. Talk to the cops, then pack."

"Taran? Dude, what the fuck happened?"

Taran turned in surprise at the sound of Denardo's voice. Too tired to reprimand a beta rookie for calling him dude, he recounted the evening's events before he let the EMTs do a quick repair job in the bathroom.

He returned to the den to hear Denardo complimenting Lark on her composure, which she seemed to appreciate. Taran had noted her composure, but he didn't compliment her.

He never complimented her, he mused.

"Hey, Danny," he said loudly, "how'd you know I was over here?"

"When Lark called it in—" the beta put his hand on her shoulder as he said her name, and Taran very consciously refrained from growling, "—she told the dispatcher who you were. I was at the precinct when we heard about an officer down. You going to the hospital now?"

"No," he said shortly. "Don't need to. He missed the important parts." You could pump a beta with whiskey and speed, but you couldn't make him a decent knife fighter. "They gave me an antibiotic shot. I'll just stay off it a day or so." He couldn't protect her from a hospital bed. He'd feel like shit for a couple days, but he'd recover shortly.

"Look, werewolf, I don't mean to tell you what to do," his trainee said diffidently, "but you look like hell."

"He's right," Lark said. He almost told her to back off, but she put her hands to his face, feeling his cheeks and his forehead, so he stood quietly and soaked in her touch.

"Taran, you're cold," she fretted. "You've got silver poisoning. You need a doctor."

He looked at her eyes. She lowered her gaze, but not before he'd seen the worry there—worry for him.

"I'll be fine for tonight, silly brat." he said softly, venturing a quick kiss on her forehead. She jumped a little, smiled nervously, and gave him a quick hug before backing away. They looked at each other uncertainly for a moment.

Taran cleared his throat. "I called Nick while the EMTs worked on me. He's sending a couple of guys over here to put your door back up."

"Thank you."

"Lark says she doesn't recognize the dead guy," Denardo said.

"No, I don't," she confirmed. "That's sort of scary. I mean, he could be one of them," she continued, pointing at the corpse still face down on the door in a small pool of blood, "or I could run into one of them on the street, and I wouldn't even know it."

"Which is another reason for you to stay at my place, till we get a bead on these assholes," Taran said.

"It's the drug," Denardo said to Lark. "GHB wipes out memory of everything that happens after you take it. That's why it's a date rape drug. I'm surprised you remember anything at all. You need anything from me?" he asked Taran.

"Nah, I can drive."

They both looked at him incredulously.

"Taran, you really shouldn't—" began Denardo.

"No way," Lark said. "I'm driving you."

"I'll follow and help get you settled," Denardo chimed in.

"Goddamn it," Taran said, "I'm not that wounded. I don't need help getting to bed."

"Taran…" Lark crossed her arms, this time not in a fearful, hunched up way but in a bossy, female way, "…if you don't let us help you, I'm telling your mother you got stabbed."

He couldn't answer that. At least the beta had sense enough not to laugh.

Chapter Three

She pulled up to Taran's isolated Memorial home around midnight, Danny right behind her. Taran didn't speak during the short trip, and he didn't watch her every move as she drove his car, so she knew he was exhausted and in pain.

Werewolves ran fevers when ill, except for silver poisoning, which lowered their body temperature. It indicated infection, and she hoped the antibiotic got it. If his temperature still ran low in the morning, she'd call Nick, who'd order Taran to the doctor.

She gave in to temptation and pressed her palm to his left cheek. He felt marginally warmer than a while ago.

He opened his eyes and looked at her.

Before she could snatch her hand back, he pressed it to his shoulder with his cheek. He turned his head and lightly kissed her wrist.

"You all right?" she asked in a shaky whisper.

He nodded against her palm. "Yeah. I just want to sleep."

He looked about to say something else, but Danny appeared at Taran's window.

"Is he okay?"

Lark sighed and got out. Danny helped him into the house and to bed.

Taran insisted she take his room. She refused—she couldn't handle sleeping in his bed, even if he weren't hurt. Denardo went home, Taran fell asleep, and Lark unpacked her stuff. Then she lay awake in a guest bedroom until about four o'clock in the morning.

✧

Lark loved the rambling, one-story ranch-style house built in the fifties. This had been Taran's childhood home, before his wealthy father passed away and his mother married Uncle David. He'd thoroughly remodeled and updated it when he left the Army and returned to Houston. He'd left some of the original features intact, including the brick walls, exposed ceiling beams and huge stone fireplace in the den.

She sat at the breakfast table in the huge kitchen Monday morning, enjoying an unhurried mug of coffee. Taran walked in, dressed for work in another fitted sweater, this one black, and a pair of dark blue jeans. Lark still wore the purple and white striped rugby shirt and purple sweats she'd slept in.

"You going in late?" he asked as he poured coffee for himself. She noted his slight limp and the barely perceptible wince when he lowered himself into a chair across from her.

"Nope. Not going in at all," she said cheerfully. "I didn't fall asleep until about, oh—" she glanced at her watch, "—three hours ago. I lay there thinking, you know what? I had a hell of a weekend. Someone else can take depositions for a few days."

"I think that's wise." He stood to pull a key and a piece of paper from his pocket. He slid both of them across the table to her. "Here's the key, here's the code to the alarm system. I want you to check in with me every three hours."

"*What??*" she exclaimed, appalled. "You're not serious."

"Hell I'm not," he said mildly, forcing her to drop her gaze by staring her in the eye.

Fucking arrogant alpha dominance bullshit.

"I can't get you full protection. But I *can* get an unmarked car to drive by here during the day, and I can make you stay in touch with me. Until we figure out who those assholes are, I'm keeping tabs on you."

"But how would they even know I'm here?"

"How'd they know where you lived?" he asked quietly.

"I don't...I guess..." She trailed off, flustered.

"I don't know either, Lark, but they did. Did Eloise give them your full name?"

"I don't remember," she whispered.

"Lark's not a common name. She may have told them y'all

worked together, and I'm sure they knew where she worked. However they did it, they found you, and I'm not going to assume they can't find you again. So you're keeping in touch with me. Every three hours. You can call or you can text, it's up to you. And if you leave the house, you text me where you're going."

"Well, shit," she muttered, "why don't you just put a GPS locator on me?"

"Don't tempt me." He smiled and rose to leave.

"Hey, what about the doctor?"

"What doctor?"

"You're going to the doctor about your leg, right? You're limping and wincing."

He rolled his eyes. "Fine. I'll call the doctor. Every three hours, Lark, and I mean it."

She followed him to the front door.

"Fine," she said. "Come home with a doctor's note, or I'm telling Aunt Meg."

He'd just opened the door, and now he turned to her with a look of amused amazement. "Are you fucking kidding me?" He laughed.

"I'm not," she smiled, delighted. She hadn't seen him laugh like that in years. "I'm as serious as you are, werewolf. Get that leg looked at and don't come home till you do."

He was still shaking his head as he got into his car and drove away.

Chapter Four

"Holy fuck, what happened to you?" Taran asked when the rookie beta walked into the squad room Wednesday afternoon.

Danny tried to grin, but it came out a grimace. "Bike. Took a turn doing ninety and planted my face in some gravel."

The shiner on his right eye and cuts and scrapes on both cheeks made him look like he'd lost a fight, and not a close one. He winced, favoring his right side as he sat down at his desk across the aisle from Taran's.

"That's a shitty way to spend your day off. Think you broke anything?"

"Nah," Denardo replied. "Just bruised all over and stiff as hell."

Betas didn't heal as fast as alphas.

Denardo sat down at his desk and logged into his computer before continuing, "Hope it's gone by this weekend; I'm standing up in my buddy Luc's wedding, in Vegas. I leave tomorrow, come back Sunday. Unless you think I need to stick around for the case?"

"I don't see why. If anything breaks I'll call you, but I'm sure I can handle it. Hey, wait a minute." Taran looked up from his computer. "Luc. He wouldn't be a French guy, would he?"

Denardo seemed startled. "Uh, yeah. French Canadian, actually. Why?"

"Huh. I showed Lark some pictures I found at Eloise Catrera's place, and she ID'd a French wolf named Luc Deviger. Said Eloise went to Vegas with him a few times."

The beta frowned thoughtfully. "Yeah, that's him. Weird. I don't remember Luc ever mentioning her, but then he used to juggle three or four females at a time."

Taran nodded. "Yeah, Lark said Eloise had a thing for wolves." He paused for a minute, thinking, and then he shrugged. "Well. Ask Luc, see if he knew anything about a Czech wolf she was seeing."

"A Czech wolf?" Denardo asked sharply. "What's that about?"

"I got prints back on the beta Monday. We might have a lead here."

"Why didn't you call me?" The beta smelled distressed.

Taran laughed. "You spent all day Monday following Gossen and you were off yesterday. Relax, wolf. It could wait. Days off are important. Anyway. Take a look at your email and you'll see what I got."

Neither the dead beta nor the comatose alpha carried any identification, and they'd been driving a stolen car. Taran had pinned all his hopes on fingerprints, and he got lucky. Maybe.

Denardo opened his email. "Stephan Navratil, Czech, expired visa, last known address Miami," he read aloud.

"Yeah. And you know what they got in Miami."

"Cubans?"

"And gambling, guns and girls. It's a great place for bringing women in and out of the States. Navratil's got priors there. He worked as an enforcer for another Czech, a werewolf named Dominik Kuba. Kuba ran some big poker games in South Beach, attracted high rollers. Miami-Dade thinks he ran call girls down there, too, but he got spooked and left town just as they started to collect some good intel. They think a fed tipped him off. An agent in the office there has a gambling problem, looks like he was into Kuba for a lot of money and paid him off with tips. Miami-Dade sent us everything they've got on Kuba—including photos."

"What's all that got to do with our case?" The rookie frowned.

"Lark says the werewolf Eloise met at Le Monde was named Dominik, *and* he was Czech." Taran leaned back in his chair and gave his trainee a triumphant grin.

"She remember anything else? Any of the other werewolves there?"

"No." He sighed. "Says she can't remember faces or anything else, just El telling her Dominik was Czech."

"That's not much to go on. Even if we have pictures of this Kuba guy, there are five million people in Houston."

"Yeah, but only five hundred wolves. I've already sent his photo to Nick to get it out to everyone in the pack. And I'm hoping Dominik and his picture show up in one of the other women's photos or emails or something."

"When?" Denardo asked shortly.

"Huh?" Taran replied as he looked over notes on another case.

"When did you send Kuba's pictures to Nick?"

"Monday, soon as I got them from Miami."

"I see."

They didn't speak for a while as each wolf attended to his own work. Then Denardo cleared his throat.

"How's Lark? Still at your place?"

"Yeah, at least for a few more days. She can't stay there forever, though, and if we don't get a break on this thing..." Actually, Lark could stay there forever, if only she wanted to. "The alpha's still in a coma and the doctors don't think he'll make it. Navratil's file is helpful, but I'd still rather have him to question. I should've left one of the assholes alive."

"You were protecting your cousin. Any wolf would've done the same thing, especially after the beta pulled the knife on you."

"I still should've kept my head." If it had been anyone but Lark in danger, he wouldn't have let rage cloud his thinking.

His cell phone vibrated—Lark, checking in by text. He didn't read it—it'd be another *still alive. 18r.* Sometimes she included *RME.* He'd needed someone to explain that it meant "rolling my eyes".

"Okay." He stood and put on his jacket. "I've got to interview a witness in one of my other cases. I'll see you tomorrow."

Danny didn't reply. Taran walked out, leaving the novice staring at the information on Stephan Navratil.

On Thursday afternoon, in a feat typical of Houston's bipolar winters, the temperature plummeted from the mid seventies to the mid forties in three hours. Lark had expected to get home before the cold front blew in, but she lingered too long in the grocery store. When she stepped out around four-thirty in her flannel lounge pants and her long-sleeved thermal Astros shirt, the wind seemed to cut her in two. She squealed in chilly shock as she jogged with the cart to her car.

Back at Taran's she headed straight for the fireplace. When she had a nice crackling blaze going, she put away the groceries. Then she poured herself a stiff brandy and took it with her to the bathtub.

She'd seen little of Taran over the last three days. He went to work in the morning and came home late at night, undoubtedly avoiding her. In spite of what he'd said, he probably felt crowded. She'd been checking in with him via text as ordered.

His protectiveness thrilled her, but she wouldn't lie to herself—he cared for her like a big brother, nothing like the way she cared for him. It made living under the same roof bittersweet. She needed to go home before her heartache worsened.

She lolled in the bathtub until after six. Then she towel dried her hair, put on clean lounge pants and a long-sleeved T-shirt and headed for the kitchen at the other end of the house. She stopped in the den to poke at the fire and sip from the brandy she still nursed. When she glanced over her shoulder, she started to shake.

A lamp on the loveseat end table glowed. She hadn't touched it. She turned to look at the sliding glass door that led to the backyard; closed and locked when she went to take a shower, it now stood partially open. She hadn't touched the light on the deck, either, yet it blazed in the darkness. Anyone creeping around the backyard could see her perfectly, and she couldn't see them.

Her heart began to trip like a jackhammer at the sound of paws scrabbling on wood. Her throat tightened in fear. She forced herself to exhale, fighting blind panic.

An enormous brown shape materialized out of the darkness into the pool of light on the deck. She recognized Taran at the last minute and clapped a hand over her mouth to stop the scream. They stared at each other through the open door. He turned and ran back out of the light. She slowly sank into the couch in front of the fire, the glass of brandy still in her hand. She took a big swig and set it on the end table.

Oh shit, that was stupid, she thought as smooth fire flowed down her throat and burned in her chest. Tears poured from her eyes and she doubled over, choking and coughing. She started to laugh, which made her cough more, which made her eyes water more. She didn't hear Taran come in until he kneeled in front of her, murmuring into her hair.

"Lark? Lark! I'm sorry, I didn't know you were there. I didn't mean to scare you, baby..."

"No, it's okay, I'm laughing, I'm—wait. Huh? Did you just call me *baby?*"

Only in her dreams did he ever call her anything other than her name. One little word sent a new fire, this one slow like honey, coursing through her veins. She felt a hot flush in her chest and up the back of her neck.

She gasped as he cupped her head in his hands and tilted it back, brushing the hair away from her face. She ventured a peek at his eyes, surprised at the fear and worry in his expression. What on earth could scare *him*?

"Taran? Are you okay?"

"No," he muttered hoarsely, his mouth hovering over hers. "Not really."

Glimpsing a flash of lustrous green as he raised his eyes, she immediately dropped her gaze. She stared at the vein twitching in his jaw.

He'd thrown on jeans, but nothing else. She always took care not to stare at him overtly, lest he notice, but now her eyes feasted on the smooth golden expanse of his shoulders, the rippling biceps and wide chest inches away from her.

He rubbed his thumb across her cheek, skimmed it down her nose and dragged it slowly straight down over her bottom lip. She couldn't breathe. Though his huge hand traced her face as softly as a breath, her skin tingled everywhere his fingers wandered. The currents ran all the way down her spine, and she closed her eyes as a small sigh escaped her.

His body vibrated with leashed tension, belying the controlled precision of his movements. Afraid to break whatever spell possessed him, she tried not to move, but she couldn't sit still beneath his touch. She turned her head to kiss his hand, and impulsively ran her tongue across his palm. He jerked, and when his mouth came down on hers, it wasn't gentle at all.

He wrapped one hand in her hair as his tongue plundered her mouth. With his other hand, he caressed the side of her neck, his thumb stroking hypnotically up and down over her throat, and she purred at the delicious tremors he ignited.

She parted her legs to pull him closer, smiling against his lips when he shuddered. None of her dreams compared to the reality of his hot, greedy mouth on hers, the rough sweetness of his tongue, the hard strength of his hands on her skin and in her hair. She half-expected to wake up any second.

Slowly she slid her hands up his arms, around his broad shoulders and over his back, delighting in his skin and his muscles and his pulse beneath her palms. She'd wanted him more than anything in her life. She'd never thought she could have him, and now that she held him in her arms, her mind almost refused to accept it, even as her body burned and rejoiced.

Taran buried his face in her neck with a muffled groan. The powerful alpha—so much bigger, so much stronger than her—wrapped his arms around her waist so tentatively she thought her heart would break.

He still smelled a little of his cologne and the indefinable, unmistakable odor of a changing or just-changed wolf. She likened the scent to clean soil and fresh leaves, with a hint of pine.

Taran breathed heavily as she trailed her open mouth across his shoulder and up his neck. His skin was hot against her tongue. "You want me," she breathed. "*You* want *me*."

"Fuck, Lark, yes," he groaned. "I can't even... Christ, baby, I'm sorry."

"Why?" She ran a finger down the scar on his cheek. The vein in his jaw began to twitch again. "What's there to apologize for?" she asked softly.

He started to answer, but she crushed her mouth to his. She'd never taken a man's mouth like that before. She twisted her fingers in his silky amber locks as she raked the roof of his mouth with her tongue and arched against him.

She whimpered in protest when he suddenly broke the kiss, resting his forehead against hers.

"Tell me to stop," he rasped. "Tell me this is a mistake, and we need to stop, and I will."

"Why?" she asked angrily. Hurt and confused at his sudden hesitation, she drew back. "You're the big bad alpha! You started it, damn it. You think it's such a mistake, stop it yourself."

She cried out when he slid his hands under her, cupping her ass and pulling her hard against him, his stiff cock pressing into her stomach. His hot breath stirred her hair. She felt him smile.

"Are you challenging me, silly brat?" he growled.

His hands burned through her lounge pants. She hadn't put on panties after her bath, and she squirmed at the sensation of soaking wet flannel between her legs.

"I'm serious, Taran." Her voice shook. So did her fingers as they drifted through the curly golden hair of his chest and stomach. "You can't start something like this and then act like you didn't mean to do it. And you can't call me 'silly brat' while you're squeezing my ass."

He laughed softly into her hair.

"That's not a joke. Shit," she muttered into his chest, startled to find herself close to tears. "You never laugh when I say something funny, now you think I'm funny when I'm not joking."

"Wait a minute. You're upset? What'd I do?" He put a hand under her chin to turn her face up, but she yanked her head away.

"You kiss me and apologize, you kiss me again and tell me to stop you, then you treat me like a little girl. Do you want me or not, Taran?"

He tensed, going perfectly still. "Lark, if you knew how much I wanted you, you'd run like hell."

"You don't know that," she scoffed.

His voice took on a familiar hard edge, the one he got when he lectured her. "I just mean there are things you don't know, things I haven't told—"

"So? There are things you don't know about me. You don't know what I think or what I feel, you just assume you do."

"I'm trying to protect you."

"What, *now*? Taran, you idiot, once you stick your tongue down my throat and grab my ass, you don't get to play big brother any more. We're not that kind of rednecks."

She stood up, pushing at his shoulders. He didn't move. Legs awkwardly akimbo, she found herself trapped between him and the couch.

She shivered when he growled softly, his face just inches away from her sex. His breath warmed her belly. He rubbed his cheek against her stomach, sandpaper stubble tickling her skin through the thin T-shirt, and she gasped to realize she'd thrust her hips against him.

A hot rush of desire turned her legs to liquid. She would've crumpled if he hadn't taken hold of her at the exquisitely sensitive spot just below her butt. His hands were so large his fingers wrapped around the inside of her thighs. The thought of him sliding his hands up just a fraction of an inch brought a new flood of wetness. She heard him draw a deep breath, and she knew he smelled her arousal. She bit her lip and whimpered at the ache between her legs. He growled deep in his throat and squeezed her thighs.

Are you challenging me, silly brat? She hadn't just challenged him, she reflected; she'd teased and taunted and insulted him. She'd played chicken with an alpha, and she'd lost.

Or not.

"Sit down, Lark," he said in a dangerously soft voice, his mouth moving against her stomach. She obeyed, because even with his assistance her legs would no longer support her.

She collapsed to the couch. He slid one hand into her hair and pulled her head back, gripping her chin with the other hand before slowly, with agonizing thoroughness, running his tongue across her top and bottom lips, over and over till she was dizzy, her body suffused with heat and trembling. He bit her bottom lip and sucked on it, hard.

The burning knot of desire in her belly got hotter, and the heat spread lower. Her sex throbbed with wet fire, her spread thighs making the torture so much worse, and she clenched and unclenched her lower muscles in a desperate, fruitless attempt to ease the ache.

He thrust his thumb just inside her lips and ran it over her bottom teeth, smiling slightly when she gently bit it. His tongue replaced his thumb, and she moaned under the onslaught of his kisses.

"Stay here," he said against her mouth. His voice vibrated

inside her chest. He stepped away, and she suppressed a groan as she pressed her thighs together with relief. She sat stupefied, fighting to get her breath back while he walked to the glass doors and drew the curtains shut, then wandered to the loveseat, picking up her brandy glass on the way.

She watched him prowl the room, enthralled with his supple grace and the wild beauty of his body. He turned out the lamp on the end table. The fire behind him cast shadows and highlights across his brawny arms and shoulders, his strapping chest and the flat planes of his stomach. Her mouth went dry as she stared at the fine line of downy blond hair that tapered and disappeared into his blue jeans, tight and straining with his erection.

He was teasing her, she knew, revving her motor and making her wait for the downshift.

She looked up when he nudged her legs apart with his knee. Brandy glass in one hand, he gripped her thigh with his other hand as he smoothly knelt in front of her again. He stared at her lap as he pushed her leg aside, and when his eyes returned to her face, his slow, wicked smile of lust and promise drew a shuddering moan of need she didn't even try to hide.

He tipped the brandy glass to wet his index finger in the golden amber liquid—the same color as his hair, she noted dreamily—and rubbed it on her lips. He repeated the process, and put his finger between her lips, watching her mouth as she sucked. "Harder," he murmured, and she obeyed, swirling her tongue around his rough skin. He smiled at the faint *pop* when he pulled his finger out, and he held the glass up to her lips.

She took a small sip. He licked the excess off her lip before he reached over to put the glass on the coffee table.

"Raise your arms."

Shaking, weak with wanting, she stretched her arms above her head. She closed her eyes and whimpered softly as he began to push the T-shirt up over her ribcage. Her nipples throbbed, already unbearably tight and tingling in anticipation of his touch, and she cried out in torment when his thumbs brushed over them and kept going. Her breath came in short, labored gasps.

"Open your eyes, Lark. I want to see you looking at me."

She stared at the familiar, beloved face and saw a stranger whose hands and mouth had set her body on fire, a fire he now stoked slowly and relentlessly while she burned from the inside out. She shuddered with every breath she drew, waiting for him to finish pulling the shirt over her head and past her fingertips. When at last it came off, she gasped as air flowed across her breasts.

"Put your hands behind your head, baby," he said in a low, ragged rasp.

She bent her elbows behind her head and arched her back. The rough hunger in his face and his harsh, uneven breaths sent a primal thrill coursing through her as she realized he burned for her just as she did for him. But his masterful control never wavered. She, not he, sobbed with pleasure when he cupped her breasts in his feverish hands and flicked his thumbs across the taut, diamond-hard nipples.

She put her head back. Instead of kissing her, he took her throat with his mouth, a declaration of dominance. He slid his teeth up and down, his tongue tracing her veins while his fingers traced her areolae. She shivered at the delicious friction of calloused hands against delicate tissue.

He chuckled when she sank her fingers in his hair and pushed his head down to her breast. His scalding, wet mouth closed on her nipple and every time he sucked, she felt an answering throb between her legs. She scooted closer to the edge of the couch, tightening her legs around his, urgently and helplessly thrusting against him.

"I've wanted this so long." His mouth moved to her other breast, his teeth teasing her nipple, his tongue soothing the bites. "I can't stop, baby. I can't stop."

"I don't want you to," she breathed.

She screamed when he slid his hand between their bodies and squeezed her mound. His fingers pressed the flannel fabric between her swollen lips, rubbing it back and forth against her folds while his thumb made slow circles on her clit.

She writhed against his hand and struggled to breathe through the moans racking her body.

"Look at me, Lark."

She dug her fingernails into his shoulders and gazed, eyes half-closed, at his ravaged angel countenance. He stared at her, rapt.

"You're beautiful like this," he growled. "You know how many times I pictured you like this? In my dreams, you look like this when you come."

"Taran, I'm so hot. I can't—please..."

He groaned and shuddered, for the first time clearly struggling to maintain his own control while driving her into a frenzy. When he stood to unbutton his jeans, she reached up to stop him.

"Me. Let me," she said hoarsely. He stilled, panting, gazing at her with an adoration even her sweetest dreams had never envisioned, and she undid each snap with trembling fingers. She ran her palms across the hard, flat expanse of his abdomen, her thumbs stroking his obliques, and she smiled when his muscles spasmed and jumped beneath her hand. His hips jerked, and he grabbed her wrists with a ragged laugh.

"Baby, don't," he said unsteadily. "Don't make an alpha embarrass himself."

Her mouth went dry and she moaned, tugging the jeans over his hips to free his long, engorged cock. The velvety smooth shaft seared her skin as she ran her hands down the length of it, tenderly caressing the head as she watched his face. Taran closed his eyes, taking quick, shallow breaths. The vein in his jaw jumped erratically, his neck and shoulder muscles taut and strained. She would never forget the sight of him like that, or the fierce euphoria of knowing she did it to him. When she tried to take him into her mouth, he pushed her back.

"No way." He laughed raggedly, "I'll never make it."

"Taran," she pleaded, "*Now.*"

He stripped her pants off in one fluid motion. With that same wicked smile, he picked up her foot and gently kissed her ankle with his open mouth. Then her calf, then her knee, and then he stopped kissing and just ran his mouth the rest of the way up, and she writhed, shivering with pleasure as his whiskers abraded the soft skin of her inner thighs.

He put his hands beneath her ass and lifted her sex up to his mouth. He licked slowly once, twice, and took her clit in his mouth to suck. Her fingers dug into the plush couch cushions and she held on for dear life as he pulled and licked and teased, and when his tongue dove into her passage she almost levitated off the couch. Her heels dug into his hard back and she screamed as his greedy tongue probed and swirled. She drew in short, shallow gulps as her climax built and she ground her hips against his mouth, desperately pleading for release.

"Oh God, Taran, I—" She sobbed, and she screamed, and she came. And she kept coming, harder and for longer than she could ever remember as his mouth never left her clit, relentlessly riding the waves of her climax until she shattered.

Before she could draw another breath, he pulled her off the couch and onto his lap as he sat back on the floor. Still weak and shaky from the aftershocks of her orgasm, she steadied herself on her knees as he guided his cock into her. She moaned his name softly as she impaled herself on the full, rigid length of him, and he filled her.

"I can't..."

His tongue laved the hollow of her throat. He began to thrust. "You can't what, baby?" he asked in a voice so low she strained to hear it.

"I can't believe you're inside me," she sighed, and they moved together, his hot hands on her ass holding her tight as he drove into her, each thrust harder and longer than the last, and she murmured little aching cries of need while he fucked her harder and faster.

He reached down to stroke her clit with his thumb, and even though she knew she couldn't come again, not so soon after that earthquake, she did. A sweet little orgasm rocked her softly and she wrapped her arms around his head, his face buried in her neck.

He pumped hard a few more times. Then he too shuddered and came, more quietly but powerfully. Her heart soared at the way he softly shouted her name, squeezing her so tightly she lost her breath. He fell back on the carpet with her atop him, and they didn't move or speak for a long, long time.

Eventually, when she could breathe again and it felt like her mouth might work, she cleared her throat and whispered against his neck, "I thought I'd had sex before, but maybe I was wrong."

He lay on his back with one arm flung across the carpet, his other hand roaming her back, and she heard his smile as he said sleepily, "I'd kinda forgotten about it myself."

"What?" Her hand stilled on his stomach. "Do you mean you don't—I mean, you haven't been..."

With an odd, sardonic laugh he said, "I haven't been a busy wolf lately, no."

She kept quiet, so as not to let on how he'd flabbergasted

her. Taran had had women, and spare women, stashed around the city as long as she could remember. He never had steady girlfriends, and he'd never shacked up with anyone, but the idea of an even temporarily celibate Taran just didn't compute.

"Well," she lightly, "I guess it really is like riding a bicycle, huh? Hey. You taught me to ride a bicycle, didn't you?" Long, uncomfortable pause. "Not that we need to think about that right now. It's kind of squicky to think about, isn't it. I mean, you taught me how to ride a horse, too, and...wait." She felt him shaking beneath her; she was pretty sure he was laughing. "Shit." She sighed. Yeah, he was laughing. "God, I'm babbling. Make me stop babbling."

"Okay," he said softly, and rolled her onto her side, sliding his hand up into her hair and kissing her, slow and deep and gentle. She nibbled along his chin and jaw, because the feel of his stubble beneath her tongue made her tingle. He groaned contentedly and pulled her close, tucking her head beneath his chin.

"We need to get off the floor."

She snuggled against him. "I don't think I can walk yet. And I like the fire."

"Okay. Couch then."

"No, I don't wanna get up..." she whined as he stood up, and she whooped in surprise when he reached down and scooped her up. He slid in under her on the enormous sofa and pulled a fleece throw blanket over them.

She lay warm and drowsy between Taran's burning body and the blanket, and as her hand drifted lazily across his stomach, and his hand softly wandered through her hair, she remembered a game she had played with herself as a young girl. When she found herself somewhere she really wanted to be, or doing something she loved doing, or just feeling generally elated, she'd hold her breath and pretend that as long as she didn't breathe, time would stop and that moment would last as long as she wanted. She distinctly remembered playing the game as late as the age of twelve, when Taran taught her to ride a horse. He was a twenty-two year old Army Ranger, home on leave, and her worship of him approached idolatry. She didn't fall in love with him for another five or six years, but that afternoon at the stable in Sugar Land had been a harbinger of the longing she'd carried for him ever since.

"Lark?" he said quietly.

"What?"

"You okay?"

"I think so. It's just weird."

After a moment he asked, "Weird good, or weird bad?"

The big badass alpha sounded a little scared. She wanted to throw her arm around him and reassure him; but to do that would be to acknowledge his insecurity, and one didn't do that with alphas. She certainly couldn't tell him she loved him. So she said simply, "Weird good, of course, but still weird."

"Okay. I just don't want you to regret it."

She laughed softly. "Never."

She thought he'd fallen asleep when he said, "I've thought about this a long, long time."

"I have, too. For years."

"Really."

"Yes, really. Why?" Rising up on her elbow to smile down at him, she ran a fingernail over his ribs till he laughed. "I told you there were things you didn't know about me," she said more seriously.

"Like what?"

"Like, you gave me my first orgasm."

"Lark!" he exclaimed tenderly, and put a hand to her face. "Baby, I didn't know you'd never—"

"Not tonight!" She laughed, dropping a kiss on his broad chest. She lingered there, distracted by the sweet salty flavor of the smooth brown skin, and her fingers skipped across the top of his washboard abs. She grinned as his cock, just below her hand, began to notice.

"Lark," he said in a low voice, and grabbed her hand. "Your first orgasm...?"

"Oh, yeah." She kissed his ear and slid her leg between his, his cock hard and hot against her skin like a curling iron. "I was sixteen or seventeen when I figured out how to masturbate. The first time I got off, I was thinking about you."

"You're making that up," he breathed in an awestruck tone.

"Nope. I swear it's true." She nipped at his jaw again.

"God help me," he groaned.

He rolled over on top of her, and for a minute she was squished into the crack of the couch. A second later, she was on her back, Taran braced on his elbows above her. She gave a throaty, contented sigh, dug her fingers into his biceps, and raised her hips to open herself to him, wrapping her long legs around his waist. He dove into her with a mighty groan, and when he began to move inside her, she threw her arms around his neck, crushing his mouth to hers, loving the feel of his tongue thrusting in her mouth as his cock thrust into her slick passage.

She didn't come that time, but she didn't care. She couldn't help the tears. If he noticed them, he didn't say so.

Chapter Five

I have to tell her tonight, he thought on the way home from work Friday.

She might go psycho on him at first, but once he explained it to her, made it clear she didn't owe him anything and she could take all the time she needed, she'd understand. He tried to tell her last night. She'd want to know why he didn't try harder. He'd never confess the humiliating truth—simple fear.

After years of silent yearning, his self-control had hardened into a barrier of tempered glass. Almost losing her put a sizeable chip in that glass, and the cracks had steadily spread. Last night, the flick of her tongue across his palm shattered the whole goddamned thing. He'd needed her too much, and for too long, to say anything to make her pause.

He wouldn't apologize for what he couldn't regret.

As soon as he turned onto his street, he saw Nick's Range Rover sitting in his driveway.

He hadn't told his Alpha about last night; he didn't know if Lark talked to TJ or anyone else.

Nick, don't say anything. Help a wolf out, Alpha.

Surely, she'd understand. She acted as if she loved him. She could handle it. Together they'd figure out how to tell the family.

When he walked into the silent living room, he knew how badly he'd fucked up.

Nick stood looking out the sliding glass doors with his hands crammed in his pockets, apparently fascinated with something in the back yard. But Taran knew his best friend of twenty years better than that. The set of his jaw, his heavy-lidded gaze, his ramrod posture instead of his customary insouciant slouch all indicated the alpha's anger.

Lark huddled in the love seat with her head down and her arms wrapped around her knees. She didn't look up when he walked in.

After an agonizing minute of silence, Nick turned to him and said quietly, "I dropped by to talk to you about Kuba. Lark was here. As soon as I realized she was yours, I told her how happy it made me, for both of you. She didn't know what I was talking about. Taran—what the fuck were you thinking, wolf?"

He cleared his throat, started to answer, and found he had no words. A dull roaring sound filled his ears. He stared at Nick, silently begging for a life ring. Nick returned the stare with an expression part ire and part sorrow. It seemed to acknowledge yes, he could see Taran drowning but no, he couldn't—wouldn't?—pull him out.

Taran turned to look at his mate. His mate, whose scent he still wore, whose skin he still tasted, who'd come so sweet and frantic in his arms only this morning and wouldn't look at him now.

"Lark? I meant to talk to you tonight about this—"

"You claimed me?" She finally raised her head to look at him, her face streaked with tears. "You *claimed* me, and you didn't tell me? You bonded to me without telling me. How long have you known I'm your mate, Taran?"

He'd expected anger, but the anguish in her voice stunned him.

"*How long?*" she shouted.

"Three years," he said quietly.

"Three years," she whispered. "Three years." She nodded, looked up at the ceiling, back at him. "Three years. You've known for three years, and you never said anything. Three years you've treated me like you treated me all my life, either ignoring me or criticizing me, and you never bothered to mention that *I'm your fucking mate.*" Her voice got louder and harder with each word. She uncurled and put her feet on the floor, hugging herself tightly and leaning forward. In a voice so full of contempt he flinched she said, "What changed your mind, Taran? What made you decide it was time to fuck me?"

He gaped at her. "What are you talking about? That's not what happened—"

"It's not? You didn't plan last night?"

"How could I plan that? You think I wanted that to happen?"

"What, you didn't?"

"Yes! But, but—no, I mean—goddamn it, Lark!" He ran a hand through his hair, tugging at it in frustration as he began to pace. "I've thought about it for years, but I never did anything because—because it was *you*, and it seemed wrong, and I thought—I thought there was no way, I'm like your big brother, and half the time you hated me—"

"I never hated you—"

"And I'd never be able to explain it to Myall, or Mom or David, but then last night happened, and, and—"

"And and what?" she mocked.

He spun around to advance on her, pointing a finger. "I didn't rape you, Lark. I asked you if you wanted to stop and you said no. You wanted it as much as I did, every time last night and this morning. You still remember this morning, don't you?"

She blushed furiously. Belatedly he remembered Nick behind him, witnessing all of this. Lark sprang to her feet, arms still crossed tightly against her chest, hunching her shoulders the way she did whenever she got angry or sad or scared, just as she'd done ever since she was a little girl.

"No, I haven't forgotten anything," she snarled. "Have *you* forgotten all the times last night and this morning you could have stopped to say 'oh by the way, Lark, you're my mate, and now I'm bonded to you for life, and every wolf who sees you will know you belong to a wolf and if you don't spend the rest of your life with me I'll be alone and, and'—fuck you, Taran! I thought you *wanted* me!"

"Are you crazy?" he exploded. "Of course I want you! I've always wanted you!"

"Yeah, because I'm your mate! How long have you been waiting for a chance to claim me?"

Could she act any crazier? This made no sense at all.

"Shut the fuck up and listen to me! That's what I'm trying to tell you—I never planned to claim you, I never planned to fuck you, last night just happened, and once it started I couldn't stop it—I didn't want to stop it—*neither did you!* I wanted to tell you, but I couldn't think of a way to say it, and I decided to tell you when I got home tonight."

"Really?" she sneered. "Last night and this morning, even when we were making love, you never looked me in the eye—you're telling me that was a coincidence? You didn't want me to realize I could look you in the eye because then I'd know, and you didn't want me to know!"

"I wanted you to find out the right way—"

"The right way was before you seduced me!"

"*Seduced* you?" he roared. "You think I seduced you? *I can't stop, Lark. I don't want you to.*

I can't believe you're inside me.

As he remembered last night—Lark's sighs, her moans and her kisses, her fierce satisfaction in knowing what she did to him—he almost wanted to throw himself at her feet and beg her forgiveness. He almost thought he'd do anything to make it right, to make it like it was this morning when they kissed goodbye after making love one more time in his bed.

Almost, but not quite.

An alpha didn't grovel, not even to his mate, especially when he'd done nothing wrong and she was behaving like a spoiled child.

"You think you're some kind of victim here? Grow up, Lark." He hadn't meant to shout, but he didn't care if it scared her. She acted as if he'd forced her, or tricked her, into making love with him. Bullshit. They'd thrown themselves into the fire with equal abandon, and he wouldn't let her forget it.

"You lied to me!" she raged. "You—you tried to trap me, you act like I don't have a choice, like...like...you can just decide my future! I'm not ready for this, I didn't..."

"What did you expect, Lark? Casual dating? A fuck buddy? Is that what you wanted?"

"No, you asshole! That's not what I wanted! I don't know what I wanted! I didn't expect any of it to happen! I didn't expect you to want me, and when you did, I couldn't stop it, I just couldn't..."

"Don't you mean you didn't want to stop it?" he shouted.

"Yes! That's what I mean! I didn't want to stop, I always wanted—but I never thought you'd—and then—"

"Lark, listen to me." He took her by the arms and drew her to him, trying to calm her.

But she flailed at him, knocking his hands away. Her elbow

caught his chin in a glancing blow and he staggered back with a shocked snarl. She stumbled and fell on the couch, one hand on her mouth and her shoulders shaking as she stared up at him with huge tears pooling in her eyes.

"I'm not staying here," she blubbered. "I'm leaving. Now."

"For God's sake, Lark, get a hold of yourself! Drop the hysterical bullshit and listen to me. I'm not trying to push you, I'm not telling you what to do, I just—"

"Taran."

"We need to discuss this like adults and you need to take responsibility for what happened. And you can't leave as long as we don't—"

"Taran!" his Alpha bellowed.

His head whipped around like Nick had jerked it on a choke chain.

"Go outside for a minute and let me talk to her."

"This is my house, Nick," he growled.

"I'm your Alpha, wolf. Get your tail outside. *Now.*"

He balked, but then he thought—fuck. What good would it do? He'd only make her more hysterical if he tried to talk to her while this pissed off himself. He went outside to prowl the deck. Nick joined him ten minutes later.

"All right," his Alpha sighed. "She's going to TJ's house for the night. I couldn't get her to promise me anything more."

"What do you mean you couldn't get her to—"

He didn't finish the sentence. Nick calmly grabbed him by the throat and applied just enough pressure to make breathing iffy and vision blurry. Just for good measure, he picked him up off the deck a couple inches. Nick was three inches shorter and thirty pounds lighter than Taran, but he lifted him as if picking up a broom, which explained why he was a Pack Alpha and Taran wasn't. Taran dropped his head in submission. Nick let go and set him back on his feet.

"Bro, you know how much I love you," Nick said grimly. "I feel for you, I really do, and I think I understand what happened. But that female is madder than hell, and there's nothing you can do about it right now. I won't force her to stay here, and neither will you. Think of another way to keep her safe."

He could breathe normally again. He put his hands on his

hips and scuffed his cowboy boot against the patio table.

"All right," he muttered. "All right. Can you ask TJ to try to make her stay at her place?" "

"Absolutely."

"I already put a GPS locator on her car, so I'll know where she is when she's not with TJ."

Nick snickered. "I shouldn't be surprised. When did you do it?"

He grinned bitterly. "Monday morning."

"I'm assuming she doesn't know."

"Nope."

"If you think she's pissed at you now..."

He shrugged. "What's she gonna do? Hate me more?"

"Taran. She doesn't hate you. You scared her, wolf. You just altered her life, and it's gonna take some time for her to adjust."

"I was trying to tell her she could have all the time she needed. She doesn't want me, Nick, I think that's pretty obvious."

"Don't be stupid. Sounds like she wanted you all night, and I think she's wanted you a long time. She just needs—"

"You said you came over here to talk about Kuba."

He probably shouldn't interrupt his Alpha so abruptly. Nick fixed him with a narrow-eyed stare for a beat, clearly trying to decide if it warranted a more thorough throat-crushing, but he crossed his arms and raised an eyebrow. "What?"

"Kuba. The Czech wolf. You said you came over to talk about him."

"So we're not going to talk about your mate anymore?"

"No point. It's over, I'll deal with it." Cracks had been repaired, the barrier restored.

He'd let the pain seep through later, a bit at a time. "What about Kuba?"

Nick shook his head and sighed with resignation. "Okay, fine. A wolf out in Channelview says one of his buddies saw the Czech wolf in a dive bar. He snapped a picture of Kuba on his phone."

"Nick, that's huge!" He eagerly latched on to the one thing that could push Lark out of his mind for a bit. "Who was it? You have the photo? When did—"

His Alpha held up a hand. "Whoa, hold up. I don't have anything yet—I'm still waiting to hear from the wolf himself; he's a roughneck, moves around a lot, he's supposed to call me."

"When did he see Kuba?"

"From what I was told, the day I sent out the photo you gave me, so what—Monday? Yeah, I think so. But there's more. Another wolf who doesn't want me to give his name plays in some big poker games around town—he's an attorney, and there are a few high stakes games around right now."

"Yeah, yeah, I know—I wouldn't try to bust one up or anything."

"That's what I told him. Anyway, he's pretty sure he saw Kuba at a game this week. Naturally he didn't try to take a picture or anything, but he said it looked like the picture I sent out, and the guy had a thick accent and played huge—he walked away with something like fifteen grand that night."

"Okay, that's good. That's good," Taran said half to himself, mind racing. He felt the itch coming on—the wholly irrational but highly accurate signal telling him a case was moving, clues were popping, maybe this thing had some legs after all. He started to prowl restlessly across the deck again. "Your guy's gotta me get into one of those games, Nick."

Nick started to say something, and Taran cut him off.

"Tell your guy I don't give a shit about the poker game. My captain won't, either—if I bring Kuba in, no one's gonna care where I found him. Would you talk to your wolf and tell him I want in? I know they're always looking for more players and I'll spend money. No one will know I'm a cop."

Nick nodded. "He'll do it if I tell him to. I want these assholes off the streets and out of my town."

"I wonder if I should take someone along. Maybe Denardo."

"Who?"

"Rookie, officer from Oklahoma. Wants to get on SIU. He hasn't been here long, so he wouldn't be recognized either."

"Oh yeah, I've talked to him on the phone but we haven't met yet."

Any wolf moving into an area with an established pack had to meet with the Alpha at least once, to pay respects and acknowledge the Alpha's authority, even if the wolf chose not to join the pack. In cities like Houston, with large wolf populations, the process was much more informal than in smaller cities.

"He seems like an honorable wolf, real dedicated." He stretched and sighed. "All right. Shit. I need a drink. Can I go back in my house now?"

Nick laughed shortly and threw an arm around him. "Yes. I'll go see if I can help Lark out of here, and then you and I can get drunk for a little bit, if that's what you want."

"Yeah. Yeah, I think it is."

When they went back inside, they found Lark gone.

TJ had the margaritas ready when she got there. She dumped her things in the apartment's tiny second bedroom and threw herself down in the vintage eighties Papasan chair TJ wouldn't throw out no matter how many people pointed and giggled.

Mumbling her thanks when TJ put the glass in her hand, she waited while her best friend settled on the sofa. She closed her eyes, but she felt TJ's stare and sensed her anticipation.

"Well," TJ eventually said softly, "I always figured if you and Taran got together, you'd call me, we'd giggle and squee, and then we'd analyze every single thing he said and try to figure out what would happen next."

She didn't answer.

"We still need to figure out what happens next, don't we?" TJ continued.

She nodded.

"Lark, sweetie, you have to say something here."

"He told me I'd run," she mumbled.

"What did he mean by that?"

"He said if I knew how much he wanted me, I'd run like hell." Her voice quavered as her throat tightened. "He was right."

"Can you tell me how you feel? Are you sad, scared, pissed off, confused?"

"Yes."

TJ smiled. "Okay. Are you even a little happy? The guy you've been in love with for ten years wants you, and—"

"Yes. It makes me happy. It made me happy; I mean, for about twenty hours it made me delirious. I thought my whole life had changed." She laughed bitterly. "And I was right."

"So. You're happy he loves you, pissed off and scared because you didn't have any warning—"

"Who said he loves me? I'm his mate. He doesn't have a choice; it's not like he picked me for *me*."

On her way to the kitchen for refills, TJ stopped and turned around. With one hand holding the pitcher and the other one planted on her hip, she said, "Please tell me that's not what flipped you out. Please tell me you understand the difference between a man and a werewolf."

"Werewolves fall in love with women who aren't their mates, don't they?"

"Sure, all the time. Most wolves never even find a mate," TJ called over the blender. "But wolves who *do* find mates say it's love—it looks like love and feels like love and hurts like love. Only difference is, a mate bond lasts forever, and human love often doesn't. Scientists say even for humans, love is partly a physiological reaction, so do you really want to get hung up on details?"

TJ poured her a new 'rita and sat back down on the couch, sipping her own.

She didn't pick up her glass right away. She sat cross-legged and cross-armed in the large chair, growing more morose and annoyed by the minute as she realized her most trusted adviser insisted on approaching this whole issue rationally.

"I don't consider it just 'details,' Teej. I've known him almost my whole life, and he's never acted like he wanted me, or even liked me. He's always treated me like an irritating little sister and now he figures out I'm his mate, all of a—"

TJ slammed her glass down on the coffee table so hard some of the icy green concoction jumped the rim and puddled on the finished wood. She paid no attention to the mess.

"Lark. Are you going to argue with *me* about wolves and love and bonding?"

She blinked in surprise. "Oh, my God." Her heart dropped down to her shoes, and her face burned with shame. "I'm a selfish fucking bitch," she said through her hands. "I'm a stupid, insensitive asshole. I can't believe I didn't even stop to think about you and Josh. Oh, Teej..."

"Stop it, sweetie. Just stop," TJ murmured, sighing. "I wasn't trying to make you feel like shit. I was reminding you I know something about this. I want you to look at this calmly. You need to figure out what you're really feeling here."

She raised her head to see TJ looking at her with love and sympathy, and she wondered what she'd done to deserve such a best friend.

"You don't think I'm a bitch for freaking out about Taran claiming me, even though you lost your boyfriend when he found his mate?"

TJ took a couple deep breaths, staring into space for a minute. "You're not a bitch, baby. I'm your best friend; you're supposed to come to me when you're unhappy. I lost Josh seven years ago. I've healed."

"You're healed, but you refuse to date werewolves?"

"Yes," TJ said firmly. "Losing Josh hurt like hell. But it hurt mostly *because* it wasn't his fault. And once it happens to you, you want to make damned sure it never happens again. Josh loved me—he really loved me, I know that—and then Melissa showed up, and it wasn't his fault or her fault. It just felt so fucking random."

"Some werewolves don't leave their girlfriends, or their wives, when they meet their mates."

"True. But they end up miserable. If a wolf's in love with a woman and his mate shows up, he's screwed either way."

"But since it's so rare for a wolf to even find a mate," Lark said gently, "the odds of it happening to you again are, like, nonexistent. So you *could*—"

"Lark, I'm not discussing Nick. Not today, not tomorrow, never. We're talking about Taran."

"Okay. Sorry."

"Forgiven."

Lark knew she meant it.

"Now. Can we agree having the wolf you've loved for ten years wind up bonded to you is maybe not the worst thing you've ever experienced?"

She sighed. "Oh, hell. I guess so."

"All right. That leaves what? Anger at him for not telling you before he claimed you."

"Right. It feels like he trapped me."

"But he can't. He can't force you to stay with him. He's fucked if you don't want him. He's bonded to you, body and soul, for the rest of his life, so if he committed some great sin, he'll be doing penance forever."

"Yeah, but for the rest of *my* life, there's a wolf out there who can sense me, can find me, can never forget about me... I mean, there are some really scary stories about bonded wolves whose mates rejected them."

"And none of them apply to y'all. He'll never hurt you, he'll never go crazy on you. Like you said, he's never acted like he wanted you. You really think it's because he didn't?"

She frowned. "What? You mean like, he wanted me and purposely acted like an asshole so I wouldn't know?"

TJ rolled her eyes. "Duh. And why do little boys chase little girls and hit them with their backpacks?"

"I hadn't thought about it like that." She recalled something Taran said last night. "Oh. Oh, wow."

TJ raised her eyebrows.

"Last night, after...after we made love. He said something about forgetting what it was like. He said he hadn't been a busy wolf lately, and I was surprised, because he's always had women, you know? So that would mean..."

"That would mean he hasn't had sex in a while because you're his mate. He probably hasn't wanted anyone else. Even when he's horny, being with other women would just make him unhappy."

The implications staggered her. She leaned forward, resting her chin on her hands. "Holy shit. What if he's been feeling like this for years? What if he's been suffering as much as me? I mean—"

"How was it, by the way?"

"Huh?"

"The sex, Lark. How was the sex?"

"Oh. Um, unfuckingbelievable."

TJ grinned slowly. "Really."

"Yeah. Scary good."

"Well, no wonder you're so pissed off. Y'all could've been having heart attack sex all this time."

She snorted her margarita. It burned her nose. "That's not what I'm really worried about right now, but yeah, I guess."

"So. What you're really upset about is his not telling you first, because now you feel trapped."

"Yeah. I feel responsible for him. He asked me if I'd expected a fuck buddy."

TJ damned near snorted her own drink. "Shit. He said that? Did you punch him?"

"No! I was too upset to even notice. Hey. *Could* I punch him?"

"Oh hell yeah. He's bonded—he's yours. Look him in the eye, tell him to go to hell, throw something at him, alpha don't mean shit after this. I don't know why they refer to a wolf claiming his mate, when he's the one who gets shackled, but oh well. So, you felt trapped..."

"Yeah. I always fantasized about him wanting me, or..."

"Falling desperately, head over heels in love with you..."

"Yeah. And then we'd have wonderful sex and be together. But I never tried to imagine the rest of it—explaining it to the family, dating like normal people. Get married? Break up? I mean, when you think about it, the complications could be horrible."

"Well, yeah, I'd say so. Y'all never lived together, did you? I mean when you lived with Meg and David. I can't remember."

"No. Taran joined the Army a year before my folks died."

They each sipped their margaritas, lost in their own thoughts.

"I'm getting buzzed here," Lark said after a while.

"I'm getting bombed." TJ smiled. "Wanna give me the details on the sexy sexy?"

"I'll need another 'rita before I can do that." She laughed. She found it weird and difficult to dish personal dirt on sex, even to her closest friend in the world. "Teej?"

"Yeah?"

"I feel bonded to him. You think it's my imagination? I haven't felt this way before. With the other guys, after the first time we made love—I didn't feel this—this pull, this tether. I just feel like we're connected, and I don't..." She trailed off, unable to explain it any better.

"They say it's a two way thing," TJ mused. "Scientists, I mean. They're not sure how it works. They've just observed in a lot of cases—and I mean, like, a maj—maj—most of the time—"

she hiccupped, and they both giggled, "—when a wolf bonds to a woman it's recip—she bonds back, you know? Nature's way, I guess." She hiccupped again. "Someday when I'm not trashed I'll tell you all about the werewolf's limbic system."

"The wha-huh?"

"Limbic syst—the brain, you know? Controls emotion, memory, the primal stuff. 'S where the mate switch is, they think."

"He tried to tell me," Lark mumbled.

"'Scuse me?" TJ demanded. "What'd you say?"

"I said, I think he tried to tell me. He ashked me—he ask*ed* me to stop him, or make him stop, or if I wanted to st—whatever, you know? Like he felt guilty. I thought it washh just the big brother thing, like he wash—was—trying to protect me. Cause he does that, you know. Really pisses me off. Always Mr. Bossy."

"Um, alpha, shweetie."

"Well, that's no way to run a relashunship. Mr. Sensitive he ain't."

"But now you're his mate, you can do something about that. You can't really change him, and he'll shtill be a-a alpha—crap, I think I've had enough."

Lark sighed drunkenly. "Me too. I can't go to bed like this."

"Me neither."

"We need to eat. Wanna order pizza?"

"Sounds good. You call." TJ managed to lurch into the kitchen with an armload of glass and no bumps or bleeding. She called from the kitchen a minute later.

"Hey, Lark?"

"Yeah?" she replied as she wiped the margarita rings off the table.

"There's a big brown werewolf across the street, shtaring—*staring* straight at my kitchen window."

She sat down on the couch. "Okay. Is that shtalking, or is that guarding?"

"Let's call it guarding, and let's ignore it. Call for pizza."

"Okay." She pulled out her cell, but didn't dial. "Teej?" she wailed. "I don't wanna call Papa John's! I wanna call Taran. Like right now, and tell him I'm sorry, and I love him, and—"

TJ staggered back into the living room. "NO. Lark Manning,

no. Drunk dialing ish not what you need to do right now. Even I know that, and I'm drunker than you. Here." She held out her hand. "Gimmee your cell phone."

"I could just call him from your phone, you know."

"Oh. Yeah. Okay, don't. Bad idea." She stood up, swayed, righted herself. "Lish—listen to me. You need to take a few days and think this over, sweetie. He's not going anywhere. This is a huge change in your life. Don't act on impulsh—" She hiccupped. "I'm drunk, but I'm right. Sleep on this a while. Get ushed to it before you call."

"I know, I know, you're right," she said miserably.

Her every nerve screamed to call him, run to him. On the other hand, she'd acted on pure emotion earlier, and look where it got her. She needed to get her head straight before she poured her heart out.

He spent the next six nights on four feet outside TJ's apartment, enlisting friends always willing to help a wolf guard his mate. Maintaining a discreet stance in the shadows of the office complex across the street, someone kept an eye on Lark's arrivals and departures from dusk to daybreak. Between the apartment surveillance and the GPS tracker on her car, he covered her as well as he could hope.

She could see her uninvited security detail, but so what. He didn't do it to goad her into communicating; he did it to protect her life.

He'd anticipated complaints from people in the area. Even in a twenty-first century metroplex, many people recoiled at werewolves loitering about in public. After dropping a couple hints to the rent-a-cop who drove the little golf cart—he didn't explicitly call it a stakeout, but if the rent-a-cop got that idea, Taran wouldn't disabuse him of the notion—no one approached him or his buddies.

It reminded him of stories older werewolves told, of the days before werewolves came out. Everyone knew certain parts of the city and surrounding countryside—Memorial, Katy, Sugar Land—experienced less crime than other areas. Most people assumed higher incomes made safer neighborhoods. Residents knew better. Even the roughest working class parts of Sugar

Land suffered little crime. Something besides money or fear of cops protected those neighborhoods. Years later, everyone learned it was werewolves. Good werewolves ate bad guys.

He called Nick three times a day, to see if the roughneck had emailed the could-be photo of Kuba and if the lawyer had called about a poker game. By Monday, Nick quit answering his phone. Taran started calling from other people's numbers, but TJ started taking Nick's calls, and he couldn't bring himself to talk to her. Once, after answering the phone and hearing nothing for a few seconds, she said, "Taran, do you want to talk? We could talk."

He could handle a hell of a lot—Army Ranger training, live combat, gang violence, formal challenges, his mother's attempts to fix him up, his first unsolvable case, even his mate's rejection. He couldn't handle Tyler Jean Turner's sympathy. He hung up on her.

Nick finally called on Thursday afternoon as Taran drove back to headquarters after making arrests in a moonshine ring. He could still solve cases, just not his most important one.

"Hail, Alpha. This humble wolf is grateful for your attention."

"Watch the 'tude, wolf. You want to talk about Lark, I'm listening. I just got tired of telling you I hadn't heard from my wolves."

"Oh well, at least TJ is doing real secretarial work for a change."

"TJ's my assistant, not my secretary, she works her ass off, and that's the last attitude warning you're getting." Nick paused for a minute. "She's worried about you."

"I'm not comfortable with that."

"She's worried about both of you. Lark is—"

"I can't talk about Lark, Nick. Not attitude, just fact. You calling about my case?"

Nick exhaled sharply, and he steeled himself for another tongue-lashing, perhaps a command to submit for discipline. But after another pause, Nick said only, "Yeah. Lawyer's name is Petri. He'll meet you tomorrow night at seven. Warehouse downtown, 7000 block of McKinney, white brick with red trim. There's a goth club in the front of the building. Go around to the back, gray door, tell them Petri sent you, password is Brunson."

He laughed in spite of himself. "Fuck. It's like an old speakeasy. If the cops show up do all the tables slide into the floor or something?"

"No idea," Nick replied drily. "What do you expect, with the dumbass gambling laws we have? Petri will meet you inside. Tall, blonde, yuppie, radiates lawyerness. He's nervous as hell about bringing a cop, but I told him you're my best friend. You better just hope Vice doesn't have a raid planned tonight."

"I'll make certain they don't. Thank you, Nick. This could be the break I need."

"Don't thank me. You're my wolf, and I want these curs brought down. Talk to you later."

They hung up. On impulse, and before he had a chance to come to his senses, he dialed Lark's cell phone. As expected, he got her voicemail. He wouldn't hang up; alphas didn't hang up. They just talked real fast when they had something difficult to say.

"Look. I don't expect you to call me back. Christmas is gonna be hell, it's my fault and I'll worry about it. Shit, I'll probably have to leave town." He took a deep breath. "I should've tried harder to tell you. I just wanted you too much. I'm sorry I yelled at you. I'm sorry I told you to grow up and, and—everything else. I didn't mean to—no, scratch that. I lied. I'm sorry I hurt you, I'm sorry I scared you, I'm sorry I yelled. I'm not sorry I claimed you. I wanted you before I knew you were my mate. I think I loved you before then, and I know I love you now. I'm no—"

Beeep.

Goddamn it. The first and only humiliating apology of his life—getting cut off in the middle of it didn't do much for his self-esteem.

Alphas didn't have self-esteem. Alphas *were* self-esteem.

Fuck it. He dialed again.

"You need to understand something, Lark. I'm never gonna regret fucking you, hear me? It was the best night of my life, and it was the best night of yours. I'm gonna think about it every day single day." He felt himself growing hard just saying this out loud. Maybe he really was an asshole; he'd live with it. "I'm gonna think about how you looked, how you smelled, what you did, the way you begged me to make you come. And when we see each other—because we will—you remember this—I'll be thinking about it whenever I look at you." He stopped, panting heavily. "I love you."

He hung up.

Chapter Six

She always turned her cell phone off when she worked. Sometimes she forgot to turn it back on till long after she got home—or, in the present case, TJ's apartment. Around nine-thirty Thursday night she saw she had six missed calls, including two from Taran. Hands trembling, she looked to see if he'd left a voicemail.

She stared at the screen for five minutes before she pressed "send" to listen. The first message set her pulse racing, her stomach flipping and turning itself in knots. The second message turned her legs to jelly and she had to sit down, because her body ached and burned like he was in the damned room, saying all those things in person.

She listened to it at least a dozen times, turned on and trembling. Then she started to panic with the (largely) irrational fear someone could get hold of her phone, hack her password, and listen to the message. She emailed the voicemail to herself and then erased it. When she got home, she'd print the email from her computer and add it to the Taran Box, which no one, not even TJ, knew about.

It contained every item, memento, or, most rarely, gift she ever received from him, including the ticket stub from the showing of *Beauty and the Beast*. He had taken her and two girlfriends to see it the first time he came home on leave following her parents' death. After the movie he took them to Bennigan's for dinner, three giggly eight-year-old girls and one gorgeous eighteen-year-old wolf. Their constant squealing, he said later, made his ears ring for days. Over the years, she'd filled the box with silly shit like that. Nothing like the message, though. That message was the hottest thing any guy had ever said to her. *"I'm glad I fucked you; I'll remember it every day of my life; I love you."* It was probably as close to romantic as Taran could get, and it was all she needed.

He stopped by the office Friday night to confirm plans with his captain: no raids on the party, nobody cared if he won money, and a couple guys in the unit hanging out in a bar one block away from the warehouse in case Kuba showed. Taran would send a prearranged text, they'd show up and take the Czech downtown for questioning. Given Kuba's rap sheet and the information from Miami, they could hold him at least twenty-four hours without a warrant for his arrest.

Taran wouldn't talk about Kuba or Eurowolves at the game. Someone there might know Kuba and tell him people were asking about him. A wolf like Kuba didn't like people asking about him. Taran would watch, wait, listen and hope. Mostly hope, because this shot was miles fucking long.

He'd just shut down his computer and put on his leather jacket when Denardo walked in.

"Hey!" The rookie was clearly surprised to see him, "Why are you here so late?" They hadn't spoken since Denardo got back from Vegas.

"I'm about to go play poker," Taran replied with a frown. "Wolf, maybe you should give up the bike. It's not for everyone, you know."

The bruise beneath Denardo's right eye was almost as dark as his iris. Once again, he limped. He had a split upper lip and contusions on his cheek.

"Not the bike this time," Danny muttered, reddening. "The reception got a little out of hand. A fight broke out in the hotel bar."

"Did your side win?" He grinned.

"I don't even remember," replied the beta, easing into his chair. "I'm just lucky I didn't end up in jail."

Taran stopped and turned when Denardo said, "Wait a minute. Poker? You're going to play poker?"

"All in the line of duty. Nick heard from a wolf who thinks he played with Dominik Kuba at a big game downtown. He's getting me in tonight. Wanna come along? Real undercover work, plus you get to gamble and drink."

"Um, no thanks. I don't play, and I'm still kinda sore. I was gonna check my messages, then go home and sleep till noon."

"I'll let you know if anything shakes out."

"Good luck," Denardo replied quietly as Taran walked out.

The two large rooms in the back of the recently renovated warehouse featured surprisingly comfortable furnishings, including custom made poker tables and easy chairs for players to relax and visit between games. The soundproofed walls blocked the noise from the goth club so well even wolves could barely hear it. Taran thought he recognized the anonymously catered food from one of Houston's hippest restaurants. Whoever ran this game had a lot of money and wanted players who did, too.

"Three hundred to you, Tom," the dealer said, using the name Taran had adopted for tonight. He didn't see anyone he knew, but as the only Taran in the Houston pack, he couldn't risk someone blowing his cover.

Down by a thousand bucks so far, he didn't care because he enjoyed poker. He'd decided to stay all night in case Kuba showed. Petri the Lawyer (there couldn't be another Petri in the Houston pack either, but Taran assured him they'd probably never talk again) promised to point him out. Two hours in and no sign of wolves with accents, Slavic or otherwise.

About fifty wolves played tonight. Most humans wouldn't play poker with wolves, who didn't need to read tells when they could smell fear, excitement, happiness and anger.

Folding his measly pair of sixes, he sat back and waited for the hand of five-card stud to end. Everyone else folded as well. The guy who'd opened, a Jersey wolf calling himself Tonio, bought the thirty-five hundred dollar pot.

As Tonio raked in his chips and the dealer shuffled the new deck, another wolf whose name he hadn't gotten said, "Anyone heard from the Russian wolves? I was hoping I might get some of my money back."

Taran took a sip of water and sat back in his chair with a

yawn, thankful to be an alpha and one unusually good at controlling his reflexes and pheromones.

The dealer, a strong beta, replied, "I don't know, George. I like the ones who throw the money around, but those guys were a little too hardcore. We get enough big fish here; we don't need Russian mobsters or shit like that."

"Dominic's an Italian name, isn't it?" said another player. "I never heard of Russians named Dominic."

Taran feigned an interested frown, as if considering the ethnic origins of "Dominic". Mentally, he high-fived Nick, Petri the Lawyer, Tonio, and the wolf who'd just named Kuba.

Tonio chimed in, "Those guys weren't Russian, they were Czech."

Bingo. Hallelujah. Where the fuck was Kuba?

"Russian, Czech, Italian, I don't give a rat's ass," grunted the dealer. "My bosses like friendly little thousand dollar buy-ins where you get killed for normal reasons, not because some KGB type lost too much money."

The dealer had a point, Taran reflected as he maintained his bored expression. If you put fifty wolves in a small space, gave them alcohol and pitted them against each other in a series of pissing contests, you didn't really need genuine psychos to make it dangerous.

"Don't matter anyway," Tonio said flatly. "They were coming, now they're not. One of the first guys here tonight said he talked to a guy in the Czech's crew—something spooked him. He changed his mind."

An unseen fist punched Taran in the gut.

The dealer halted mid-shuffle. "Spooked?" he barked. "What does spooked mean?"

It means someone tipped Kuba off, it means we have a leak, just like they did in Miami.

Tonio shrugged. "Fuck should I know? Something made the Czech guy not wanna come after all. Who cares?"

"Well, Tonio," the dealer said with sarcastic solicitude, "*we* might care if we were about to get busted. There's a lot of money on the tables here."

Conversation skidded and crashed in both rooms, the only remaining sound the muffled thump of bass-heavy music through the walls of the goth club.

The air thickened with the scent of stress, fear and anxiety. He didn't expect an imminent panic, but he shifted slightly in his seat so he'd have easy access to his gun.

An alpha in the next room—a dealer, probably—said firmly, "There's no reason to think we're getting uninvited guests tonight, gentlemen. We maintain excellent relations with the authorities." Taran assumed he meant someone on the force tipped them in advance. "Play will continue until four, as normal. Anyone who cares to cash out when the current hand is finished is free to do so. But I'm sure everyone will remain calm, and I hope most of you choose to stay."

Another second passed. The alphas dialed down their own tension. Conversation quietly resumed. A more restrained mood prevailed with slower play—no more boisterous joking and bragging, just serious poker.

The players at his table elected to take a break. He maintained his relaxed façade, professing not to care if they stopped for a while or not. Inside he seethed.

Who had tipped Kuba?

If he could've attended without telling anyone, finding and bringing Kuba in by himself, he would have done so. Investigations didn't work that way. A cop couldn't show up at an illegal poker game without a word to his superiors, not if he wanted to keep his badge. He'd had to tell his captain. The captain had to make sure Vice wouldn't raid this particular game on this particular night.

The wolves waiting at the bar down the street. Petri the Lawyer. Whomever Petri the Lawyer may have told. Fact was, the list of people who knew about Kuba being at this game, and about Taran attending tonight, was not short.

A big, black, dangerous funk hovered on the edge of his consciousness. Tomorrow it would turn into rage.

No reason to stick around for another hand now; he needed to release his backup. He got up to mix himself a scotch and soda—his first alcohol of the evening—and sat down in an easy chair to send the text and check his messages.

He had several missed calls, one of them from Lark.

He took a sip of scotch as he stared at her name and number on the screen. A wolf walking by said with a laugh, "Bro. You having a seizure?"

"Huh?" He didn't look up.

"You been staring at that phone like it's flashing strobe lights."

"Oh. No. No, just a call I wasn't expecting." He still didn't look up. The wolf took the hint and walked away.

He looked in his voicemail. One from Lark.

He forced himself to text his backup before he listened to the message, noting with disgust how his hands shook slightly. Once he'd sent the text ("no kuba go home"), he returned to the voicemail list and stared at it some more. Took another sip of scotch. Considered walking outside to listen to the message. Stayed in his chair, unsure whether his legs would shake as badly as his hands.

Apparently, getting bonded to your mate made you act like a chick.

He hit Send and entered his code.

Beep.

"It's me, I, um—" Her voice paused, took a breath. Just one little breath, but it wafted through the phone and he sucked it in and closed his eyes, breathless at his body's immediate fierce response. His pulse throbbed in his throat, his gut churned, his dick ached. He growled softly.

"I got your message, and—I never—I didn't think I..." Her hesitancy, the shakiness of her voice, shredded his heart. "I didn't call you back sooner because I was scared. Not—not of you, I mean, but that you might be mad or—or hurt, really, cause I was such a bitch. I mean, you scared me. But I should've handled it better. Shit." She paused, and he heard her swallow. "I've been thinking about this all week. I feel like a dog that finally caught a car, you know? I have no goddamned idea what to do with it now."

He barked once in startled laughter, and every wolf in the room stared. Embarrassed, he turned his attention back to the message. "...a long, long time. God, for so long Taran, and it hurt so bad..." He could hear her trying not to cry. It killed him. "You were right," she whispered hoarsely, "it *was* the best night of my life, and I acted like a spoiled brat. I'm not sorry we did it, and I'm not sorry I'm your mate, and I need a little time to get used it to but—" the words tumbled out in a rush now, "—I *will* get used to it, I want to, I—if you don't hate me, if you still want me, I love you. I just—I love you."

Beep.

He played the message again.

He swallowed, took another sip of scotch, and played it again. Then again, then once more, forcing himself to breathe slowly and block out every sound around him till nothing existed but her voice in his ear, her sighs, her pauses, the unshed tears behind the words "if you don't hate me," the way her breath caught before she said "I love you."

The dealer touched him lightly on the shoulder. He jumped out of his skin.

"Sorry, Tom, but I've been calling the table back for five minutes. You never looked up."

"Ah." He shook his head. "I...I think I need to leave."

The dealer smirked at him. "Yeah, I think you do too, wolf."

When he stood, the room swam. Not like when he drank too much, because he hadn't. Not like when Nick's dad caught them in his porn stash and flung them into opposite corners of the room. Not even like when he bled out two pints of blood after close quarters combat.

No. He reeled from nothing less than pure, euphoric, I-thought-the-rest-of-my-life-was-going-to-suck-but-maybe-it-won't lightheaded wooziness.

He didn't worry about falling down; he worried about floating away.

He staggered out of the warehouse into the crisp night air with a goofy-assed grin plastered on his face. Catcalls followed him, accompanied by filthy suggestions from jealous wolves about what to do when he caught up to her.

His body screamed with need, urging him west, toward her, the pull of his bonded mate as accurate, and far more powerful, than the GPS locator he'd put in her car. The strain of resisting that pull threatened an involuntary change, but he couldn't afford to get four-footed right now. To keep from howling in the middle of the parking lot, he clenched his jaw till he heard his teeth grind.

As a wolf, he needed his mate. As a cop, he needed to determine who'd betrayed his investigation. "My mate called and said she loved me" would elicit sympathy, but it wouldn't excuse dereliction of duty.

First to headquarters, then to Lark.

He drove to the nondescript building housing SHIU on the other side of downtown, obeying all posted speed limits and stopping at all red lights despite the urge to get to his mate as fast as he possibly could. A thirty-six-year-old alpha didn't lose control, no matter the circumstances.

Right.

He allowed himself to dial Lark's cell before he got out of the car. It went straight to voicemail. His vocal chords locked up. He wheezed into the phone like some kind of stalker, and he wondered if the sound of his breath could seize command of her body, as hers had done to him.

"Lark," he croaked. He cleared his throat and began again. "Baby, don't you think I've already tried to hate you? Silly brat. I mean..." He stopped, laughed a little. "Shit. I've tried everything to get you out of my system. I gave up a long time ago. You weren't—you didn't do—it doesn't matter, okay? None of it matters. If you love me."

He stopped again, unsure how to continue, unable to hang up.

"I'll find you tonight. Call me, but even if you don't—I'll find you. I love you."

He didn't see his captain at headquarters. Andy Gossen entered the squad room as Taran logged into his computer.

"What are you doing here?"

"Trying to figure out who fucked up my investigation. You?"

"Captain said he'd have my throat if I didn't do my paperwork." Gossen grinned, then sobered as he realized what Taran had just said. "What happened?"

He sighed and leaned back in his chair, stretching his arms over his head. "You know about the missing fae women?"

"Yeah. We still like the Euros for it?"

He nodded. "The wolf behind it's a big poker player, was supposed to be at a game tonight, right here downtown. Nick had someone get me in. But someone at the game said the perp got spooked and changed his mind.

"Think he was tipped off?"

"Had to be," Taran grimaced. "And I gotta know who did it."

"Sucks, bro." Gossen began typing at his own computer.

Taran completed his email to the captain and looked through his notes.

"Hey," Gossen said suddenly. "Why don't you ask Denardo about other rich games? Can't be that many."

He turned in his chair to look at the other detective, confused. "Why?"

"Danny's a big poker player."

Ice ran up his spine and into his scalp. He closed his eyes against a sudden, vicious attack of vertigo.

"Taran? Bro, what's wrong?"

"I asked Denardo if he wanted to ride along tonight." He opened his eyes. "Said he didn't play."

Gossen raised an eyebrow. "That's not what I heard," he said slowly.

"Denardo tell you he played?"

"No. I know a cop in Oklahoma—said everyone knew Danny was a big player. His dad was a pro."

"Y'all ever talk about it?"

Gossen shook his head.

"So," Taran said after a few minutes' silence. "Think of a good reason why he'd lie about that."

"Can't."

"Me neither."

He stood up to pace, the scent of his anxiety filling the room as he ran the past weeks' events backward in his mind. The faster his mind raced, the harder his heart pounded. The harder his heart pounded, the more pheromones he shed.

Gossen, a beta, grew progressively more agitated until he finally barked, "What is it?"

"You know my cousin got drugged at Le Monde?"

Gossen nodded.

"Danny was there that night."

"That doesn't mean anything."

"Right. I took her home from the hospital the next day, told Denardo I was doing it. That night, she gets attacked again. Denardo shows up; says he was here when dispatch got the officer down call."

"What night was this?"

"Two weeks ago Sunday."

"I'm going into the duty and access log." Gossen looked up from his monitor, a grim expression on his face. "Denardo wasn't in the building that day."

Taran took a deep breath. "I need to find him."

"Could be a coincidence."

"Danny knew everything I had on Kuba. He's been acting weird. Miami lost Kuba to an agent with a gambling problem." He felt in his pockets, then looked on his desk. "Shit. My phone's in my car. I need to—I need to call Lark, tell her to—I need to find her. Now."

It felt like Le Monde all over again: the unfamiliar, queasy sensation of helplessness, made worse by the fact he couldn't protect her this time, couldn't even locate her. Now that he'd bonded to her, any threat to her elicited instant reaction from him. It had already started. He smelled the change, felt the bones in his hand rippling as he tried to dial her cell phone from his desk.

"Taran? Dude, are you *changing?*" Gossen sounded horrified.

"She's...my mate," Taran panted as he listened to Lark's phone ring. "Don't—" he swallowed, drew a deep breath and let it out slowly, "—don't freak. I can control it. I have to control it—"

"Taran?" Lark's voice—soft, happy, surprised—ran through him like cool wine. He shivered with relief, falling back into his chair.

"Where are you?" he asked huskily.

"Cowgirls. I met TJ and the girls, but they had to leave. I was gonna see, if, um, you wanted to meet me? If you're not working, or busy or, you know? I got your message." He could hear her blushing.

"Why are you whispering?"

"Because I'm not alone."

"So? How can anyone hear—Lark, who's with you?" But somehow, he already knew.

"Danny."

Gossen gasped.

"You know, your rookie?" she said when he didn't answer. "He came in a few minutes ago. He reminds me of someone. I can't figure out who. He says he just has that kind of face."

A brief moment of sweaty, nauseated, near-howling dread, and then—nothing. He exhaled. His vision cleared, his bones stopped morphing, intellect evicted emotion, and he shifted smoothly into combat mode. Mind over instinct.

"Danny's there? With you?" He kept his voice level.

"Yeah," she said uncertainly. "Why?"

Denardo could hear everything Taran said.

"I need to see you, baby. I want to see you—right away." He needed her out of there. "Go to my place." He snapped his fingers at Gossen, who nodded and picked up the phone. Gossen quietly ordered a unit to his house as Taran continued, "Tell Danny I need my mate and he'd better not get in my way." He said it lightly, but if Denardo had done what Taran thought he had, he'd understand.

She laughed throatily. "Okay, that's kind of embarrassing, but I like it. Do you—"

"Leave now, Lark. *Now*. Call me when you're in your car, hear me? I love you. *Go*."

He hung up.

"You want me to come with you?" asked Gossen.

"No. I want a unit at Cowgirls. And nobody stopping me on my way home."

Racing through red lights toward I-10, he reached for his cell phone on the front seat and punched in Nick's number on speed dial.

"Did you get my text?" Nick asked in lieu of "hello".

"Wha—no, you send me one?"

"Yeah. The roughneck finally sent me the picture. Sure looks like Kuba to me."

"Okay. I'll look at it in a minute."

"Do you—"

"I got a problem here, Alpha." He filled Nick in.

"You're not sure about Denardo?"

"No. It's just a hunch."

"You have good hunches. What do you need me to do?"

"Call Cowgirls." The managers and bartenders were all wolves. "If Denardo's there, tell them to watch and track him. Lark's driving to my place. If—" his voice cracked for a second, "—if she got out of there all right, and he's not with her, she's fine. I just need to know where she is, where he is. Hanging up."

He drove with one hand as he raced onto the freeway. With

the other he pulled up Nick's message and attached photo.

It was Kuba, all right, a good frontal shot of the Czech wolf sitting at a table. Another guy at the table sat with his profile to the camera. He couldn't tell for certain, looking at his phone in the dark of his car, but it sure as hell looked like Danny Denardo.

He punched the accelerator and hit speed dial for Lark. It went to voicemail.

"Baby, I told you to call me. Do it now."

The GPS receiver showed her car headed northwest—the right direction—but who drove it? Was she alone?

He hit redial, got voicemail. "Lark? Where the fuck are you?"

Traffic slowed as he approached Washington and stopped altogether at the Loop, all four lanes locked solid. Self-control slipping, cool melting, his emotions pounded at the door and demanded readmittance. Intellect gave way.

He smelled it, heard it, felt it under his skin. He quit trying to fight it and pulled the car over. Just as well—he'd get there faster on four feet than on four wheels anyway. Let Fast Tow take the car.

He unbuckled and jumped out just in time. Wolves didn't strip and change in public very often, certainly not on the shoulders of major freeways. He'd probably show up in the *Chronicle* tomorrow, maybe even with a pho...

...shaking his head and howling as the last human thought evaporated, the wolf raced for home and mate.

Chapter Seven

She watched her rearview mirror all the way from Cowgirls, but no car followed her. Maybe Danny Denardo didn't realize she'd remembered him.

No—surely he smelled her fear. For some reason, he let her get away.

When she saw the cop car in Taran's driveway, she parked under the streetlamp in front of his house. Turning off the engine and resting her head on the steering wheel, she gave in to tears and shakes.

She didn't see anyone outside gawking at the red and blue lights. Taran's house was one of only four on the small cul-de-sac; his neighbors might well all be out on this Friday night.

He'd arrive any minute, crazy with worry or furious at her for not calling. Probably both. She assumed Danny took her cell phone.

She got out and shut the door behind her. Then she looked up and screamed.

Danny Denardo stood in the middle of the street.

The cop—probably a werewolf—yelled, "Ma'am? Ma'am! Get out of the way!"

Too late. Denardo slammed into her, pinning her against the car with his hands on her shoulders. He looked past her to the cop.

"Put the gun down. Don't touch your radio. I don't want to hurt her."

"You don't?" she asked tightly. "That's not why you're here?"

Danny stepped back but didn't let go of her shoulders. He

trembled as badly as she did. His battered face, sallow beneath the streetlight, wore a miserable expression and his dark, haunted eyes searched hers—looking for what, she didn't know.

"I've never hurt a woman before."

"You didn't kill Eloise?"

"No. I just told Kuba about her. He did the rest."

"Why?" She had to keep him talking. The cop could only stand and watch.

"I owed him money. Gambling." He paused. "I used to be an honorable wolf. I swear to God."

"I believe you."

They regarded each other in silence.

"Why'd you let me leave Cowgirls?"

"Was that the first time you remembered me?"

She swallowed, nodded. "Yeah. When I was walking back from the bar, you turned to look at me, and it clicked. You were standing just like that at the table at Le Monde that night."

"You weren't supposed to remember anything after we put the GHB in your drink."

"Sorry," she whispered. "Why'd you do it?"

"Because Eloise was supposed to show up alone. They said if I didn't help get rid of you, they'd kill me. But then I realized you were Taran's cousin, and I met you later, and I liked you, and I like him, and now you're his mate, and..." He closed his eyes and shuddered.

"Did you take my cell phone?"

He laughed humorlessly. "Yeah. You left your purse when you went to pay the tab. You really need to be more careful in bars, Lark."

"Are you gonna give me the chance, Danny?"

A tear slid down his cheek. "I don't know what to do. Kuba's gonna kill me."

"Taran's gonna kill you first. You can kill me and the cop, but Taran's on his way and he's not gonna—"

"I know. I *know*!" he agonized. "What do I *do*?"

"Give yourself up." She prayed the scent of her fear wouldn't push him over the edge. "The police will protect you."

"I could get life!"

"Not if you testify against Kuba. He's big. They'll deal for him."

She waited on a knife's edge of apprehension. Sirens wailed nearby.

He blinked, nodded and stepped back further, releasing her shoulders.

"You're right," he said dully. "I can't get out of this, and I'm not a killer."

She heard movement behind her and held up a hand.

"Wait!" she called to the cop. "Don't shoot. He's surrendering."

Danny put his hands up and smiled sadly. "Thank you," he mouthed.

She nodded. Together they turned toward the driveway where the cop waited, gun aimed at Danny.

Not only did werewolves run too fast for human eyes to track, they ran too quietly for human ears to hear.

Danny jumped, gasped and vanished from her side. She felt a stroke of fur and rush of wind as a large dark shape sailed through the air and bore Danny with it across the street into the neighbor's yard.

The cop flew after them.

Fangs snapped, flesh ripped. She froze. Then Taran's howls and Danny's screams and the cop's shouts shattered her paralysis.

"*Taran! Stop!*" She didn't know she could scream like that. Every werewolf in Memorial heard her.

His head came up and swiveled to her. Another cop car and an ambulance streaked around the corner, lighting up the cul-de-sac like a football field. She stared at her love, his wide yellow eyes shining in the headlights, blood dripping from his gaping jaws, his chest heaving.

Their gazes locked.

"Stop," she whimpered, "please, baby, stop."

He didn't move, and she didn't take her eyes off him, as a policeman approached from the side.

"Miss," he said in low, urgent voice, "are you Detective Lloyd's mate?"

She nodded mutely.

"Would you please go to him? We need to get to Officer Denardo, and Detective Lloyd smells very close to loco, ma'am."

She tried to move, found she couldn't.

"I'm scared." Her voice sounded strangled. Her heart felt like it, too.

The cop kept his voice low and soothing. "I promise you, ma'am, he won't hurt you. You're the only one who can approach him right now, and we need to get to Denardo before he bleeds out."

"Danny wanted to surrender," she whispered wretchedly.

"Yes, ma'am. We can save him, if you'll go to your wolf."

Her werewolf. He needed his mate.

She wobbled across the cul de sac on shamefully unsteady legs. He didn't move, made no sound as she approached. She stopped a few feet away from Danny's body. Forcing herself not to look, she stared fixedly at Taran instead.

"I'm all right, baby. See? I'm fine." Tears poured down her face, but she didn't flinch as he crept slowly to her. She'd never been this close to him when he was furry; his back came level with her waist, his head just below her breasts. "I'm sorry I did something stupid and freaked you out. You really love me, don't you?" She held her hand out; he sniffed it uncertainly and leaned into her. "Shit, you're a horse," she gasped, sniffling a laugh. "You said I'd have time to get used to all this."

He pressed his head against her ribs and whined softly, quivering from nose to tail. She stroked the thick, stiff fur of his neck. When she sank to her knees, he stretched out on the grass beside her. She murmured nonsense with all the love she could push into her voice and slowly, slowly, his body relaxed and his breathing returned to normal.

The cops and the EMTs moved in to pick up Danny's body. She stayed in the grass with Taran and stroked his flank until the ambulance took off, sirens blaring. Maybe twenty minutes had passed; it felt like they'd been there for hours.

"Lark?"

Taran raised his head, and she turned to see Nick standing a couple feet away. She started blubbering in earnest and rose to her feet.

"No, Lark, don't," he said softly. "Stay there. I'll come to y'all."

Taran whined softly to see his Alpha.

"I couldn't do that," she snuffled.

"Do what, honey?" Nick replied as he stroked Taran's head

and made alpha-sounding noises.

"Touch his head. The blood and stuff—it's squicking me out."

Nick laughed, loudly, and it jarred something loose inside her. She could breathe freely again.

"Yeah, there's quite a bit of squick around here, isn't there? That's what happens when a wolf thinks someone's about to hurt his mate. Werewolves can be icky, says TJ."

She snorted, then hiccupped. "Hey. Where'd the cops go?"

"Huh? Oh, I sent them on," Nick said casually as he pulled at Taran's ears. "Y'all can give statements and everything tomorrow. Or Sunday. Whenever."

She gaped at him. "The cops do what you tell them to? I mean, I know they're werewolves, but still…"

He shrugged. "I didn't tell them what to do, I just suggested it. Come on, pretty girl, why don't you go inside and get some sleep."

"I can't sleep after all this!"

"Honey, you're about to pass out. I want you to do it in his bed, not out here."

"What about Taran?" she protested as Nick took her hand and pulled her up.

"I'll stay with him. He won't change for a while yet, and he'll need me when he does. Take a shower and go to bed."

"Oh. Shit. I don't have my stuff here anymore."

"Your bag's in my car. I picked it up from TJ's."

She stared at him in wonder. "You're incredible."

Nick sighed. "Yeah. That's what I keep telling TJ."

Chapter Eight

He awoke with a brutal jolt; asleep one minute, awake the next, and for one terrifying moment he didn't know who or where he was.

The clock said three p.m.

He closed his eyes as scenes from last night floated through his head. A wolf's human memory of time spent on four feet varied depending on mood, circumstance, and emotion. More sensate than factual, impressions rather than events, remembering what happened while furry felt to a wolf like watching a movie with earplugs and a see-through blindfold. You could follow the plot, but it felt distant and removed.

Where was Lark?

She'd been here, asleep, when he finally fell into bed in the wee hours of the morning. Nick had stayed with him while he changed, then helped him into the house. He'd showered, careful not to wake her. She lay curled up in those damned flannel pants and T-shirt, smelling of apples and girl soap and Lark and love. He'd tucked the blanket around her and run a hand through her still-damp hair before Nick softly called him out to the kitchen to eat.

Lingering in the shower, he stretched as scalding water ran over his aching shoulders. Two showers, three showers, four might still not work out the soreness and stress of the last two weeks.

He finally relaxed when he heard Lark moving about in the bedroom. A part of him had worried she'd fled again.

The bar on the outside of the shower door was empty when he put his hand out for his towel. He stepped out, dripping water on the carpet.

Lark leaned against the counter, towel in hand, naked but for tiny lace panties and seriously high, spiked heels. Her hair hung loose about her shoulders, still smelling like apples.

Instantly his cock stiffened and rose. His mouth watered at the sight of her hard, rosy nipples and the dark, neatly trimmed patch peeking through the lace of her purple panties. He could still taste her in his memory.

He swallowed. "Have you been running around like that?"

The pulse in his throat jumped at her slow half-grin.

"I need my towel, please." His voice shook, and he knew she heard it.

"If you come over here, I'll dry you off," she said huskily. "You look like you could use some help." Her hand drifted across her stomach, down to the waistband of her panties.

He smelled her heat, heard her heart. His blood turned to fire as it raced through his veins. His dick throbbed and pointed straight at her—*go! that way!*—but he stood rooted in place, paralyzed with lust, hands dangling at his side.

The look she gave him—hot, sultry, straight in the eye—left him gasping for breath. He didn't know this Lark, this cocky, confident woman who stared at him as if she owned him and could make him do what she wanted. She did, and she could, and it scared the shit out of him.

"Where have you been?"

"I went to see Meg."

"You saw my mom?"

"Yes."

"What the fuck for?"

"I'll tell you later."

He knew he'd lost control of the situation; he just didn't know how.

"You'll tell me now."

"No, I won't." Her laughter filled the bathroom and tickled the pit of his stomach. She held his gaze. "You're still wet, and so am I." Her hand dipped into her panties, and his whole body shuddered. "If you come over here right now, I promise to leave the heels on," she whispered.

His body finally wrested control from his mind. He stumbled over to her. She pushed away from the counter to lay her hands lightly on his chest, and he bent his head, expecting a kiss. His lips met her hair. He gasped as she sucked the water off his skin. Her hands fluttered down his sternum, and she dragged her thumbnails across his obliques as she licked more droplets from his torso.

"I love your stomach," she purred against his chest, pressing her palms flat against his belly. "I dream about your stomach. I'm gonna curl up and go to sleep on your stomach." She pulled her head back to look up at him with a smirk. "You know what? I think carpet in a bathroom is a wonderful thing."

He closed his eyes and fought for air. Desire wracked his body, his blood pounding in his ears. He growled with need. He tried to put his hands on her ass, to pull her tight, but she sank to her knees, her soft tits slowly sliding down his body and over his aching, iron hard dick.

"Lark," he moaned, "what are doing to me..."

"Shh," she said. "Look in the mirror."

His eyes flew open to see her head poised before his groin. She rubbed her cheek against his dick, and he reached down to gather chestnut silk in his hands. His stomach muscles spasmed as her fingers followed the hair running down his belly until they met her mouth.

She stroked his balls with one warm, supple hand and wrapped the other around the base of his swollen dick. He shuddered and sucked in his breath when she licked up the vein on the underside of the shaft. Then she took the head in her mouth and suckled, swirling her tongue around and around.

"God, yes," he breathed between clenched teeth, "baby, that's...fuck, that's perfect, Lark, that feels so good."

He felt her smile around the knob of his dick before she slid the rest of it into her mouth as far as it would go, until it touched the back of her throat. He gasped with awe and pleasure. Slowly she pulled it out, keeping her mouth tight around it like a popsicle. She laved the head with her sweet, hot tongue again, then took it all the way back into her mouth. Her hands stroked at a firm and steady pace with her mouth, working his shaft as she sucked.

He watched the mirror as his hips jerked rhythmically against her mouth. Taking care not to push her head, he ran the silk of her hair between his fingers.

"Put your other hand between my legs, baby, please," he begged. She slid her fingers behind his balls, pressing up. He shuddered again. "That's it, that's so good," he panted.

He couldn't hold on much longer. She'd milk him until he came, but suddenly he needed to be inside her.

He put his hands beneath her chin and gently pulled out of her mouth.

"What's wrong?" she cried, looking up in confusion. The love in her eyes warmed him till he glowed.

"Nothing's wrong," he growled, stroking her face as he pulled her up. "It's perfect. You're perfect."

He held her chin and lowered his mouth to hers, tasting himself as he sucked her tongue. Before she could wrap her arms around his neck, he forced them back to her sides and spun her around with a shaky laugh.

"Taran!" she mewled, "what are you—" She moaned as he bent her over the counter.

Covering her body with his, he whispered in her ear, "I need to come inside you. You can look in the mirror if you want."

She did, her lovely face flushed with desire, lips wet and parted, eyes half closed. He watched her face as he spread her arms and flattened her hands against the counter, making sure she was braced. She shivered as he rubbed his chest against her back, his stiff cock pressing against the crack of her sweet, round ass.

She cried out when he grabbed her panties and yanked them down. He held her feet steady to pull the panties all the way off, smiling in triumph when he saw her legs shaking.

"I love it like this," she whimpered. "Hard. I love it hard like this."

He crouched to grasp her cheeks with both hands, reveling in the hot, firm flesh, and she shrieked when he nipped at one side and licked the sting away.

"Do it again," she moaned, and he obeyed.

He slid two fingers inside her, finding her hotter and wetter than he'd even imagined. Her muscles squeezed his fingers. She let out a long wail of pleasure. He slowly spread his fingers, stretching her, and she sobbed when he pulled them out and plunged them back in.

"Are you about to come, baby?" he breathed.

Another sob was all the answer he needed.

He guided his cock into her, groaning long and hard as he finally found the warm, wet shelter he'd sought. They were perfectly aligned, perfectly fitted for this. He grabbed her hips and dug his fingers into her flesh, pulling her ass back against him so she didn't have to take all the weight on her arms. Finally deep within her, he abandoned control and began to pump, letting his body do what it needed. She met his every thrust.

"Harder," she whimpered. "Do it harder."

He did, closing his eyes and losing himself in her slick warmth, letting the noise of her ecstasy wash away the remnants of his fear and doubt, sure at last that she was his not because he'd claimed her, but because she'd chosen him.

He smiled, delighted, when she reached back to grab his hand and press it between her legs. The edge of the counter bit into the back of his hand as she ground against his palm. She screamed when his middle finger found her clit and seconds later she came, wet and hot and screaming his name. Her screams died away into little half sobs, and his body began to jerk as the orgasm seized him.

He heard himself shout, telling her he loved her, saying things he'd never said to any female before. Hard and helplessly he came, and he collapsed across her back, burying his face in her hair, resting in the scent of his mate.

"Taran," she whispered. "Sweetie. I can't stand up. You have to get off me." She giggled a little hysterically. Her ankles were wobbling in the four inch spikes, his body pressing her down against the ice cold granite.

He laughed into her hair. "I'm sorry, baby. One sec." He raised himself off her, bracing his hands on the vanity and taking a couple deep breaths. "Okay."

Smoothly, and with no apparent effort, he swept her up in his arms and carried her to his bed, letting her drop with a thud. He laughed at her "oof!" of surprise. Then he tenderly unstrapped her heels and tossed them away before falling down atop her.

"Oh. Sorry, I'm too heavy—"

"Shh, it's okay." Rolling him over onto his back, she laid

her head against his stomach and drew the blanket up. She tucked her hand beneath his butt and breathed in the scent of his seed, the both of them still wet and warm and sticky. She shivered as he played with her hair.

"La Perla," he said sleepily.

"Huh?"

"It's—"

"I know what La Perla is, Taran. It's expensive lingerie. What about it?"

"I'm buying you some. A lot."

"You don't want me in flannel?"

"I'd fuck you in burlap, baby. But I want to see you in satin and silk too."

"Bought a lot of La Perla, have you?"

"No. But Nick buys it for all his females."

"Ew."

His hands stopped in her hair for a moment. "What ew?"

"Nothing."

"Bullshit nothing. Why do you care what Nick buys for his women?" he asked belligerently.

Alarmed, she raised up on her elbow to look at him. "I don't care," she said softly. "Other people might, that's all."

He frowned at her for a long minute, and she would've laughed at his eventual shock of comprehension if it hadn't been such a sad subject.

"You mean TJ...?"

"Let's forget I said anything, okay? Please. I didn't mean to spoil the afterglow. I'll wear whatever you buy me." She put her head back down. "Play with my hair some more."

"How about those corset things?" he asked eventually.

"Corset things?"

"You know. The ones that go around your waist, but not over your tits. You wear them with garters and panties."

"That's more sex boutique than La Perla but sure, I can do that. I can do anything."

His laughter stopped abruptly, and his hand paused in her hair again. "You can? Like, what're we talking about here? What've you done?"

"I don't mean I *will* do anything," she sighed patiently. "I haven't done everything; I'm just open to ideas. Okay?"

251

"You give damned good head." He was quiet for a minute. "Where'd you learn that?"

"The Dummy's Guide to Blowjobs," she said drily.

She could sense his dismay.

"Taran." She rolled over on top of him, resting her chin on his stomach. "I'm twenty-six. I would've waited for you if I'd known you wanted me, but come on."

"I haven't slept with anyone in a long time," he whispered. "That's how bad I've needed you."

"But I still haven't slept with nearly as many people as you have altogether. It doesn't really matter, since we'll never sleep with anyone else again. Right?"

He nodded contritely. "Right. You're right."

"Okay, then." She laid her cheek against his belly once more.

She'd just dozed off when he asked, "What did you talk to my mom about?"

"Us. Danny. The whole thing."

"How'd she know about the whole thing?"

"Oh. Right, I haven't told you."

She rolled off and crawled up to lay her head on the pillow next to him. He pulled her hand back over and pressed it to his stomach. She remembered TJ telling her how deeply wolves craved touching and holding, and her heart ached to think how long he'd been without it. The touch of friends and family couldn't substitute for a mate's. She resolved to hold and caress him every second she could.

Snuggling into him she whispered, "Well, big guy, you were in the *Chronicle* this morning."

"I was? Why—oh, shit..."

"Yeah. Big Ass Werewolf Races Down I-10 In Midst of Traffic Pileup, or something like that. Not sure why so many people saw you. That late at night, and you moving so fast, I'd have thought you'd be some kind of blur, but apparently you ran across the tops of a few cars."

"Fuck." He shot up. "Lark! *Did I hurt anyone??*"

"Of course not, baby, I'd have told you already if you did! Lie down." Once he'd settled back, she wrapped her arm around him. "No. You scared the hell out of a bunch of people, but you missed the cheap cars—you only hit the big stuff. Left some dents and scratches. So far, the department's only said it was a police officer in pursuit of a dangerous suspect, and they'll reimburse all vehicle owners for damage. So it's good. Your name might not even get out there."

"Nick didn't mention any of that last night."

"I think he was more concerned with you."

"About TJ..."

"No, Taran. No about TJ. That one's off limits." She laid a hand against his cheek, looked into his eye. "Swear to me, baby. No word to anyone."

"Yes, ma'am."

"God..." she groaned in ecstasy, "...I love it when you do what I tell you. If I'd known all these years I could boss you around like this, I would've been so...*Taran!*"

She shrieked as he flipped her on her back, held both her hands above her head in one of his giant paws, and tickled her mercilessly under her arms and on her sides. She screamed and thrashed but she couldn't very well move with three hundred pounds of werewolf on top of her.

"Good Lord, little girl!" he shouted. "Where the fuck did you learn language like that?" He had to stop tickling her because he was laughing too hard.

She lay beneath him, gasping for breath. "Taran Lloyd, you fucking asshole," she panted, "every time you tickle me like that, there's gonna be consequences. You hear me? Big, big consequences."

"I think there already are," he rumbled into her ear. He still held her hands imprisoned above her head, and now his other hand dipped into her folds, stroking the fresh wetness. "See? I think you liked it." He rested his hand there and stared at her, daring her to move, his mouth an inch above hers.

"So. You want to know what Meg and I talked about?"

He grinned wickedly. "You trying to embarrass me? You think I can't make love to you if you bring up my mom? I've been having dirty dreams about my cousin for years. Nothing embarrasses me." He lowered his mouth to stroke his tongue across her nipple, so lightly she wasn't even sure he'd done it, and she arched against him with a needy little cry.

"What'd she say?" he asked casually and began to suckle the whole areola.

"Aunt Meg said..." she gasped and ground her hips against his, "...she said...oh thank heavens finally."

"Wait. Huh? Was that you saying that, or her?" He lifted his head, and she giggled at the confusion on his face.

"Her exact words. 'Oh thank heavens, finally.' Said she'd always suspected we felt that way and she just prayed we'd figure it out one of these days. I asked her why the hell she hadn't said something, and she said—" she slipped into her Aunt Meg voice, "—'Well, sweetie, I just didn't know what to say. You know I don't like to pry.'"

"She loves to pry! She lives to pry!" He roared with laughter and she did too, but he didn't let go of her hands. She wrapped her legs around his waist and began grinding against him again.

"She said something else."

"What?" he grinned against her neck.

"She said you had to marry me. She can't wait to be the mother of the bride AND the groom. I think she's already planned the whole thing."

He lifted his head to gaze down at her. "You'll marry me, right?"

"Oh, baby," she breathed, her heart breaking once again at the question in his eyes. "Let go of my hands."

Brushing his hair from his eyes, she traced his scar with a finger, reveling in the heat and the love and the tenderness on his face. She slid her fingers into his hair and brought his mouth down to hers.

"Of course I'll marry you. I'm yours, Taran. I've always been yours."

About the Author

Kinsey W. Holley lives in Houston with the Hub and the Tomboy Diva, who are jealous of her laptop. She's been a law librarian for over ten years, and she loves her job, but if she awoke to find herself the JR Ward of werewolves one day, she'd give her notice the next.

For years she's had people talking in her head—only to each other, never to her (the distinction matters). When it got too crowded up there, she started writing about them. She's not sure what she'd do if anyone from her church or the Diva's school found out she wrote sexy romance; she just hopes no one does.

When she's not writing, she enjoys spending time with friends and family (the two groups overlap a lot), chatting on the Internet with close friends she's never met, and hanging out with the Tomboy Diva, who shares her mother's love of reading and propensity for daydreaming.

You can visit Kinsey Holley (and see pictures of the Diva!) at www.kinseyholley.com.

GREAT CHEAP FUN

Discover eBooks!

THE FASTEST WAY TO GET THE HOTTEST NAMES

Get your favorite authors on your favorite reader, long before they're out in print! Ebooks from Samhain go wherever you go, and work with whatever you carry—Palm, PDF, Mobi, and more.

LaVergne, TN USA
23 March 2010
176864LV00011B/5/P